PRAISE FOR JEFF LINDSAY

"[A] breath of fresh air blowing across all crime-novel conventions..."

—*The Denver Post*

"Lindsay's original, cockeyed view of the world is alive and well... [His] dark, comedic fiction is an alternate universe once removed."

— *Angeles Times*

"Lindsay keeps the blood flowing —

g Free Press

"Any writer who can n ⋯ be doing something right."

—*USA Today*

PRAISE FU ... DEXTER SERIES

"A macabre tour-de-force... so snappy and smart."

—*The New York Times Book Review*

"With chills like this, you can skip the air-conditioning."

—*Time*

"A dark comedy with a creative twist."

—*The Miami Herald*

"Wonderful... Darkly amusing... Our handsome murderer may consider himself emotionless, but his sheer joie de vivre—or joie de mourir—is both obvious and contagious."

—*The Boston Globe*

"Dexter is a fascinating character, though he's not the kind of guy you'd like to invite to dinner."

—*Chicago Sun-Times*

"Mordantly funny."

—*New York Post*

"Maybe the first serial killer who unabashedly solicits our love."

—*Entertainment Weekly*

"Wonderfully fresh and packed with just the right amount of grotesquerie and wry wit."

—*USA Today*

RED TIDE

A BILLY KNIGHT THRILLER

JEFF LINDSAY

DIVERSIONBOOKS

More Billy Knight Thrillers

Tropical Depression

Diversion Books
A Division of Diversion Publishing Corp.
443 Park Avenue South, Suite 1008
New York, New York 10016
www.DiversionBooks.com

For more information, email info@diversionbooks.com

First Diversion Books edition October 2015.
Print ISBN: 978-1-62681-721-0
eBook ISBN: 978-1-62681-720-3

CHAPTER ONE

Things were not going well that last slow month of summer. Business had fallen to an all-time low in the hard and stupid heat of August. People still came down to the docks, but no one wanted to go fishing. Instead, they would amble sideways down to my boat to gawk, scratch their necks and ask, how much? And when I told them $450 a day some of them would look unhappy for a moment, and some would grin strangely, and some would just stare, and then they would all look behind them, take a funny little step to the side, and wander away with a shy half glance over their shoulder like they were hoping I hadn't noticed them.

Art, the 350-pound ex-biker dockmaster, said it was the same with people who called his shack on the phone. They would clear their throats three or four times, ask the price, and promise to get right back to him, but they never did.

Art said things would get better soon, but Art always said that. I guess he felt like he had to keep up the morale of the handful of guides that worked out of his dock.

It wasn't working. My morale was bad, and it wasn't all because business was slow.

Things were not going any better away from the docks. The court had finally awarded me salvage rights to BATTLE, a lush 54-foot Alden sailboat I had taken from a guy named Doyle who

5

thought he was the reincarnation of Adolf Hitler. He was dead, blasted to bits by lightning, and nobody else had come forward to claim the boat. So I could count on a nice chunk of money when I sold it. That should have solved a lot of problems. But there seems to be a special rule of life that whenever you have money, everything else goes wrong, and it all did.

Nancy had moved out a few months earlier, saying she just needed some space for a while and it didn't really mean anything, but we both knew it did.

She had moved to Key West from L.A. because working as a nurse in a small ghetto clinic had started to turn her sour—and because, I still thought, maybe we had something.

And maybe we had. We had tried hard to make it work and for the first few months together, it had worked magically. Even in my small and battered cottage, there was room for two of us and everything we needed because we were in love. Or at least, we thought we were in love, and maybe that counts for the same thing until the fairy dust wears off.

There is nothing quite like being in love in Key West. Just walking down Duval Street can make you feel more alive than you have ever felt before, like God loves you more than other people and everything you do will always turn out all right. You can almost hear the music playing and you begin to believe that you are Gene Kelly.

And when the fairy dust wears off there's nothing worse than love dying in Key West. On the passionate canvas of the tropics the brush strokes are brighter, harder-edged. They hurt more. Everyone holds hands in Key West, and if your hand is empty you feel it more.

But Nancy and I had not broken up; we had simply moved apart. We would spend an evening together, and Nancy still kept some of her stuff in a closet at my house. Of course that made it harder; if we had just agreed it was over I could get on with life. Instead, the ending was dragging on indefinitely as the relationship twitched into temporary life from time to time, bringing the illusion of hope into a thing that was already as dead as it could be.

The illusions didn't last long. The final killing blow came in a way that might not have been able to happen at all, except in that searing, stupefying August heat.

• • •

The Moonlight Room was a back street dive. Every waterfront town has one. There are no signs posted to tell you, but it's for members only. To be a member you have to live in town and work the boats.

The membership at the Moonlight Room was made up of Key West's sports-fishing community and a good handful of the commercial fishermen. Any evening would find the place full of guides, charter captains, mates, and shrimpers—and their wives, girlfriends, and families. If an outsider wandered in by mistake, the odds were pretty good they'd get the message quickly and wander out again. If they didn't take a hint they'd better either buy a round for the house or know how to use their fists.

You almost had to duck under the small neon sign to get through the door. Once inside you were never sure it was worth it. There were three small tables, a couple of barely-padded high-backed booths, and a row of stools along the bar. At the back was a small hallway, only slighter deeper than a broom closet, with a telephone, a cigarette machine, and a unisex restroom.

I don't know where the term "Happy Hour" comes from. I've never seen one that wasn't two hours long and pathetic. Happy Hour at the Moonlight Room was so standard, it might have been a Norman Rockwell, if Rockwell had ever painted All-American shabby degenerate drunken resignation. A handful of idle captains, mates, and retired drunks sat on stools and in booths and just drank with a concentration you could almost call sober.

With Nancy avoiding me and my future with her uncertain, I had taken to spending the last of the late afternoon heat in the dark and moldy coolness of a booth. After the first few times, the residents stopped glaring at me when I came in. I was starting to fit in. I wasn't sure how to feel about that.

Draft beer was fifty cents and there was usually a ball game on the television. I would have two or three beers, watch the game, sulk for a while, and then head out into the evening, my mild buzz a shield against the dying heat of the day.

Sometimes I would find Nancy and we would eat dinner, talk a little, fight a little, and then either make up and make love or separate to stew in our separate bitter puddings. The next day it would start all over again and I was at the point where I couldn't tell one day from any other, which is something that happens in Key West anyway, but now it was worse.

I had learned that Nancy was one of those people who needs to fight. Not out of any sense of meanness, but from a feeling of worth. If she couldn't argue about something, the thing had no value. She would take great satisfaction from fighting until terrible things were said and then she'd make up in the face of this new "honesty."

I was just the opposite. Nancy thought fighting was a sign of a healthy relationship; I thought it meant something was wrong. Neither one of us could shake these convictions. So the fighting went on, Nancy always pushing at my refusal to fight until she got too frustrated to stand it any longer and left, or I got too mad and gave her the fight she craved.

And so it had gradually dawned on us that we were even farther apart than we thought. The distance between us grew, and the silence. By now I knew that it was going to take a very big effort to keep the relationship alive. I was willing. I wanted it to work. But Nancy began working later shifts, forgetting to return my calls, staying away sometimes for three days at a stretch.

She always apologized, saying that her work schedule at the hospital was worse than usual. Or maybe she took somebody else's shift in the ER as a favor. And when I said she should have called, it would launch us on another three-hour screaming match.

When you are in love with someone and they don't see you or call you for three days—unless you are a complete idiot—you begin to think they don't care for you as much as you care for them. And also—unless you are a complete idiot—you realize that there is not a damned thing you can do about it.

So with nothing else to do and no work to distract me, I glided into the routine of Happy Hours at the Moonlight Room.

It wasn't so bad. Everybody else in the place at that time of day had something they pitied themselves for, so it was quiet. Every so often somebody would play a song on the jukebox, which had somehow been loaded by mistake with a bunch of old songs made up of actual melodies and words that meant something.

Between the songs and the ball games and the fifty-cent draft, life was full again.

This evening was no different. There was a game on the blurry old TV set above the bar. The Marlins were losing again. The same happy crowd hunched over the same half-empty glasses. They barely blinked as I came in. I grabbed a draft and found my regular booth in the back of the room.

Maybe Nancy would find me. Maybe she had forgiven me. Maybe she would even tell me what she was forgiving me for.

I sat in my booth, trying not to notice the smell from the back room. Apparently they'd just poured some new pine-scented stuff into the toilet, and they figured that ought to do instead of flushing. On top of that, somebody in the small kitchen had found something washed up on the beach and decided to fry it in transmission oil from a Packard they'd pulled out of a canal.

And if that wasn't enough, the Marlins were down seven runs in the fifth inning and suddenly my glass was empty. Something had to give.

I stood and walked over to the bar. There were a couple of boney, rangy guys sitting at the end of the bar, shrimpers from the tough, unwashed look of them. Neither one of them looked up from his glass as I passed by. That didn't mean anything. I hadn't seen either one look up from a glass in all the time I'd been coming here. They just sat there, two feet apart, and drank. Never talked, never moved at all except for the slight bend of the elbow as they raised their glasses without moving their heads. So far they hadn't even gone to the bathroom.

A very large woman with short hair and an ornate tattoo on her arm refilled my glass without looking up and without saying a word. Maybe she was related to the shrimpers.

As I headed back to my booth there was a blinding burst of light and the front door swung open. I squinted in its direction.

Nancy stood just inside, blinking as her eyes adjusted. She looked like a deer caught in the headlights of a car, except a deer never made me feel weak in the knees. She looked so good that the two shrimpers moved their heads an inch and a half each just to look at her.

"Billy," she said, as she was finally able to see in the gloom and caught sight of me gaping at her. I felt warm.

"Hi."

Key West had been good to her. She seemed more relaxed than when I first met her. The smile lines that bracketed her mouth had grown gentler and there was a glow of health under her flawless olive skin. She still had a ripe mouth and the most perfect neck I had ever seen.

Her hair was pulled back now in what she called her "working do" and even the awful hospital whites could not make her figure look chunky. It flowed like a piece of sculpture, begging for hands to run over it and feel its curves and textures.

My mouth felt dry. I kissed her lightly and she smiled.

The door opened again. Two charter captains I knew came in with their mates, three women and two other guys I didn't know. One of them, a guy with a deep tan and a shifty, uncertain look to him, started yelling that drinks for the house were on him. They all pushed past us to the bar, cheering and talking all at the same time.

I smiled at Nancy. "Have a seat."

She looked around the room and then arched a perfect eyebrow at me. "If you're sure I'm not interrupting anything—"

"But you are," I said. "And just in time, too."

I settled Nancy in my booth and went to get her a drink. I came back with her spritzer and slid into the booth across from her. That meant I had to sit with my back to the door.

No man who grew up in America dreaming about cowboys

is comfortable sitting with his back to the door. That's how Wild Bill Hickok was killed, and we're all half-convinced some cowardly desperado will slink in the door and blaze away at your back. It happens all the time—look at Jesse James.

Most of that uneasiness faded when Nancy locked her eyes onto mine. "Billy," she said. "I'm sorry I've been so—" she fluttered a hand. It was strong, sleek, and smooth, the nails short and clean. "I guess off-and-on is the phrase. I'm sorry."

"So am I." I took her hand.

I held Nancy's hand and she didn't pull it away and we hadn't started our evening's fight yet. Who knows what might have happened next.

"Hey," she said softly in a voice I hadn't heard for a while. The rum and honey sound of it sent goose bumps up my arms.

I squeezed her hand. "Hey yourself."

"I haven't seen that smile for a while."

I thought of a lot of things I could say to that—that it hadn't been around, that she hadn't been looking for it. But I settled for, "It's been here. It's always here for you."

She pulled her hand away and I wondered what I'd done wrong this time. She looked up over my shoulder and a voice boomed out behind me.

"Well," said the voice, "do I smell bacon?"

I could only think, at least it wasn't something I said. "Hello, Tiny."

"Hello, Bacon," he said in his annoying voice. "Bacon" as in ex-cop, burned-out pig. He thought that was pretty funny. Tiny had a surprisingly high-pitched voice with a thick Pittsburgh accent that always seemed to pour sarcasm out of his twisted mouth. It kept him talking from the left side. His hairline just missed merging with his eyebrows and his small blue eyes always seemed filled with stupid suspicion. He reminded me of a hornless pink rhinoceros.

He had been sniping at me for a while, taking cheap shots whenever he got the chance, and they had started to get to me, to eat away at my careful self-control, in that slow, sullen August heat.

Sooner or later I knew he would catch me when I was worn down by the heat and the dull desperation of the summer, and then I would hurt him.

But this wasn't the time. Not with Nancy here in front of me, smiling and not looking for a fight for the first time in months.

I turned back to Nancy, but I could tell by her expression that Tiny hadn't moved.

I looked. He still stood there, staring down at me with stupid delight.

"Bar's over there, Tiny."

He curled his lip an extra inch higher. Maybe he thought it made him look like Elvis. It didn't. "Thanks," he said. "I didn't know that."

I nodded. "That's what I thought."

"Billy—" Nancy said with a warning tone in her voice.

Tiny pushed his head toward me. "What's that s'posed to mean, Bacon?"

"It means you couldn't find a fish even if it was in your pants, and you can't find anything better to do than drool on my shoulder."

Nancy stood up. "That's enough, Billy. Let's go."

Tiny put a hand on my shoulder and leaned down. "Blow me," he said.

It wasn't much as an insult. It was about what you could expect from Tiny. But something about the combination of the stupid retort, the sharp words from Nancy, the beer, the lousy ball game, and that damned August heat made it seem a lot worse. Whatever it was, I'd had enough.

I threw a sharp elbow into Tiny's groin and slid out of the booth. By the time he half-straightened I was already standing. "Son of a bitch," he said, his teeth showing. I hit him again, in the gut this time, and he folded some more.

"God *damn* it, Billy," said Nancy. "If you think—"

I didn't think. There wasn't time. Tiny gave a high-pitched gurgle and charged me. His head went into my mid-section, just above the belt, and drove me backwards.

I had about three steps back before I was going to slam into the wall. I used one of them to move sideways. Tiny kept going straight until his head smacked the wall with a dull bong. He sat down hard and just blinked a few times.

I turned to Nancy. "I'm sorry," I said. "Do you want to leave now?"

She looked at me, shaking her head. Then she turned away and headed for the door.

"Nancy. Wait." I caught her just two steps short of the door. "Nancy, look—" I started.

She turned to me. "Billy," she snapped. Then her eyes widened. "Duck!"

I heard a slight scuffling sound behind me. I grabbed Nancy and swung her away, turning just in time to see a chair fly through the space we had been standing in.

Tiny was up and charging again. A table got in his way. He knocked it over. The thick glass ashtray flew sideways and smacked one of the shrimpers. He turned his head and glared at his partner. "God damn," he said, and swung a haymaker at his buddy.

The second shrimper flew backwards and landed on the table occupied by the charter captains and their wives. Their drinks spilled on them as the table collapsed.

One of the captains, a bald guy with a beard and a diamond earring, stood up grinning. "Ya-HOO!" he bellowed and belted the shrimper.

In a moment a full-scale bar fight was raging. I wrestled Tiny to the floor, but as I stood up the bearded captain's mate stepped over and slugged me. "Son of a bitch!" he yelled.

I stepped back and Tiny bit my ankle.

I kicked Tiny in the face. His nose broke and blood poured over my shoe. Then the mate was on me again. I hit him hard in the stomach. He bent over and threw up on Tiny.

I turned to Nancy, who was half-crouched against the wall. "Can we just—" I said, but that's as far as I got.

"You bastard!" a voice shrilled at me, and somebody jumped on my back. Long red fingernails clawed at my cheeks; it was the mate's girlfriend. "You bastard!" she repeated. "You leave Bobby alone!"

She clawed again and I felt the blood start to trickle down my face. I have a life-long prejudice against hitting women. So I turned quickly and backed into the wall, just hard enough to knock the wind out of her. "Ucck—" she said and slid off my back.

"Jeannie!" Bobby bellowed, and charged me again. Luckily he ran into Tiny, who had the same idea. The two of them glared at each other as they bumped. Tiny swung first. Bobby ducked under the punch and slapped Tiny hard on the side of the face. Tiny grabbed for Bobby, but Bobby stepped back and fell over his girlfriend. So Tiny grabbed the uncertain-looking guy with the tan who was standing with his back against the wall. Tiny got him in a bear hug and lifted him off the floor, grunting with the effort of his rib-cracking squeeze.

I stepped close to Tiny and hooked him in the kidney, hard; once, twice, and he dropped the uncertain guy and turned on me with a sound like a wild boar charging. But Bobby sat up just then and Tiny stumbled over him, coming to his feet a moment later with a grip on Bobby's throat.

The bald captain brought a chair down on Tiny's head from the rear. Tiny dropped Bobby, shook his head, and charged at me again.

Wondering what the hell his head was made of, I hit Tiny three times as he got his arms around me. He pulled me in to his chest and started to squeeze. I rammed the heel of my hand under his chin and then brought my forehead into his broken nose as hard as I could.

Tiny took a half step backward and glared at me. I hit him again, right on the chin, as hard as I could hit. He shook his head at me. "Son of a—" he said, and fell over.

I took a deep breath, which was a bad idea. My shirt was covered with blood and vomit from Tiny's bear hug. I took the shirt off and tossed it on Tiny. I hoped he'd gotten what he wanted out of all this. I hadn't. But at least it was over.

"You killed him, you son of a bitch!" said Bobby, and swung at my head.

I ducked the punch and threw Bobby back to the center of the room. He stumbled over a chair, spun, and bumped one of the shrimpers, who slugged him to the floor without even looking.

I looked at Nancy. She had worked herself into the corner and was holding half a chair. She looked ready to use it, her lips pressed together and her eyes flicking angrily around the room.

"I'm sorry about this," I said, raising my voice over the uproar.

She glared at me and opened her mouth to say something. Before she could say it the door crashed open. "Police! Freeze, all of you!"

I turned to look. Four cops stood just inside the door with their nightsticks ready.

I looked back at Nancy.

"Damn you, Billy," she said.

CHAPTER TWO

The Key West jail doesn't look like much. It can't. It has to keep a low profile and look quiet and clean on the outside so it won't scare tourists. Most people don't even know it's the jail when they go past. They think it's a parking garage.

The inside isn't bad, considering. Even the drunk tank seems like it was built with repeat business in mind. After all, we have some very important visiting drunks here, and it doesn't pay to offend them.

That night there had been few enough drunks when we arrived at the station, so they'd stuck us all into the tank instead of into separate cells. Maybe the arresting officers thought that was funny, cooping up a bunch of guys who had just torn up a bar. Maybe they thought we'd keep the fight going in there so whoever pulled the late shift would have to keep breaking us up. That would seem like a pretty good joke to a lot of cops.

It didn't work out that way. Tiny might have had enough, and maybe all the hard whacks on his head had had some kind of cumulative effect. Or maybe he was just tired. Whatever it was, Tiny had no more fight in him. He just stretched out on the floor and snored all night.

They'd let Nancy go on her own recognizance right after booking her. Being in a nurse's uniform had probably helped. She hadn't said another word to me. She hadn't even looked in my direction.

The last I saw of her as they herded us back to the cell, she was sitting on a bench staring with disgust at the ink on her fingertips. I guess she'd never been fingerprinted before. I wanted to tell her that the ink wore off after a while, but the cop behind me poked me with his clipboard. "Let's go, killer," he said.

For the rest of the gladiators, it was over; it had never been personal for them, just something to do in between fishing trips. It was part of the lifestyle, and everybody understood that when the cops come it's over.

The two shrimpers sat down and went to sleep propped against the wall. Bobby wasn't feeling well; he just huddled on the floor and moaned himself to sleep. I moved to a corner where the floor looked clean and sat. I closed my eyes, not tired so much as feeling stupid.

After only half a minute of some pretty good self-pity I heard the soft scrape of a shoe nearby. I opened my eyes and looked up. It was a good shoe, one I knew cost as much as a good fly rod. I craned my neck.

The guy with the deep-water tan was standing in front of me looking tanned and uncertain. "Uh," he said, with a twitch of a smile. I raised an eyebrow at him and he looked sideways, then squatted down beside me. "Rick Pearl," he said, and held out his hand.

I decided he meant that Rick Pearl was his name, so I shook his hand and said, "Billy Knight."

"Um," he said. "I wanted to, you know. Ah, thank you?"

"You're welcome," I said. "But for what?"

"Come on," he said. "You saved my life. That guy would have killed me." And he nodded across the room to where Tiny sprawled in a snoring heap.

I squinted at Rick. He could be drunker than he looked, or he might be pulling my leg. But I couldn't remember saving anybody's life lately. Not even my own.

"Are you drunk, Rick?"

"What? No." He flushed a little, mad or embarrassed, I couldn't tell which. "In the bar. You took the guy off me in the bar," he said, and I vaguely remembered hitting Tiny when he was squeezing Rick.

"I mean it," he went on, "that guy was scary. It's—I've never seen anything like it before. Like—like some kind of wild animal charging. I, uh—I mean, I'm not a pussy or anything, but—" He shook his head. "Whoa. Talk about needing an attitude adjustment." And he gave a small hoarse cough of laughter.

I decided he was serious. His laugh, the way he talked, his uncertainty—I'd seen his behavior before. It was the mark of the rich kid out of place, what my mother would have called a slumming playboy. And then I remembered his name, Pearl, and the last piece fell into place.

"You said Pearl? Like Pearl's Department Store?"

He blushed. This time it was definitely embarrassment. "I don't have much to do with the store. My dad mostly runs things."

I was right. For somebody so good at figuring out people, I was sure screwing up my own life.

"I really do mean it," he went on. "I'm really, uh, you know. Thanks a lot. Um, thank you."

"Forget it," I said. "Tiny's been wanting this for a long time."

"Tiny? His name is *Tiny*?"

"Yeah. I think it refers to brain size."

He snickered. "He's got a little evolving to do, that's for sure."

"Have a seat, Rick," I said. "It's going to be a long night."

Rick settled down beside me. "Um, actually, I probably won't be here very long," he said. "Which is why—you know."

"Let it go, Rick," I said, getting just a little tired of the ponderous gratitude. It's not something spoiled rich kids are good at, so they generally tend to overdo it.

"Sure," he said. "Just—sure."

It turned out he got the deep tan from ocean racing. It was a rich man's sport, running the massive floating engines across the Gulf Stream to the Bahamas and back at impossible speeds. I'd made one of those runs with a friend once, as a last minute substitute for a drunken navigator, and for a week afterwards I walked bent over, my back twisted and throbbing from the pounding waves give you at that speed.

Some people like that. Rick was one of them. His uncertainty dropped off when he talked about his boat, the way he positioned the big fuel tanks to improve the trim, a new way to get more from his carburetor.

After about forty-five minutes of ocean racing a guard appeared on the better side of the bars. "Richard Pearl?" he called.

Rick stood up, looking embarrassed again. "My dad's got some pretty good lawyers," he said.

"I guess so."

He shifted his weight from foot to foot for a moment. "I'm sorry I can't spring you," he said. "But if there's ever anything I can do—I mean, I definitely owe you one."

"Forget it," I said.

"No," he told me, looking very serious. "I mean it. I owe you. You ever need anything, I owe you. Anything at all. Look me up." He flashed a smile. "There's only one Pearl in these waters," he said, using the slogan from his dad's store. "On Star Island."

"Come on, Pearl," the guard said, and Rick was gone, turning at the last minute to add, "I mean it." Then he was gone down the hall with the guard.

I leaned back and closed my eyes again, sinking right back into thinking of the mess I'd made with Nancy.

The night seemed to last a lot longer than it was supposed to. My hand was throbbing along the knuckles, and I was cold without my shirt. I'd left it on the floor of the bar. I had known the holding cell would be air-conditioned to a frosty 68 degrees, but at the time, cold had seemed better than wearing a vomit-soaked shirt all night. Now I wasn't so sure.

I was too cold to sleep so I sat and thought. After a while I got up and paced the cell, hoping the walking might keep me warm.

I thought about a big turtle I'd seen a week and a half ago. He'd come up just ahead of my boat and I'd almost lost my charter over the side when I turned fast to dodge him.

And I thought about Nancy, how things had turned bad and

what I might be able to do to make them right again. I wondered if maybe she would be willing to consider all that had happened as meaningful dialogue. It didn't seem likely. I wondered if I would ever see her again.

I remembered my trip to Los Angeles last year when I'd met her. I'd ended up in the drunk tank there, too. I'd been framed for drunk and disorderly by a corrupt cop, and as I sat in a much dirtier cell I had thought about Nancy then, too. It seemed to me I'd spent way too much time sitting in drunk tanks thinking about Nancy Hoffman. I wondered if it meant anything. It probably did. I thought about asking the bald captain but he was still asleep. But what the hell. If it did mean something I probably wouldn't like it.

They let us out early the next day. The court appearance was a month away. We all promised we'd be there. I shook hands with the bald charter captain. Tiny was still trying to fit his belt back into his pants. I figured it would be a bad idea to offer to help. I left.

At this early hour of the morning Key West was deserted, almost as if a plague had swept through and taken away all the people, leaving only stray dogs and cats and the smell of stale beer. In the half hour it took me to walk home I saw nobody except a few joggers, and from the serious and strained looks on their faces as they jogged by, they might have been running from the plague.

Nancy was mad. I knew she was mad, but maybe what had happened to make her mad was good. Maybe it would give us a starting place to really talk out our differences. After all, the main reason I was hanging out in the Moonlight Room was that I was not happy with our relationship. Now that this had happened she would know that. We had something definite to talk about.

I wondered what I could say to Nancy to make it right. I remembered reading somewhere that every great disaster is actually a blessing in disguise. You just have to know how to look at it the right way, to turn your disadvantage into a strength. It might have been Sun Tzu, that wise old man who wrote *The Art of War*. Maybe I could do that with the bar fight, turn it into a new strength. Sun Tzu was always right about these things.

I got home. I walked across my small yard, part rock and part weed, and climbed up the three cement steps. I wasn't inside long enough to sit when I heard a pounding on the door. It was a loud, frantic pounding, sounding like a gang of bikers trying to get into a room filled with beer and teenaged girls. I figured it had to be Nicky.

I opened the door. Nicky Cameron roared past me, nearly five feet of non-stop energy. "Bloody fucking hell, Billy! Where have you been, eh?" He spun and fixed me with his gigantic eyes.

"Hello, Nicky," I said. "What's up?"

Even as I spoke he was cocking his head to one side and then, almost faster than I could follow with my tired eyes, he circled around me, sniffing. "Well, well," he said. "Well well well well well. Lumbered again, eh Billy? What'd they cop you for this time, mate? Loitering?"

"Drunk and disorderly. How did you guess?"

He stood squarely in front of me, hands on his hips and feet planted wide. "Guess. *Guess*!? Is that what you think, Billy? That this is *guess*work I do? Oh, mate, you bloody fucking wrong me." He tapped his nose with a finger. "The Beak knows all, Billy."

I shook my head, tired and cranky but intrigued. "You're saying you smelled it on me."

He winked. "That and your chart. You see, mate, your rising sign right now is on a cusp. This means change, trouble with authority— there's lots of water in there too, mate, travel and conflict over water. And a snake. I haven't figured that bit out yet."

"I'm sure you will, Nicky."

"'Course I will, mate. I'm working a new chart for you now. That's not the point—"

"So there's a point to this?"

"Too right there's a point. I came by last night to warn you. Soon as I started your chart and saw—oh." He stopped suddenly as something else occurred to him and looked thoughtful. I didn't feel like hearing his thoughts. I was suddenly too tired, too fed up with everything, and all I wanted was a shower. I pushed past him.

"Billy, lad, slow down, hang on a bit." He grabbed my arm.

"Nancy was here last night."

I blinked. "Okay."

"She went in empty-handed and came out with a couple of bags of stuff. I didn't figure she was absconding with the silver or I'd have stopped her."

"You were probably right. Her silver's better than mine. What did the bags look like?"

He shrugged. "One of 'em was that bright red fishing tournament thing. You know."

I knew. I remembered the bag well. I had given it to Nancy and she had used it to carry some personal stuff over to my house. It had been in my closet for six months. If she took it now, then—

I closed my eyes and leaned against the wall, exhausted and feeling slightly sick. It was over. Nancy had moved her stuff out. She was slamming the door shut on any chance I had of working things out with her.

Sun Tzu was wrong.

CHAPTER THREE

The next few days were hard. Nancy would not see me. She didn't answer her phone and she wasn't home when I went over. Just before I went out to the hospital to lie down in front of her car, something pulled me back and I decided to let her alone for a while. Let her cool down, think things out, get over her anger.

But the waiting, the not knowing, took its toll on me. I stayed up late and watched too much television. I let my personal routines slide. And eventually the Key West New Age Emotional Rescue Committee kicked into high gear to rescue me from myself.

The K.W.N.A.E.R.C. consists of one person: Nicky Cameron. He's the Executive Administrative Board as well as the Chief Field Operative. He monitored carefully, and when my aura finally drooped into an unhealthy color he swooped in.

Nicky, just a bottle cap taller than five feet, looks at the world through a pair of enormous, pale brown eyes. They are set under a rapidly retreating hairline, above a large hooked nose and a receding chin.

Taken one feature at a time he was a lost cause. But there was so much energy pouring out of those eyes that nobody ever noticed he was an ugly dwarf. I have seen fashion models well over six feet tall fall helplessly into Nicky's eyes and follow him around with a soft and devoted look. He ran the New Age store in town and was probably the Keys' greatest expert on aroma therapy, past life regression, channeling, crystal healing, and astrology, although I was never sure he really believed all that stuff.

He was also the Keys' greatest expert on beer. I couldn't remember ever seeing him without at least one in his hand.

Nicky found things for me to do. He took me to parties where I drank too much and, too often, found myself goggling at odd-looking strangers from a corner where the light was too harsh and all the angles seemed slightly off.

I became his summer project. And at the end of that first week, it worked. I got so sick of his non-stop cheerfulness that I snuck away and pedaled over to check on my boat.

I chained my bike to a sign and went into the dockmaster's shack. Art kept it about forty degrees colder than the outside temperature and stepping inside was like dropping into suspended animation. You could almost hear the bones in your forehead grating as they contracted, and your chest hurt if you breathed too deeply.

"Billy!" came the phlegmy roar as Art saw me. "The hell, brother."

"Hey, Art."

He sat behind an incredible clutter of merchandise. There was so much stuff hanging and stacked that it was almost possible to miss seeing Art. That was quite a trick, since he weighed over 300 pounds and looked like a cross between a pink Dalmatian and Jabba the Hutt.

Art had ridden his Harley into town one day maybe thirty years back and never left, but there was still a little bit of the biker to him. He was still big, but most of it had gone soft and hung off him in gently wobbling waves. His skin was mottled from a life in the outdoors, with dozens of bright pink patches marking the skin cancers he'd already had burned off.

He looked up at my face like he was looking for pimples. After a minute he nodded and grunted.

"Am I okay?"

He grunted again. "Heard about your dust-up at the Moonlight.

Wanted to see if that shitweasel Tiny got a mark on you."

"You're kidding."

He gave me a sour look and shook his head. His three extra chins swirled like a tide pool. "You're losing it, brother. Been losing it for a couple months now. Maybe you pull out, maybe you crash and burn."

He leaned a huge, soft knuckle on the counter and shoved his face at me, suddenly roaring. "But if you let a butt-sucker like Tiny put a fist on you, you've gone way too fucking far and I'm coming outta here and kicking your little pink ass!" He glared at me and slapped his arm on the counter for emphasis. It sounded like water balloons hitting the kitchen floor.

"Okay." I didn't know what else to say. "Any calls?"

Art glared at me for a minute, making sure his warning sank in. Then he leaned back and shook his head, sending three or four chins crashing into each other. "Nothin'. Not even the fuckbags who say they're gonna call back. It's D-E-D-D dead, brother."

"All right," I turned to go.

"Oh," Art grunted. "That old dyke was in here. Wants to see you."

'That old dyke' was Art's name for Betty Fleming. She was only forty-five, and she wasn't a dyke, but Art didn't like women messing around with boats. And Betty was single, strong, self-reliant, and smart, making her life and her living with sailboats. I think Art secretly realized Betty was a lot tougher than he was, and it made him nervous.

"She say what she wanted?"

Art waved an arm. A wall of blubber the size of the Sunday *Times* swung back and forth from his triceps. "Aw, shit, Billy, you know what she's like. Mean, cranky, stubborn old bitch. Like she got a permanent period."

"I'll go see her," I said, and hit the door.

"Who the fuck cares. Butthead old dyke," Art muttered behind me as I left.

I paused for a second on the dock outside, trying desperately to adjust from the Arctic air inside the shack to the steam bath outside. Spring-loaded sweat shot out of my pores. A drop splattered onto the dock and I thought I heard it hiss.

Betty's sailboat was in a slip opposite mine, on the far side of the marina. I walked around, wondering what she wanted from me. She wasn't exactly a social butterfly, and her disastrous marriage had turned her into someone who hated like hell to ask anybody for help, for anything. We had a comfortable, half-distant friendship; I'd given her some fish once or twice, she'd repaid on the spot with a few cold beers.

When I got to her boat, a 40-foot sloop-rigged sailboat, Betty was below in the engine compartment. A stream of profanity came up through the hatch. I wished Art had been there to hear it; he would have liked her a little better.

"Hey, Betty," I called down the hatch. A moment later she stuck her head up.

She had that permanent leathery tan the live-aboards have. Her hair, an almost colorless blonde, was pulled back into a tight ponytail. She wore a dark blue bikini top, a pair of loose cotton shorts, a wide smear of grease, and enough sweat to float a small dinghy.

"God damn all diesels anyway," she greeted me.

"Stick with outboards," I said. "When they break down they're easier to throw overboard."

She pulled herself out of the hatch and onto the deck. "Come on aboard," she said.

I stepped across onto the deck. It was scrubbed clean, as it always was. A red metal toolbox stood beside the engine hatch and a small circle of engine parts was spread around it.

I nodded towards the engine. "What's the trouble?"

She waved it off, refusing to meet my eye. "I'll fix it later," she said, and I was pretty sure she would. In any case, I knew she'd rather get out and push her boat than ask for help in fixing the engine. "Beer?"

"It's a little early," I said.

She wiped a river of sweat off her forehead. "So?"

She had a point. "Sure. Thanks."

Betty went down the hatch and I followed. It was even hotter below with no air moving through it and after the bright glare of the sun it seemed dark. Betty took two bottles of Molson's Ice from a small refrigerator under a counter and handed me one, angling her head at the small table. "Sit," she said. I sat, taking an experimental pull on the beer. It tasted okay, even this early. Maybe it was the heat. Maybe it was because I was about to crash and burn.

"What's up, Betty?"

She turned on a small fan and sat down across from me and took a long pull on her beer. "I need a hand," she said.

I stared at her in astonishment.

"I can pay," she added quickly. "You're not doing any fishing and I thought you could maybe use some extra money." She looked so defensive I didn't know what to say. "Besides, Nancy can't miss you if you're hanging around."

I've never known how the marina grapevine worked so quickly. But every now and then I got my nose rubbed in the fact that it did. The guy on the next boat probably knew more about your wife's feelings for you than you did. "Maybe you're right," I said. "But I need to talk to her first."

She turned her head and looked at me, really looked me over the way only a woman can look—thoroughly, disinterestedly, and without missing anything.

She shook her head. "Your problem is you want to suffocate a woman. You get into a relationship and you think everything is settled."

"I thought it was."

"It's never settled, Billy. Nothing's ever settled. A relationship is alive. It needs to breathe, to grow and change."

"And end?"

She shrugged. "If that's what happens."

"I thought Nancy wanted something steady. I thought that's what most women wanted."

"Sure—if it's on their terms. But if it's coming from you she'll feel crowded, trapped, pushed into something that isn't to her advantage. A woman has to feel liberated now, and that means free to choose, and that means the traditional options are all suspect."

I took a long pull from the beer and set the bottle down empty. "Pretty deep."

"You mean for a leathery old broad who lives on a boat? Yeah, I know. But I studied it. Right after Howie-the-son-of-a-bitch left me I went to the community college. I don't know what I was thinking, just kill some God damned time. Maybe learn to paint or something. Instead, I ran into this woman teaching the Women's Studies classes. We had coffee. She seemed nice. I took her classes. I started thinking about that kind of thing. Women's issues." She shrugged. "I don't know. Maybe I'm wrong."

The small fan on the wall behind her was turning back and forth, blowing a steady stream of hot air that hit me in the face and made me blink every twelve seconds. I blinked again. I didn't know what to say. Betty had asked me to stop by and suddenly we were talking about me. It was not something I was good at.

"You said you needed a hand," I said finally.

Now she blinked. "That's right. I've got a couple of sailboats over at Dinner Key in Miami. Salvage jobs from Andrew. I need to bring 'em down." She raised her bottle in an ironic toast to herself. "My new charter fleet."

"I'm not a great sailor, Betty."

She waved that off. "You're a great *boater*. These boats have engines. You want to motor the whole way that's fine."

"I don't know."

"Fifty bucks a day, plus expenses."

"If I can do it, I'll do it for free."

"Fifty bucks a day, Billy, that's final."

"I don't need the money."

"You'll take the damn money."

"God damn it, I won't."

"Then I will find somebody who *will!*"

Betty's face was flushing to a dark red. So was mine. She slammed down her bottle. The sound was very loud in the small cabin.

"Betty, for Christ's sake, it's not about money."

"Then take the fucking money!"

"God damn it, can't I just do you a *favor*?"

"No! I don't need your favors! Not from you, not from anybody!"

I opened my mouth—and then, for once that miserable August, I did something smart. I closed it again. I took a long pull on my beer. I took a deep breath. "I need a favor from you."

She glared at me suspiciously. "What's that?"

"Key West is closing in on me. Everybody's mad at me and I can't concentrate. I need to get out of town for a few days."

"Billy—"

"The thing is, I have to get away, think things through with no distractions. If there was any way in the world you could let me have a sailboat for a few days it would save my life."

"God damn it, Billy—"

"I'll pay whatever you think is fair."

"You son of a bitch—"

In the end we settled on Betty paying expenses.

CHAPTER FOUR

Early Monday morning we were at the gate of a big marina in Dinner Key, the small bay front area of Miami's Coconut Grove. Yes—we. To my surprise, I had brought Nicky along; partly because I couldn't pry him loose, and partly because I discovered I genuinely wanted company.

When I invited him, he'd screeched out an "EE-hah!", his version of what cowboys, the only *real* Americans, sounded like.

"Nicky, we'll be gone three or four days, maybe more if the weather turns bad on us."

"Perfect, mate. Ab-so-fuckin'-lutely perfect!"

He almost levitated with excitement. I couldn't figure it out. "I didn't think you'd be so happy to leave town," I said.

"Billy, old-sock-me-lad, I couldn't be happier. The shop will run itself for a few days, and I am off to sea with a hearty yo-ho!"

I looked at him, suddenly regretting the invitation. "Listen, if you're going to turn all nautical on me—"

He shook his head, winked. "No worries, chum. No Nelson at Trafalgar imitations. Just three days of cold beer, gentle breezes and working on a world class tan. Half a mo' while I pack!"

And he raced around his house and grabbed a canvas sport bag, a black plastic box, and two cases of beer.

We took the bus up to Miami and got a cab for the hop to

Dinner Key, Nicky wide-eyed at the scenery. I was looking a little hard at Miami myself. I hadn't been there for a few years and there had been some changes.

For starters, there were still signs of hurricane damage. Last season, a big one had whipped through the Dinner Key boat basin with a 16-foot tidal surge. It had taken thousands of boats moored there and dumped them inland in great untidy heaps.

Many of the heaps were still there a year later. It was startling to see the prow of a 45-foot trawler married to a 50-foot sailboat, or a small Donzi speedboat with a mast coming up through the hatch.

Half a giant cabin cruiser, Italian built, lay on one side. The other half was completely gone, whirled away to Texas by the storm. All around it lay a tangle of cable, cleats, deck chairs, coolers, marine toilets, cushions, bent engine parts, mangled fishing gear, half a fire extinguisher—all the imaginable chunks of every kind of boat, all smashed, twisted, bent double or shattered, laying in their piles as if it was a maniac's hardware store.

"Holy shit, mate," Nicky breathed. Australians don't like to let on that they're impressed, but the sight of this billion-dollar trash heap was too much for Nicky.

"And then some," I told him. I moved past the luxury dump and out into the boatyard. Nicky followed, his head swiveling among the busted miracles.

We went through the gate and found Betty's boat, *Sligo*, a French-built 42-footer, over beside the lift. The storm had picked her up and shoved a dock piling through her side, just behind the forward cabin. She had been a total write-off, tossed on one of the impossibly high heaps of broken toys. A stringy, indignant man named Bert had rescued her.

"Sons-a-bitches just left her," he fumed at me. "Little hole like that, and they don't give a shit. Take the insurance money and get a new one, and the sons-a-bitches'll fuck *that* one up, too, and take the insurance money and get *another* one. God damn sons-a-bitches."

Nicky leaned in and laid a hand on the smooth side of the repaired boat. "You'd think the insurance would catch on, eh? Why don't they just refuse to pay?"

Bert cocked his head and stepped back, looking at Nicky through one squinted eye. "Not from here, are you," he said.

Nicky shook his head. "Key West," he said.

Bert spat. "Insurance company sent a fella out to look at *my* boat." He spat again. "Man was from Iowa. Never seen anything more complicated than a rowboat on a duck pond. Flew him in to help out 'cause there was too much work for the regular adjusters." He nodded at the boat I would be taking home. "Same with that one. Dumb sons-a-bitches."

Bert took a step back and turned to look at *Sligo*. She rested in a wooden cradle and Bert led us around the side to admire his work. "Go ahead," he smirked at me. "Find the patch."

We walked slowly around the boat one time. I could see nothing. Nicky gave up and wandered over to the fence, staring out again at the landscape of the marine Apocalypse.

I went around the boat again. I ran my hand along the side. One small area forward felt smoother than the rest. I paused and looked at it carefully.

"Shit," said Bert behind me. "Done it too good." He stepped in and put his hand where mine had been. "I sanded a little better than they do in the factory. I do it by hand. Can't help it. Hate to see a sloppy job. Hey, Ramon!"

A stocky muscular kid wearing a black back brace swaggered by, combing his hair. Bert jerked his head at the *Sligo*, and five minutes later the boat was lowered into the water and tied to the small wooden dock.

Bert showed us where everything was, all the various switches and compartments, always hidden and always different on a boat. Then he hopped up onto the dock, cast off my bow and stern lines, and as I motored slowly out the channel he stood there on the dock watching, head cocked and eye squinted at me, watchful of the boat he had saved.

"Keep to the channel!" he yelled just before we were out of range. "You draw four feet!"

Nicky looked up at me, suddenly anxious. "Is that good, Billy? Drawing four feet?"

"Not in Florida Bay," I said. "Average depth some places is closer to three."

"Oh," he said, looking thoughtful. "So, uh, what. We like, hit the bottom? Get stuck?"

"That's about right."

"What happens then?"

I smiled. "We walk home."

He nodded and popped a beer open. "Good to know, mate," he said. "Good to know."

I steered us straight down the channel, past the half-ruined docks of the marina and beyond a small island still littered with chunks of boat. A few people looked to be living on the islands, tarpaulins stretched between the smashed boat hulls.

The Dinner Key Channel runs a good mile out into Biscayne Bay. I kept to the middle, except for six or seven times when large motorboats came straight at us at full throttle. Then I moved to the right side, but twice they still came close enough that I could have leaned out and touched them.

Miami has this problem with its boaters. Some of them are still sane, rational, careful people—perhaps as many as three or four out of every ten thousand of them. The rest act like they escaped from the asylum, drank a bottle of vodka, snorted an ounce of coke, ate 25 or 30 downers and decided to go for a spin. Homicidal, sociopathic maniacs, wildly out of control, with not a clue that other people are actually alive, and interested in keeping it that way. To them, other boats are targets. They get in the boat knowing only two speeds: fast and blast-off.

I mentioned a few of these things to the boats that tried to kill me. I don't think they could hear me over the engine roar. One of the boats had four giant outboard motors clamped on the back; 250 horsepower each, all going at full throttle no more than six inches from *Sligo*. If I had put the boom out I would have beheaded the boat's driver. He might not have noticed.

"To get a driver's license," I said to Nicky through gritted teeth, "you have to be sixteen, take a test, and demonstrate minimal skill behind the wheel."

Nicky was busy fumbling on a bright orange life jacket, fingers trembling, and swearing under his breath.

"To drive a boat—which is just as fast, bigger, and in conditions just as crowded and usually more hazardous—you have to be able to start the motor. That's all. Just start the motor. There's something wrong with this picture, Nicky."

"There is, mate," he said. "We're in it. Can you get us out of here?"

My luck was working overtime. We had four more close scrapes—one with a huge Italian-built motor yacht that was 100 feet long, cruising down the center of the channel at a stately thirty knots, but I got us out of the channel alive and undamaged. When I cleared the last two markers and turned into the wind I told Nicky, "Okay. Raise the sails."

He stared at me for a moment. "Sure. Of course. How?"

It turned out Nicky had never been on a sailboat before. So he held the tiller while I went forward to the mast and ran the sails up. Then I jumped back into the cockpit and killed the engine.

"Home, James," said Nicky, popping two beers and handing me one. "It's been a bitch of a morning."

I took the beer and pointed our bow south.

It was a near-perfect day, with a steady, easy wind coming from the east. We sailed south at a gentle five knots, staring at the scenery. Cape Florida looked strange, embarrassed to be naked. All its trees had been stripped away by the hurricane. Farther south, the stacks of Turkey Point Nuclear Reactor stuck up into the air, visible for miles. It was a wonderful landmark for all the boaters. Just steer thataway, Ray Bob, over there towards all them glowing fishes.

* * *

The weather held. We made it down through the Keys in easy stages, staying the first two nights in small marinas along the way, rising at dawn for a lazy breakfast in the cockpit, then casting off and getting the sails up as quickly as possible. Part of the pure joy of the trip was in the sound of the wind and the lack of any kind of machine noise. We'd agreed to do without the engine whenever we could.

That turned out to be most of the time. Nicky took to sailing quickly and without effort. We fell into the rhythm of the wind and the waves so easily, so naturally, that it was like we had been doing this forever, and would keep doing it until one day we were too old and dry and simply blew gently over the rail, wafted away on a wave.

The third night we could have made it in to Key West. But we would have been docking in the dark, and working a little harder than we wanted to. So we pulled in to a small marina with plenty of time left before sunset.

Nicky used the time doing what he called rustling up grub. I don't know if that's how they say it in Australia, or if he heard it in some old John Wayne movie. From what he'd told me about Australia, there's not much difference.

I sat in the cockpit with a beer, stretched out under the blue Bimini top, and waited for Nicky to get back. I had a lot to think about, so I tried not to. But my thoughts were pretty well centered on Nancy.

It was over. It wasn't over. I should do something. I should let it take its course. It wasn't too late. It had been too late for months. Eeny meeny miny mo.

Luckily, Nicky came back before I went completely insane. He was clutching a bag of groceries and two more six packs of beer.

"Ahoy the poop," he shouted. "How 'bout a hand, mate?"

I got him safely aboard and he went below to the little kitchen. It sounded like he was trying to put a hole in the hull with an old stop sign while singing comic opera, so I stayed in the cockpit, watching the sun sink and thinking my thoughts.

There is something very special about sunset in a marina. All the people in their boats have *done* something today. They have risked something and achieved something, and it gives them all a pleasant smugness that makes them very good company at happy hour. A few hours later the people off the big sports fishermen will be loud obnoxious drunks and the couples in their small cruising sailboats will be snarling at them self-righteously from their Birkenstocks, but at sunset they are all brothers and sisters and there are very few places in the world better for watching the sun go down than from the deck of a boat tied safely in a marina after a day on the water.

I sipped a beer. I felt good, too, although my mind kept circling back to Nancy, and every time it did my mood lurched downwards. But it's hard to feel bad on a sailboat. That's one reason people still sail.

Anyway, tomorrow we would be home. I could worry about it then.

Early the next morning we were working our way towards Key West, about two miles off shore on the ocean side. We had decided on the ocean side because of the mild weather. With the prevailing wind from the east, we would have a better sail on the outside, instead of in the calmer waters of the Gulf on the inside of the Keys.

And because the weather was so mild, we went out a little further than usual. Nicky was curious about the Gulf Stream, which runs close to the Keys. I put us onto its edge, and by early afternoon we were only a few miles out of Key West.

Nicky had dragged up his black plastic box and, surprise, pulled out a large handgun.

Like a lot of other foreigners who settle in the USA, Nicky had become a gun nut. He was not dangerous, or no more dangerous than he was at the dinner table. In fact he had become an expert shot and a fast draw. The fast draw part had seemed important to him out of all proportion to how much it really mattered. I put it down to the horrors of growing up a runt in Australia.

Somehow Nicky managed to rationalize his new love for guns with his philosophy of All-Things-Are-One brotherhood. "Simple, mate," he'd said with a wink, "I'm working out a past life karmic burden."

"Horseshit."

"All right then, I just *like* the bloody things. How's that?"

Nicky had a new gun. He wanted to fire off a *few* clips and get the feel of it. Since we were out in the Stream and the nearest boat was almost invisible on the horizon, I didn't see any reason why not. So Nicky shoved in a clip and got ready to fire his lovely new toy.

It was a nine millimeter Sig Sauer, an elegant and expensive weapon that Nicky needed about as much as he needed a Sharp's buffalo rifle, but he had it and so far he hadn't blown off his foot with it. I was hoping he would stay lucky.

"Ahoy, mate," called Nicky, pointing the gun off to the south, "thar she blows."

I turned to follow his point. A bleach bottle was sailing slowly out into the Gulf Stream.

"Come on," Nicky urged, "pedal to the metal, mate."

I tightened the main sheet and turned the boat slightly to give him a clear shot and Nicky opened up. He fired rapidly and well. The bleach bottle leaped into the air and he plugged it twice more before it came down again. He sent it flying across the water until the clip was empty and the bottle, full of holes, started to settle under.

I chased down the bottle and hooked it out with a boathook before it sank from sight. There's enough crap in the ocean. Nicky was already shoving in a fresh clip.

"Onward, my man," he told me, slamming home the clip and letting out a high, raucous, "Eeee-HAH!" as he opened a new beer.

We were moving out further than we should have, maybe, out into the Gulf Stream. It's easy to know when you're there. You see a very abrupt color change, which is just what it sounds like: the water suddenly changes from a gunmetal green to a luminous blue. The edge where the change happens is as hard and startling as a knife-edge.

"Ahoy, matey," Nicky called again, pointing out beyond the color change, and I headed out into the Gulf Stream for the new target.

"Coconut!" Nicky called with excitement as we got closer. It was his favorite target. He loved the way they exploded when he hit them dead on.

I made the turn, adjusting the sheet line and again presenting our broadside, and swiveled my head to watch.

Nicky was already squinting. His hand wavered over the black nylon holster clipped to his belt. He let his muscles go slack and ready. I stared at the coconut. From fifty yards it suddenly looked wrong. The color was almost right, a greyish brown, and the dull texture seemed to fit, but—

"Hang on, Nicky," I said, "Just a second—"

But the first two shots were already smacking away, splitting the sudden quiet.

I shoved the tiller hard over and brought us into the wind. The boat lurched and made Nicky miss his second shot. He looked at me with an expression of annoyance. I nodded at his target. He had hit the coconut dead center with the first shot. It should have leapt out of the water in a spectacular explosion. It hadn't. The impact of the shot pushed it slowly, sluggishly through the water and we could both see it clearly now.

It wasn't a coconut. Not at all.

It was a human head.

CHAPTER FIVE

A lot of people have gotten into the habit of bad-mouthing the Coast Guard, but let me say this in their favor: they really know how to handle a dead body that's been in the water a week, nibbled by sea-life, and then shot in the head.

It was only about half an hour from the time I raised them on my radio to the time the Coasties were sliding the black body bag up into a French-built helicopter, and whisking it away. They did it with casual efficiency, flicking off the clinging sea life without losing any body parts.

Lieutenant Ray Harkness, a short guy with the square silhouette of a body-builder, was in command of the chopper. He had grown up in Key West and I knew him slightly. When the body was loaded he leaned out. "Billy," he said.

"Yeah."

"The way this works, I'm supposed to take you in. But I know you, and you're not going anywhere, right?" He looked at me a little harder than he needed to, but I guess a dead body is a good excuse.

"That's right, Ray," I said.

He nodded. "So you just get yourself in to the Sheriff's office. They're waiting on you." His eyes flicked to Nicky. "Two of you don't show up in the next couple of hours I'm in trouble. But not as much as you."

"We'll be there, Ray."

He looked at me again, then nodded. He pulled his head back into the chopper and a moment later it was whistling away towards Key West.

Under the circumstances we took the sails down and motored in. Nicky didn't have a lot to say on the ride in. He seemed shaken. He sat with his head down and for the first time since I'd known him he looked like a very small guy with no chin. When we were only about twenty minutes away from the dock he shot up suddenly, lurched his body over the side of the cockpit and threw up.

I didn't say anything. Death hits some people harder than others, and this was an ugly death, a death complete with rot and bloating. Nicky was not used to death in any form, had not seen the things I had seen, and he probably felt guilty, too, in some weird, illogical way. He had shot this man in the head and immediately afterwards seen the decomposed body. So it became his fault.

We got the boat tied up in a slip next to Betty's. Betty herself was out until sundown, according to a note tacked to the piling. So I tied off the *Sligo* fore, aft, and spring lines.

Nicky hunched over on the dock while I scrubbed down the boat. His color was a little better, but he still looked like a half-dead water rat. He tried to help at first, but he kept staring off into space and running his shoes full of water so I sat him down until the boat was clean, secure and buttoned up.

By the time we got to the sheriff's station Nicky was almost normal. He surrendered his pistol meekly. We were told to keep ourselves available for questioning and we promised we would. The cops were polite; other towns can get away with judging somebody's importance and political clout by what they wear. Key West cannot. In a town where cut-offs, T-shirts, and thongs are formal wear, anybody might be somebody.

So they stayed polite up until we were about to leave. That is, until I thought we were about to leave. Nicky had other ideas.

"Do they know anything yet?" he asked the Sergeant quietly.

"I wouldn't worry about it, Mr.—" the Sergeant glanced down

at the forms on his desk. "Mr. Cameron."

"But do they have any idea, you know. About the, uh—the body?"

Cops aren't hard-asses twenty-four hours a day. Sometimes that's a mistake. The Sergeant, seeing a meek, tiny local merchant, had a softhearted moment. "Mr. Cameron, the Coast Guard thinks this was a Haitian national. These people put to sea in things I wouldn't let my kids use in a wading pool. It's a sure bet his boat swamped and he drowned. Happens all the time."

"So you'll let us know, eh Sergeant?" Nicky asked as I was half-turned to go.

"Let you know what, sir?" the Sergeant asked, already amused.

"What happens. How it comes out. What you discover." Nicky poured his words into the increasing silence. There is nothing as quiet as a police sergeant's poker face.

"Discover about what, Mr. Cameron?"

Nicky leaned in, as though increasing his volume and intensity might drag the Sergeant out of his apathy. "You remember? There was a dead body? We found it. Man was dead." He said it in that flat Australian way nobody else seems able to copy.

The sergeant, a guy I knew very slightly, looked at me and raised an eyebrow.

"Australian idealist," I said. "Believes in truth and justice. Thinks you have a big red 'S' on the front of your shirt."

He turned back to Nicky with a tolerant, very small, smile. "There won't be much of an investigation, sir. There's a problem with jurisdiction. And this is really not that big a deal."

"It bloody well is to the dead guy."

The cop took a deep breath. I could almost see him counting to ten. It would have been funny under other circumstance. "Let me give you a word of advice, Mr. Cameron."

"I'd be de-bloody-lighted to hear it."

"Forget about this."

Nicky's mouth hung open. He blinked. He looked at me, then back at the sergeant. "Do what?"

"Forget about it. Put it out of your mind. Pretend it never happened."

Nicky took a step back. Then he started to get taller. I don't know how he does it. The sergeant's eyes got wide as he watched.

"Aw, yeah, mate, that's bloody lovely. How's about we ask the dead guy to pretend it never happened while we're at it, eh? I reckon that'll take care of the whole bloody damn shootin' match, eh? You lot'd like that. Go home and have a few cold ones and fergit it all, eh?"

"Nicky," I said, trying to slow him down. It didn't work.

"That'd be fan-fuckin'-tastic, wouldn't it, mate? Just fer-fuckin'-get the whole fuckin' thing. He's not dead! Because it never happened! That'll bring a nice stiff smile to his face, eh?"

The sergeant's face was starting to gain just a little bit of expression. It wasn't a smile.

"Nicky," I said, trying now to edge him out the door.

"Mr. Cameron," the sergeant said, leaning forward as if to make sure he really was taller than Nicky. "This is a police matter and the police will handle it."

"Like they handle everything else?" Nicky demanded.

"That's right."

"Perfect. Bloody wonderful! Case is good as solved!"

"Come on, Nicky," I said, taking him by the elbow and dragging him towards the door.

"The only thing worse than a police state—is an *incompetent* police state!" he shouted, and I got him outside.

Outside the station Nicky deflated again. We got home without saying more than three words. Unfortunately, it was the same three words, over and over. Nicky would smack his fist into his hands as though just discovering something and mutter, "Forget it! Christ!" and then grind his teeth together silently until he needed to say it again.

He wanted to do something about this. The small part of me that still thinks like a cop wanted to kid him about it. But the rest of me was a citizen now. I let him work it out for himself. Besides, I was afraid he might tear into me like he had the sergeant.

He left me at his door, still quietly smoldering.

Just before he closed the door, though, he turned back and looked me in the eye. "This hasn't ended, Billy," he said in a strange, I-Have-Been-There-And-Seen-It tone of voice. "This goes on."

I didn't have a clue what he meant. "Okay, Nicky."

"I mean it, mate. There will be more to this. Fair dinkum. See if there ain't."

"I think you better have a nice hot cup of tea, Nicky."

He rubbed his eyes, dwindling with each breath. "Yeah. And then a nice lie-down."

"I'll see you later."

"Ta, Billy."

He closed his door and I headed home.

It wasn't hard to realize in a general way what he was going through. He had found a corpse. He'd been expecting fireworks, commotion, wheels set in motion, shouting and wailing and gnashing of teeth. The cops hadn't obliged, and he was realizing that they wanted this to trail off into a few forms to fill out and maybe two lines in the paper. And then, no matter how much indignation Nicky summoned, it would be over. Life would go on. The cops wouldn't even think about it anymore.

That can be tough to accept. In a funny, finders-keepers way this was Nicky's body, and he wanted what was best for it. And when most people encounter death they feel like it should mean something. Death is impressive, and if you don't see it every day— the way I had when I was a cop—then it seems more significant than it really is and you want it to add up to something important, noble and meaningful.

It doesn't. Death makes us all a little smaller and a little cheaper. There is so much of it, more of it than of anything else, and it is all that is guaranteed to us in life. You can have your nose rubbed in that a few times and get used to the idea, go on with waiting for it.

But if you're a small Australian New Age astrologer and aromatic oil salesman, the idea takes some getting used to.

CHAPTER SIX

Life goes on. That's not always good news, but it's always true. Life. Goes. On. Terrible things happen and we wonder why the sun doesn't stop dead in the sky, but it never does. At the same time that we're staring at the broken pieces of our life, somebody else is wondering whether to have another slice of bacon or go right for the cheesecake.

Life goes on. And a big part of my life was Nancy. Or it had been. Now I wasn't sure, and I needed to be. Nicky would come to terms with his dead body, one way or another, without me.

I realized how sour that seemed. I knew I should feel some concern, try to talk to Nicky and get him straightened away, feeling better about what had happened. But I was so used to having him try to cheer me up, it didn't seem right the other way around. I wouldn't know where to start. Besides, after being cooped up with him on the sailboat, I was ready for a vacation from manic energy, beer, handguns, and cries of, "EE-hah!"

I went into my house and turned on the huge, ancient, window-mounted air conditioner. The roar of it was like being on the flight line when a wing of B-25s takes off, but after a few minutes the room was cooler and I could turn the thing down to a level that didn't threaten to rupture ear drums on Duval Street.

When I left town all I could think of was trying to call Nancy.

All that had changed. I had been out of town, in the clean air and salty water, long enough for my head to clear and for my brain to organize all my thoughts. I waited for all the thoughts to look organized—it didn't happen. All I could think about was trying to call Nancy.

So I called Nancy. There was no answer at her place, and her answering machine wasn't turned on. That wasn't like her.

Now I was worried. Key West was no longer the sleepy fishing village it had been when I was a kid. Bad things happened here. It could have happened to her. She could be lying on her floor, helpless, slowly dying, wondering why I didn't come find her.

I had to do something, anything. Either that or turn into a permanent couch cover.

I went outside and looked at my car, a two-year-old Ford Explorer. I hadn't started it since April. No, wait; I had gone to that wedding in Marathon—late June?

It wasn't that long ago. The thing might even start. I climbed in and turned the key. The motor whined at me, complained of being tired, then finally kicked over, coughed, and started.

I idled it for a few minutes, letting the engine get used to the idea of running again. Pretty soon it sounded smoother and I put it in gear.

I drove over to Nancy's apartment. Her car was not in its parking space. A plastic Winn-Dixie bag had blown into her space. A litter of leaves and gum wrappers sat on top of the bag. I walked around to the front. There was a small clutter of mail sticking out of her mailbox.

I drove out to the hospital on Stock Island. Nancy's car was in the parking lot. I parked a few rows away, closer to the exit, and turned off the engine. I waited.

I wasn't sure what I was waiting for, more than just seeing Nancy. She was inside, sooner or later she would come out. And then—

What? Force her to reason with me? Keep her from getting into her car until she admitted she still loved me? Show her my winning smile and say, "Let's start all over"?

Confrontation didn't seem like any kind of answer. She could either dodge it or win it too quickly. I didn't want that.

So what did I want? I wanted her to love me, because I loved her. I couldn't make that happen. And by confronting her I might spoil the last chance of preserving it if she did still love me.

I wanted to see her—but only if she wanted to see me. Again, if she didn't want to, she could just get in her car and go, and probably that would kill the last chance, too. If there was one.

I knew all that. I had known it for weeks. It was why I hadn't done this before. So why was I sitting in the hospital parking lot in the hot sun, watching Nancy's car? Because—I had tried to call her. And there were too many times when she wasn't home and wasn't at work.

Where was she?

There was one very good, very simple and logical, answer. I just didn't like it. So I sat in the car. I found a peppermint and a stick of gum in the glove compartment. I ate the peppermint. It had been in the car so long that most of it clung to the wrapper, a soft and warm mush of sweetness. The flavor was still okay.

I watched people going in and out of the hospital. None of them noticed me. Most people wouldn't notice a UFO in a hospital parking lot. They're too wrapped up, thinking about what might happen to their precious, irreplaceable hides, or how they're going to get through the rest of their lives without somebody who's slipping away inside, or how they will ever pay for it all.

I've always thought that hospitals must know this, know that people won't notice anything at all beyond the clutter of tubes and shininess, the gurgle of life support machines. It's a diving board into death, either your own or someone you love, and no one can see beyond that. The hospitals know that. That explains the decor in the waiting rooms.

It was almost dark when Nancy finally came out to her car. A guy came out with her. He was tall and slender and very dark-skinned, almost blue-black. He wore a green hospital jacket with a pocket protector and a stethoscope around his neck. He walked Nancy to her car; a good idea, since even Key West has joined the 21st century. We have crack, and we have rapes, robberies, assaults, smash-and-grabs. I was glad Nancy was being safe and having someone walk her out.

The two of them reached her car, stopped for a minute to say something I couldn't hear, and then Nancy opened her car door. She turned back and the guy gave her a peck on the cheek. She reached behind his head and pulled his face down to hers. They stayed like that for a long moment. Then the guy took a half step back and stroked her face before he turned and walked back into the hospital.

Nancy watched him go for a minute. He turned once and waved. She smiled at him and climbed into her car.

She drove across Stock Island and I followed her. On the far side of the island from the hospital there is a series of trailer parks. Nancy drove into one of them, not the worst. She parked in front of one of the trailers, took a key from her purse and went inside.

I guess I had known it for a while. I had not admitted it, but the knowledge had been there at the edge of my thoughts, lurking the way something evil lurks under a kid's bed. Always there, hugging the dark, the thought had just been hiding, waiting to slide out and eat me when the lights were finally all out.

Nancy had somebody else. Of course I had known that. Finding love is easy in Key West. Keeping it may be impossible, but it is always there to be found.

Nancy had found somebody else.

Somebody else. The funny thing was, I felt a sense of relief. Sure, I was hurt, mad, hollow-feeling. But I was relieved, too. Now I knew. Now I was not in doubt, wondering where the relationship was going, wondering if it was even alive anymore.

It was dead. No room for doubt. I was out, the guy in the intern's coat was in. Ballgame over, no extra innings. Case closed. No appeal.

Somebody else.

I got home and found a bottle of peppermint schnapps somebody had left in my kitchen after a party. I poured a glass. I drank it. It was the traditional thing to do. It tasted awful. I could see why somebody had left it.

It was all I could do to drink the whole bottle.

CHAPTER SEVEN

The sun came up in the wrong place. It was supposed to be on the other wall and not so far *up*. There was something wrong with my neck, too. I wasn't sure, but I thought maybe it shouldn't be at that angle. Maybe that's why it hurt so much.

A weird-looking object squatted beside me. It seemed to be an empty bottle. I moved my head to look. My stomach roared. I had to get on my feet fast. That wasn't easy. First I had to find them.

I was lying on the floor beside the bed. Most of me anyway. My feet were up, tangled in the sheets. I yanked them free and made it to the bathroom just in time, trailing a stream of bed linen behind me.

Half an hour of shower, hot as I could stand it, helped a little. So did coffee, toast, aspirin.

When I was done I took a little walk to clear my head. It didn't seem to work, but at least I wasn't nauseated anymore. I was moving in slow motion. Everything seemed to be hard-edged and far away. I had to spend a lot of time on complicated things like opening the door.

At the corner I bought a newspaper, the Key West *Citizen*, and flipped it open.

How nice, I thought. That was a very good picture of Nicky. I didn't know he owned a tie. It must be from his official immigration file.

I looked at the picture for a long time before my brain got the next message down the wires. Oh. Right. Why is Nicky's picture on the front page?

I moved my eyes. They seemed to crackle when they turned. It hurt, but I focused them, tried to read the headline. *Local Businessman Chains Self To Conch Train*, it said. Of course. That would explain it. Sure. If Nicky chained himself to the Conch Train they would almost have to put his picture in the paper.

Another slow message worked through my brain: *This is not normal—even for Nicky*. I blinked. It felt good, so I held my eyes closed for a minute. I let the breeze move over my face. That felt good, too. This was a complicated problem, but maybe if I just stood with my eyes closed for a minute I could get it.

I opened my eyes and looked down at the newspaper. It was tough work, but I read the first few lines of the story.

Yup, that explained it. He *couldn't* come tell me about it.

Nicky was in jail.

• • •

A crowd of almost five people stood outside the jail. A few held signs saying, "FREE NICKY CAMERON," and "HAITIANS ARE HUMANS."

"Disturbing the peace," the on-duty sergeant told me, "Creating a nuisance, obstructing a public vehicle, and littering."

"Littering? Nicky?"

The sergeant shrugged. "He had a couple of signs about Haitian refugees with him. The wind blew 'em off."

I nodded. "Can I see him?"

He looked me over. The only decent thing I was wearing was my tan. And that was still a little green underneath. "You a lawyer?"

"A friend."

He glanced through a file folder with Nicky's name on it. "Your name Knight?"

"Mate," Nicky said as they led him in to the visiting room.

"What kept you?"

"Bad timing, Nicky."

He peered at me a little more carefully. "Christ on a bun, look at you. Hung fucking over, eh?"

"Just a little."

"A little, he says. Green as a gator, you are. You got completely pissed. Had yourself quite a party, eh?"

"Nothing like yours, Nicky."

He cackled. "Too right. You missed a doozy, Billy."

"Why did you put my name down as counsel, Nicky?"

He looked surprised. "So you'd get involved, Billy. Think I want you as my lawyer?"

I shook my head. It still hurt. Maybe it was the lingering hangover, but he wasn't making sense. At least, I hoped he wasn't. "The sergeant says they'll let you out. You just have to pay a fine."

"I don't want out, mate. Not until I get justice."

"That could take some time."

"As may be." He set his shoulders and tried to look tough and stubborn. "The fact is I made the front page and called attention to a very bad situation. While I stay here I'm making a statement they can't ignore. Reckon I can hold out a little longer, long as I'm doing some good."

"They're going to put you out in a couple of weeks anyway, Nicky."

"I can wait."

I stood up and waved at the guard. "I already paid."

He looked stubborn. "I won't go."

"As your counsel, it is my duty to advise you that the large officer standing behind you is going to commit an act of police brutality on you if you don't get out of his jail. And there are no members of the media present."

That seemed to be the clincher. Nicky wasn't afraid of much— except maybe a virus that would kill hops—but he wanted attention for his Cause. If there wasn't any to be had, why take the lumps?

The paperwork took a few more minutes. I had never realized

how hard it is to bust somebody out of jail if they don't really want to go. But I finally bullied him into signing the last of the forms and got him out the front door.

When we stepped outside there was a small cheer from the clot of protesters, and Nicky gave them a little speech. He told them the fight wasn't over and letting him out of jail couldn't break his spirit. Then he said there would be a big rally for Haitian Awareness tomorrow night and they should spread the word.

The sound of four people clapping was thunderous, but I managed to get him safely through the crush and home.

• • •

But as I drove Nicky home it hit me that he had a master plan for getting justice, and I was a big part of it. So when he stopped talking to a take a breath, I asked him. "What is it you think I can do?"

He beamed at me. "Fix it, Billy. It's something you're good at. You'll get this whole thing straightened out."

"*What* whole thing?"

He just kept smiling. "The Haitian thing, Billy. The Haitian problem. This body I found is only the tip of the iceberg. I've checked into it. The coppers aren't interested because this is an ordinary event. Happens all the time." He whacked my arm.

"Ow," I said.

"Does that strike you as a wanky little bit bizarre, mate? There's so many of these bodies they think of it as *normal?* I mean, if the captain got hit on the head by a frog turd he'd investigate, but if seven tons of reptile shit fell from the sky he'd call it weather? Eh? That make sense to you?"

"Yes," I said. "It's the way cops work. You can put your finger in a dike. You can't put your finger in the ocean."

He waved his finger at me. "Wrongo, Billy. Hundredth monkey. We can make a difference. Every one of us. Mass murder happens because nobody can believe it's happening. Nobody thinks they can stop it. And so Hitler invades Poland—"

"Nicky, hold on. This isn't mass murder—"

"Isn't it?"

"—this is just one Haitian refugee who didn't make it. I'm sorry, but it *does* happen all the time. They sail in tiny, leaky boats, so crowded they can't float—"

"With no money, Billy? With nothing in their pockets except a picture of Saint Patrick?"

I blinked and turned to look at him. He was still smiling, but it looked a little dangerous now. A horn snarled and I turned back in time to avoid broadsiding a van filled with bright pink Canadians. "What the hell are you talking about, Nicky?"

"I saw the file, Billy. The man's pockets were empty. A refugee has some cash, something of value. He has an address of friends or relatives tucked away. Christ on a bun, mate, he has a wallet on him any road. This man didn't."

I shook my head. "That doesn't mean anything."

"Aw spit, Billy. You know it does."

"It might have fallen out. It might have been in a backpack. His wife might have been holding it. There are a hundred explanations—"

"Or one very simple one. Somebody went through his pockets before they chucked him over into the drink."

"And anyway this isn't my problem. I'm not James Bond, Nicky. I take people fishing."

Nicky just shook his head. "You can't fight it, Billy. You're already in this. You may not know it yet, but you're hooked." And he settled back with a smug look on his face.

I got a very ugly suspicion. "Nicky," I said.

"Yeah, mate?"

"Why did you get yourself arrested?"

He tried to look surprised. "To wake you up, Billy. To get your attention. To get you involved."

I felt like I was in one of those old cartoons. I was Elmer Fudd with steam coming out of my ears while Bugs Bunny calmly chewed one of my prize carrots in my face. "You went to jail just to get me involved?"

Nicky smirked. "And here you are. The hook is set. You'll fight it, but it's too late. You're in."

I came as close to hitting Nicky as I'd ever been since I'd met him. But nothing I could think of to say made a dent in his cast-iron smug certainty that I was going to get involved and fix everything.

I got him home without strangling him, but that may be because the hangover had slowed me down. I told Nicky there was a lot in what he said and I would think about it. Then I made him promise not to do anything more about making people aware of the problem without telling me first. That cheered him up. It meant I was involved. He agreed, and was happily opening a couple of beers when I closed his front door and hopped the short coral wall to my own yard.

I spent most of that day circling around my living room until I couldn't stand it any longer. I rode my bicycle over to the marina, dodging around Art's dockmaster shack. I didn't want to listen to a list of my shortcomings right now.

Nobody had stolen my boat. Nobody had cleaned the moss off the bottom, either. I sat and looked at it for a while. I could almost see the barnacles grow.

This was supposed to be what I wanted. This was why I had come here. To take a small boat out onto the flats and catch fish every day. Lately every day had turned into every now and then, but the desire to do it was still there. Wasn't it?

I didn't know. There was a hollow place where hope and desire had been carved out of me. Maybe it would grow back. Maybe it was dead, burned away by the August heat.

I wondered if Nancy was happy.

CHAPTER EIGHT

It was about an hour from sunset when I got back to my house. Nicky waited for me in my kitchen. "Mate," he said pleasantly. "Have a cold one." He generously handed me one of my own beers. "Thanks,"

"So," he said casually. "What're your plans for the evening, mate?"

"I'm off duty tonight. I don't feel up to saving the world."

Nicky gave me a look of complete and permanent innocence. It was one of his best. "What's that, eh? Did I say fetch the Batmobile? Put on the cape? Didn't I say have a beer? Your name's Billy, not Silly."

He said that last like it solved everything, with the complete satisfaction of an Australian who has ended an argument with a rhyme. I don't know why they feel that way about putting two rhyming words together, but they do. Rhymes had a magical power for Nicky and his countrymen. Even if it doesn't mean anything, an Australian hit with a rhyme will back off, mutter, "Right, sorry," and call for another round, on him. Maybe it comes from living in a place where all the towns have names like "Woolamaroo," "Kalgoorlie," and "Wollongong." In a landscape littered with impossible sounds, putting two of them together is so unlikely it must call for an automatic celebration.

"You've gone all sour," he told me, grabbing himself

another beer.

"I know," I said. "Art already told me."

"It's more than Nancy. Though that might have turned it loose. But it was already there."

"Think so?"

"Too right. I think Nancy sensed it first, and that may have had something to do with why she pulled out."

"Good to know."

"The point is," he said, after draining half the bottle, "you've lost your *zest*." He wagged a finger at me. "Can't do that, mate. Man's got to have his zest."

"I know. Grab for all the gusto you can get. I've seen the commercials."

"You can laugh if you want," he said, looking slightly hurt.

"Actually, I don't think I can."

"But the point is, you're a bloody mess."

"Are you going someplace with this?"

"Too right I am. Finish your beer."

I finished my beer. Nicky finished three in the same time. It didn't seem to affect him. I've never seen beer affect him in any way. Then he led me out the door and, to my surprise, over to Mallory Square.

Mallory Square is a small cross-section of life on earth. Nobody knows where it came from, or how it started, but it keeps growing and leaving a bigger mess. Originally the Square was a big parking lot next to an old concrete wharf. Now it's a carnival, a street fair from one of those out-of-focus Italian films. There are jugglers, a sad magician, a high-wire act, trained animals, musicians, food vendors, and because it's Key West, T-shirt salesmen. And the whole thing is supposed to be a celebration of sunset. But for me it was like going to the top of the Empire State Building if you live in Manhattan. It's strictly for tourists.

"Bet you haven't seen 'er for a while," Nicky said as we walked through the parking lot and towards the crowd at the far end.

"Why would I, for God's sake?"

He winked at me. "It's fun. Remember fun?"

"Not really," I said.

"Sour," he said again, shaking his head.

We pushed in past a row of tables selling cheap jewelry. Nicky seemed to enjoy himself. He laughed at the performers' bad jokes, clapped at the silly tricks, put dollar bills in the hat each time it was passed.

He dragged me all the way down the line, pausing for each act. I let him, stewing in a kind of uninvolved stupor. But eventually it all started to get to me.

"Nicky," I said, with a small edge of anger.

"Relax. This is just exactly what you need. Straight up, you'll see."

We pushed through the crowd. I didn't try to get too close. I had seen all the acts, practically memorized some of them, the ones that had been there the longest.

Nicky was humming happily, in spite of the constant threat of getting lost in a large crowd of steadily moving people, all a foot taller than he was. He had bought a couple of gigantic cookies and was working through them like a termite with rabies, spewing cookie dust in all directions. He always eats like that, with reckless disregard for community standards.

One small girl, about six years old, stopped to watch him eat the cookie, unable to believe that anybody was allowed to eat like that. A large hand yanked her back into the stream of gawkers.

We moved along the line of performers. There was a certain familiar rhythm to the place, like the tides. Nothing changed here; it was a look at the heart of Key West, with the steady rhythm of the people moving through, dropping their money into the stream, and disappearing again. The fact that there were new faces every night was less significant than the fact that there were always faces.

After a while I started to relax a little. Nicky was right. This was a great place to not think, and it provided just what I needed, a reminder that life goes on.

Just as I was starting to pick up the rhythm and blank my mind, I heard something new, and it jolted me out of my trance.

A crowd was gathered where there was not supposed to be a crowd. This had been a dead area on the dock. A guy with dreadlocks and a guitar had the spot staked out, and he droned half-hearted reggae to two or three people at a time. He'd been doing it as long as I could remember.

Something was different tonight. For the first time the guy sounded interested in his own music.

Normally there would be one small child watching him, clinging to the hand of an impatient adult. Now the crowd was three people deep, elbow to elbow, and they were craning their necks to see. Curious, I moved around the edge of the crowd and found a place where I could see.

A beautiful young woman with short blonde hair was doing a gymnast's floor routine, working to the reggae beat with the grace and intensity you only see in Eastern European athletes at the Olympics. I watched her do an amazingly elegant walkover, up onto her hands and then over into a perfect split. As her hands went up for applause I caught her eye, and—

"That's a whacka-toodly in the fan-doodly, eh?" said Nicky.

I stared at him. "What language is that?"

He nodded at the woman. "Bet that hurts."

I looked back at the gymnast. Her back was to me as she began another complicated series of moves. It was a good back; slim and sleek.

I must have watched her a little too long. When I looked up, Nicky was staring at me with his gigantic, gleaming eyes.

"What," I said.

"Nothin', mate. Ab-so-toodly nothin'."

Somewhere between irritation and embarrassment, I turned away and shoved through the crowd, down to the far end of the dock where they sell a pretty good conch fritter. I bought some and munched grumpily, staring out over the water at the idiots on the sunset cruise boats. Probably thought they were having fun. Bah. Humbug.

After a few minutes Nicky joined me. He went through three

or four of the fritters with the same whacked-out recklessness, making chunks fly in all directions, completely unaware that he was attracting stares.

"You should put down a hat," I told him. "Make people think you're trying to do that."

He shoved in the last chunk of fritter. I waited for applause, but the sun was gone and the crowds were thinning now. And as the last glow of the sun faded from the water and the circus trickled away, Nicky dragged me from Mallory Square and over to a battered old conch house near the cemetery in Old Town.

The house was owned by a woman who worked publicity for one of the big hotels. Like most local parties this one ignored class lines; there were cleaning crews from the hotel, writers, waiters and bartenders, hotel executives, even lawyers—every level of local society mixed together in a crazy swirl.

There were a lot of sarongs showing, most of them on women. I had a beer and ate some bad sushi. I listened to a man lecture me about the bond market before excusing himself to throw up in the back yard. A large woman in a floor-length muumuu explained to me that musical theatre was America's one great contribution to world culture and I really should see *Cats* next time I was in New York.

I had a few more beers. *So this is fun*, I thought. I edged towards the door.

"Billy! Mate!" came the small foghorn voice. I turned, cornered.

Nicky chugged at me with a beer in one hand and towing a beautiful woman with the other. I felt a strange churning somewhere inside; it was the gymnast from Mallory Square. She wore white overalls and an expression of patient embarrassment. "Billy, this is Anna."

Our eyes met. There was a sort of electric thump at the back of my head and then she looked away, blushing. "How do you do," she said. She had an accent I could not place, something middle European that sounded harsh and musical at the same time.

"Hello," I replied, still trying to figure out what I was feeling.

"Anna's new in town, Billy. Chat 'er up a bit, eh?" Nicky said, squeezing my elbow. Then he cackled and vanished into the crowd.

Anna looked embarrassed. I would have, too, except I was busy being confused, and mad at Nicky. He was ruining a perfectly good sulk.

"My name is Billy Knight," I said, sounding stiff to my own ears.

She looked me over and our eyes met. She looked away. "Yes," she said. "Anna Kovacic." She said it *ko-va-CHEECH*.

"I saw you at Mallory Square, doing your act."

There was a challenge in her blue eyes, the bluest I had ever seen. "This is no act," she said. "It is to do this, or to clean in hotel rooms."

"Where are you from?" I asked her. Not brilliant, but I wasn't expecting the reaction I got. Her head snapped back to me and her eyes were suddenly burning.

"Ukraine," she said.

"Oh." There didn't seem to be a whole lot to say to that. "How long have you been in Key West?"

Her face didn't change, but she wasn't seeing me anymore. "Since they are killing all my family there."

"I'm sorry," I said.

"Yes." She looked away again.

And that really should have been the end of it. There is really and truly nothing to say when someone tells you they have recently moved to Key West because their whole family was killed. This is where normal people scramble for an even half-graceful exit. This is where I should have run for the cover of a cold beer and another bowl of peanuts.

But something about the way she said it, like it was a challenge, made me stay and look for a way to keep the conversation going.

So what I came out with was, "How did you meet Nicky?"

She turned cold blue eyes on me. "Who?"

"The dwarf who brought you over here."

She turned briefly, looking through the party for Nicky. "He is called Nicky?" She said it *Nyecky*.

"Yeah."

"Ah," she said. "I am first meeting him just now. He is talking very hot about Haitian ruffo… rufo… How you are calling the ones who come on the boats?"

"Refugees."

"Yes, refugees. And I say, well, we are taught when I am young America is not the land of the free if you are a black person. And he is very happy I say this. And after he talks for a minute more, he is looking around and seeing you. Then he takes my arm and say, come with me, dolly. Then he is dragging me here and *poom*—" She shrugged. Her shoulders rippled.

I caught myself noticing that her shoulders rippled. I tried to remind myself that I was still trying to get over Nancy and I really shouldn't be noticing anything like that right now. It was the sign of a shallow man.

But I did notice. And I noticed the graceful line of her neck, the outline of collarbone, the sleek perfection of a figure that had started good and got better through hard work. And the clear light in her eyes, the light of intelligence, wonder, doubt, thought.

Okay, I was shallow.

"Now that you're here," I said with a deep breath, "can I get you something to drink?"

She blushed. "Thank you. But I—" She was going to say no; maybe out of habit or insecurity, but not out of indifference, I was sure. Instead, she looked at me out of the corner of her eye, hesitated, and gave me the most serious smile I had ever seen. "Perhaps one of those yellow sodas?"

I got her a Mountain Dew. She accepted it politely and drank about half in one swallow. I admired the way her throat muscles worked as she swallowed.

We talked. Anna loosened up a little with a soda in her hand. So did I. She was astonished to learn what I did for a living. "I think everybody in America is a rich lawyer," she said. "And you say to be a poor fishermen? Feh."

"Not exactly. I take other people fishing. It pays a little better than if I was fishing myself."

She looked doubtful. "In my country, fishermen is a very poor job. Very smelly."

"In your country, people won't pay $450 a day to go fishing. But the fish smell the same."

She said something with a lot of consonants. "So much! For a fish?"

"Welcome to capitalist imperialism. How did you end up in Mallory Square?"

She gave me a half-sour look. "First, is what I do now. But then—" She shrugged. Those beautiful neck muscles moved again. "When I am small, I train to do gymnastic. But by the time of 16 years, 17 years, this career is over, yes? I am too big." She made hand gestures to show how fat she was. I didn't believe it.

"So when—when I come here I work in the hotel as a maid, clean the rooms. And in this country they are making you feel to be an animal to do this work. I watch through the windows of all the rooms every day, and I see Mallory Square, and I think I can do this and not have to feel I am a dog."

She slanted a long look at me through thick lashes. "They are saying this is black girl's work, to clean rooms in a hotel. It is very hard for me to see that some things in this country are just as Putin says."

"America has a race problem," I said. "Always has. Maybe it always will. I didn't used to think so, but—"

"Is this why they send these Haitians home, as Nicky is saying? Because they are black people?"

"Nicky is not well right now on the subject of Haitians. But that's part of it."

"Why is he not well? What do you mean?"

I told her about our sailboat trip, about finding the body. "It isn't pretty. But this happens every day and the police tend to think it's somebody else's problem."

"Whose problem?"

"The Haitians."

"And what do the people say?" I must have looked confused.

"You know, the everybody."

"The everybody doesn't hear much about it, doesn't think much about it."

"And does not care because these others are black people? So if they are dying every day, this is nothing?"

I'd been hearing this from Nicky a little too much lately. On top of everything else, the subject had dropped to the bottom of my list of Things To Talk About With Beautiful Women at Parties.

But there she was, wanting to talk about it. I couldn't very well say, "Yeah, you're right—hey! Wanna see my boat?" No matter how much I wanted to do exactly that. So I said, "Well, it's a little more complicated than that."

She made a face. It looked like Avenging Justice. "So. And this is the answer of someone who will not say the truth because truth is looking too bad, hah? The answer of *politician*. The answer of so many in my country who say, but is not my problem who is killed, these are not my people."

She threw her hands up in the air. "And so nobody is doing anything because is not their problem, and by the time is their problem they are not *able* to do anything and soon *everybody* is dead, ha? Because in my country I learn. Oppression is always the problem of everybody. You must either fight for others when you can, or you become others."

She dropped the empty soda can into my hand. "Thank you for soda," she said, and turned away. My mouth was still open when she walked out the door and into the night.

There were a lot of opinions I could have had about her and her attitude. That she didn't know me and had no right to judge me like that was one. And anyway, what did I care? I was still getting over Nancy.

It was nice to see that I was finally thinking clearly. The only problem was that my body wasn't listening; it was busy following Anna out the door.

CHAPTER NINE

The night was alive with the smell of things blooming, the way it can only smell in South Florida. It is a thick heady scent of orchids and rotting vegetables on top of the faint tang of low tide and it makes the hair stand up on your arms and gives you the feeling that you could live forever if you could just keep that smell in your nose.

I looked around for Anna. I saw her walking towards the center of Old Town. Still not sure what the hell I was doing, or why, I ran after her.

I caught up with her at the corner. She didn't want to be caught. She gave me a look of icy indifference and kept walking.

"Excuse me," I said. She did not look at me again. Now I was starting to get a little mad. "Is this the way they talk about things where you come from?" I said. "You give your opinion, which is always right, and then run out the door before anyone else can say something that might not agree?"

"Oh," she said without looking. "You are now having an *opinion*. This is very good. Very much progress."

"It must be so hard on you," I said. "To understand everything. Nobody else even knows enough to congratulate you."

She stopped walking. Her shoulders went up. They did it very well. "*Feh,*" she said. "And you, to be judge of *everything*. Like all

Americans, you have this thing which says, I am in right, piss on you, hah? When you have beer, who cares that others die of thirst? Feh!"

It's funny. Sometimes even when you're mad other things filter in and hit you. Right now, instead of shouting back at her with a really snappy comeback, all I could think of was how cute she sounding saying, "peess on yoo," with that beautiful strange accent.

I stuttered. I had been about to say, "I'm not like all Americans," but that was wrong, not what I wanted to say, and then she said "Peess" so cute. What came out of my mouth was something like, "I'm nee-hi hut!"

She thought I was making fun of her, so she glared at me. I glared back. We just stood glaring under a streetlight.

I cracked first. I couldn't help it; I was suddenly swamped by an overwhelming need to laugh. I fought it hard, but I couldn't beat it. A little snorting sound came out my nose. It was followed by a big snorting sound, a cough, a short laugh, and then, when something went down my windpipe wrong, a prolonged and crippling fit of coughing.

Anna stared at me. First with anger, then scorn, then a kind of puzzled concern. And as I slowly folded to the ground to sit helpless on the curb, she stood over me, looking down, then looking around for help, then folding her arms and just standing over me.

And just as I thought I might be able to breathe again, she said, "And so when you can't win argument you try for sympathy to kill your self with coughter."

It almost killed me. I think I laughed for several minutes, choking and fighting for breath.

Anna watched me. She stood with a face like one of those Greek statues, towering above me as I crouched helpless below her. And after a few more moments she snickered. Then she made the same kind of snorting sound I had made. It caught her by surprise. She laughed. And pretty soon there were two of us rolling on the pavement choking with laughter.

And just when we began to get it under control, catch our breath a little, an elderly gentlemen in a white suit walked by, trailed by an attentive elderly Filipino. White Suit stopped and stared at us with a look of the most complete disapproval I have ever seen.

That set us off again, and as we rolled together, howling with laughter, the Filipino took White Suit by the elbow and led him away, turning once to glare at us.

It was several hours and seven uncontrollable fits of laughter later that we ended up on the end of the long wooden dock at the end of Duval Street. When you laugh that long and that hard with somebody it gives you a feeling that you've known them a long time, and we were struggling to figure out what to do about this new-old friendship.

A kind of funny tact came over us. Neither one of us wanted to say anything that would break the illusion. So we leaned on the rail side by side, talking of things that didn't matter, listening for what was behind them.

She liked dogs. But she found it impossible to turn down a cat. She thought there was nothing on American TV that wasn't bad for you, except wrestling. She loved wrestling, because for her it was like a great theatre where Good battled Evil and myths were worked out.

She had also become passionate about American peanut butter, but she thought of it as a dessert item.

Pretty soon I became aware that the bars were closing all around us and the loud music had been silent for a while. And suddenly we were in the middle of that awkward moment that comes at the end of an evening when you know it has to end but you don't want it to and the way it's going to end hasn't been worked out yet.

As I walked her home it still wasn't worked out. She lived in Old Town, in an alley off Eaton, in a guest cottage attached to one of the big old houses. She shared it with two Polish women who worked as maids at one of the hotels.

"Thank you for most interesting evening," she said in her wonderful accent, standing at the door of the small green house.

"Maybe we could have another one some time," I said.

She looked at me for a very long time and I found myself moving closer a little at a time. Just before my face touched her she said, "Perhaps," very softly, and slid away into her house.

I watched the outside of the door for a while, but it didn't tell me anything, so I walked home.

CHAPTER TEN

The last time I'd been to a demonstration I'd been in uniform, standing in front of the Iranian consulate in L.A. I'd been to a couple more before that, all of them as a cop. So Nicky's little get-together was a brand new experience for me.

I don't mind the idea of standing in the street and waving a sign while you chant cute rhymes, but I'd always looked on it as either work or a kind of spectator sport.

So it still isn't clear to me how I ended up in front of the Key West Court House carrying a sign that said *GIVE ME YOUR TIRED, YOUR POOR, YOUR WHITE MASSES* and shouting, "Haitians Are Humans." The shouting part was sort of halfhearted on my part; in fact, really only when Anna was looking.

I say it wasn't clear how I ended up there, but of course it was. I was there because I thought Anna would be there. No matter how stupid I felt doing it, the thought of seeing her again made stupid seem like a good idea.

Of course I had a lot to tell myself on the subject. I still wasn't over Nancy. And getting interested in someone else so soon was shallow, not like me, the mark of a butt-head.

But no matter what I told myself, I managed to work it around to where I should just go take a look at her and prove it to myself that I wasn't really all that interested in her. And I somehow even made that justify going to Nicky's demonstration.

And when I got there and she saw me and her face lit up, I would have gone into a snake pit to protest venom.

Bad news. I was shallow.

And so for the next couple of hours I stood around watching her profile and trying to figure out what the hell was wrong with me. I didn't come up with anything, and anyway I was distracted thinking about what was so right with her.

At the climax of the rally, Nicky stood in front of the nearly fifteen people and gave a speech. He said that he wasn't born here, and he knew some of them weren't born here, and that was part of what made the country such a great place. He managed to imply that it had been a pretty smart thing for the U.S. to let in somebody like him, so they should listen up when he said Haitians should be allowed to enter the country.

Everybody yelled and waved their signs. I saw a couple of people taking pictures, but since one of them was holding a little girl by the hand and the other was in the middle of a cluster of Japanese tourists, I figured the only media exposure Nicky was going to get was going to be in a slide show in Osaka.

The most you could say we accomplished with all that marching in circles was that I decided Anna's profile was not actually *perfect*: her chin was just a little too strong. Realizing that made me feel a lot better, like I could be objective now. Thinking in a really objective way, I decided I preferred strong chins.

When we broke up I walked Anna down to Mallory Square and watched her evening show. She got a good crowd. I kept an eye on the bucket she used to collect money. I stood beside a fat guy, from New Jersey by his accent, who thought he was funny enough to compete with Anna's act. I convinced him he was wrong without disturbing her, and his finger probably wasn't actually broken.

Afterwards we walked again. I bought her a piece of fish at a restaurant and we walked some more. We ended up outside her door again at around midnight. She was gone inside before I could even think about going beyond her smile.

The pattern held for the next few days. I got to know the outside of Anna's door really well. And I thought I was getting to know her, too, from our long talks, but it's easy to be wrong about that.

I am only a human being. I try to be better than average at it, but there are parts of the job that are bigger than all of us. When two human beings of different genders spend a lot of time together and want to spend more time together, a certain question comes up. In this case, as far as I was concerned, the only question was, "How soon?"

I appreciated the fact that Anna came from a different culture. I respected her right to make a decision, whatever it might be. And if she didn't make it soon I was going to pop a seam.

After a few more nights when nothing changed, I walked Anna home after her show. She seemed moody, withdrawn and tense. When we got to her door, she turned where she usually said good night and stared at me for a long moment. Then she launched herself at me. Her lips were all over my face and her hands fluttered all over me. Her breath came hard and fast and it took me a few fast heartbeats to realize that it wasn't passion.

I tried to step back, disengage, but she clung to me with a furious strength, pressing her cold face into the hollow of my neck and shoulder.

"Anna?" I said. She pushed her body against me tighter. "Hey, Anna?" She made a muffled sound that might have been anything. "Damn it, Anna!" I got my arms free and grabbed her in a bear hug, pinning her arms to her side.

She didn't struggle. Her body got very stiff, and seemed to increase in weight until she was as heavy as me. Then she went limp, and as I held her the light from a streetlight showed a line of tears down her face.

"Anna, for God's sake—" I started.

"They are saying me I must sex you or you go away," she said.

"What?"

"They are saying me, big handsome man who does not like boys, this is most rare in Key West and I must not let you go. And I do not want to let you go. So I must sex you."

"What the—Who said—?"

"And I am thinking only of the soldiers when I am thinking of this, I am not ready yet to sex and they are saying I must be ready, in America is quicker for ready. And with you I want to try again—I must try again—But I can think only of the soldiers—" And she collapsed into wracking, gut-wrenching crying.

It took me a few minutes. First I had to wait for Anna to pull herself together. She was not a person who could be jollied or gentled. The strength I had seen in her carried over to her emotions, which couldn't be persuaded by anyone or anything. They had to run their course.

When Anna was back in control she told me that her roommates—who had been in this country much longer than she had, more than a year now—had explained to her all about dating in America. They told her that a woman must sex the man or he would think she was a bad person. I guess they watched a lot of soap operas while they made the beds. Or maybe I'd just dated the wrong women.

And so Anna had tried. She had come to like me very much and did not want me to think she was a bad person. She did not want me to stop being with her. So she had tried to sex me. But all she could think was what happened at home when the soldiers came.

We sat there on the front step of her small bungalow and she told me things that didn't seem possible if you heard them under the moon in Key West, with the small evening breeze pulling at her fine blond hair.

It was a pretty simple story and Anna told it simply. The sobbing stopped and her voice froze over as she told me. There was no emotion in her for this.

She had been raped. Her family had been killed. The soldiers had left her for dead, too. She had lived, buried the bodies, made her way slowly to the West. Come to Key West by a sort of drifting motion that brings so many people down here.

I couldn't think of a whole lot to say. I kept one arm around her, making small circles on her back with my hand. I don't think she noticed.

When she finished telling me, Anna sat stiffly, not looking at anything. So did I.

"So," she said after a while.

"Anna," I said.

"I like you, Billy, very much. I would like to do love with you. But I am thinking of doing this and I can think only of the soldiers."

"It takes time, Anna. I understand that."

"But how are you now feeling about the soldiers?"

"I want to kill them."

"You do not think me a trash?"

"For God's sake, Anna."

She nodded. "Yes. But my friends are saying me, if I say to you what happened you are no longer wanting to be with me. Because I have been so much raped and you will no longer want to sex me."

I kept an arm around Anna. I didn't know what else to do. "I'd be happy to sex you," I said. "But only when you want to."

She would not look at me. "This is not true, this is just talk. Men have the pressure to build up and they must sex often. I will lose you."

I hadn't tried that line since high school and it hadn't worked then. Maybe I should have gone to high school in Ukraine.

"Listen," I said, "Men have the pressure build up, yes. But a man can control it. I'll wait until you're ready. You won't lose me."

Now she looked up at me. She combed my face for a sign that I was lying. I didn't think I was, and after a minute I guess she didn't think so either.

"We will see," she said at last.

"Yes," I told her. "We will."

CHAPTER ELEVEN

We did see. Over the next week I saw Anna every night, and every night I said goodnight to her outside her door. It was easy. All it took was a strong will, the memory of her story, and an ice cold shower every fifteen minutes.

I guess it could have gone on like that for the rest of that awful August and no one would have noticed that anything was wrong. But nature doesn't work that way. Wherever things are locked into existing one way, there's something chewing at the corner of the picture, trying to change it. And the change is almost never for the good.

Nicky came to my place on a Friday afternoon as I was stepping out of my third cold shower of the day and into a pair of shorts.

"Well, mate," he said. "I guess you've seen it."

I pulled on a shirt. "Seen what?"

He threw a copy of the morning paper at my head and I snatched it out of the air. "Page seven," he said.

I folded the paper open to page seven and found, halfway down, a headline that had been circled in red ink.

BODIES FOUND. I looked up at Nicky.

"Read the story, Billy," he said. "Read it."

It wasn't much of a story. Just a couple of paragraphs saying that on two different occasions, the Coast Guard had brought in three bodies. Some fishing boats had found them in the Gulf Stream off the lower Keys. All three were thought to be Haitian nationals.

I looked up at Nicky. "Haitian nationals," he said significantly.

I threw the paper back at him. "Listen," I said. "I'm sorry for the Haitian nationals. I wish these three weren't dead. But it happens a lot, Nicky. It doesn't mean anything."

He pulled out one of those charts of the Keys they give to tourists and opened it in front of my face. "This does," he said. "Look here. We found our man on a Thursday, right here." He pointed to where he had written in a big red one on the chart. "Right here, on a Friday, off Marathon, the next two. And here, right close to number one, a Thursday again."

He jammed his elbow into my ribs. "Eh? Well?"

"Well what?"

He blinked at me as if he couldn't believe anybody was so slow. "It's a schedule, Billy. Somebody is keeping an exact schedule, killing these people by the clock." He pointed to one and three on the chart. "Thursday, Thursday. And Marathon is one day's sail North."

I shook my head. "Nicky—"

"There's more, mate. All four of 'em had empty pockets, no ID, no money, nothing. Highly unusual, mate, you said so yourself."

"You've been hassling the cops again."

He looked indignant. "'Course I have. They're not doing bloody fuck-all about this. 'Course I'm hassling the bloody cops."

Nicky hadn't said a word about Haitians or murder for a week and I had been dumb enough to think it meant he had let the whole thing slip away into his New Age Conspiracy network. But he had obviously been spending the time building his case instead.

"Why?"

He blinked. "Eh?"

"Why hassle the cops? Why hassle me?"

He looked at me with real pity. "Somebody's gettin' away with wholesale murder. Isn't that the sort of thing we're all supposed to try and stop?"

"There's no evidence of murder."

"There's four dead bodies, mate. All found in the Stream, all with empty pockets. And if they've found four, how many you reckon they've missed, eh?"

"That doesn't prove—"

"Prove is a word for lawyers. We're not lawyers. Just simple human fuckin' beings. Just like the ones turning up dead. Get your fuckin' head out of the sand, mate."

And he was away out the door, madder than I could remember seeing him before.

It wasn't right to say I didn't know what had gotten into him. I did; I just hadn't known it had gotten that *far* into him,

And anyway, what the hell was I supposed to do about it? Even if he was right—even if some cold-blooded maniac, for whatever reason, was killing Haitians and dumping them in the Gulf Stream—what did Nicky think I could do to stop it?

I knew he had a warped picture of me as a sleepy, sun-dazed killer. Nicky saw me as a kind of human alligator, dozing until lashed up by the smell of meat. He had an almost supernatural confidence in my ability to handle anything physical.

But this was far beyond anything he had ever expected from me before. Find a hypothetical killer working on a hypothetical ship somewhere in the Atlantic Ocean—this wasn't even a job for Superman. He would politely decline and ask for a little more evidence first. Because damn it, the world didn't work that way.

Besides, I had come to Key West to retire. The only thing I wanted to find was fish.

I explained all that to Anna that evening. I laid it all out for her, almost word for word, telling her exactly what had happened and trying to tell it in a light, funny way. It was hard to get her to smile, but it was worth it and I was hoping she would try it when she heard of Nicky's innocence.

We were sitting at a small table overlooking the water. It was Friday night, after all, and I was celebrating. Spending money I didn't really have on an unclear relationship to celebrate the end of a week in which I had done no real work; Friday night in America.

I had pulled out all the stops and taken Anna over to Louie's Back Yard, one of the classiest restaurants in the Keys. Anna had been so impressed she had even had half of a glass of white wine.

But a slow flush was climbing up her neck and onto her face. I trickled to a stop.

"Why is this funny?" she said slowly.

"It's not funny," I said. "Nicky's funny."

"He is having very high opinion of you, of what you can do."

"He is wrong."

She looked at me for just a moment, then pushed back her chair. "Yes," she said. "I think so, too." And before I could do more than drop my jaw she got up and walked out of the restaurant.

I found her on the small spit of sand next to the restaurant. She was looking out over the water and throwing rocks with a controlled fury. A light, easy chop moved across the water and Anna skipped a rock across the top of a whitecap. It seemed like a good idea not to say anything, so I didn't. She didn't look up or acknowledge that I was there, just threw a couple more rocks.

"You are most furyfying man I am knowing ever," she said at last. She flung another rock far out into the water. "I am now knowing what is inside you, I think. Nicky is knowing this too, better as you. Inside you is wonderful strong man who can do what no one else can do. But you are not knowing this. Instead you are acting as the little boy. Instead you are saying, is too big the problem and too small the me. Is nothing that can be done by me. And this is cow shits."

"What is it you think I should do?"

She turned to me, a look of angry surprise on her face. "But how am I knowing this? If I am knowing, I am doing it. You are once a policeman, you have guns and boats. Why do you not stop the killings?"

A little light flickered on in the back of my head. "You've been talking to Nicky," I said.

"Yes? And this is now bad to talk to him?"

"Only if you believe him."

She turned away again, stooping to pick up some rocks. She threw one. "What I believe—is there are dead bodies. If is by accident they are dead, fine. You will find this out, feh—" she made a kind of final gesture with one hand, "—is over."

She flung down the rocks and turned to me, stamping her foot. "But God-damness, if is not accident, it is an evil. A killing of so many—! And you must stop it."

"There are police to do that. Not me. I'm just a fishing guide, I don't—"

"No. Listen. I come here to this country to escape a very bad thing. And it is getting very bad there because everyone is saying the same. This is not my problem. This has to do with those others, not with me. I know this because I am saying it. And of a sudden are the soldiers there, inside my house, killing my family."

"This is different."

She shrugged. "Is always different. And so is always the same."

I picked up a rock and threw it. It went further than Anna's. That was one thing I could feel good about. "Yes, but—" I started, and then I stopped again. I didn't know what to say that wouldn't hurt. "This isn't like what happened to you," I said.

"And how can you say so?"

"Because there are no armies and no cities. There are Haitians every day who try to cross to America. In tiny boats, inner tubes, anything that floats. Some of them don't make it. And there's nothing to say that these bodies were any different. There's no sign of violence. There's not even any footprints. Only a few bodies and a big ocean."

"And so you do not even try?"

"Let me finish. Just say for a minute that you and Nicky are right, that somebody is routinely killing Haitian refugees."

"Yes, we are right."

"Fine. Exactly what is it you want me to do?"

She shook her head at me like I was stupid. I was beginning to feel like I was. "You will find them and stop them," she said.

"Find 'em and stop 'em. Sure, that sounds easy."

She spun on me, very fast, and threw a punch. She did not hit like a girl. I rubbed my arm and looked at her. "If was it easy, Nicky would doing it. Jesus shit, you are the one who is knowing this things, why do you behave so? To fail at this, okay, too bad, I am sorry but something was done about it. But to not try because is looking too difficult, when people are being killed and no one is caring—feh!"

"To fail at this, I will be killed," I said.

"Then you must not fail," she said. "I will not let you."

"I'll take a look," I said. "No promises, no hero stuff. Just a few questions to see what's going on."

She frowned, then nodded. "Good," she said. "That will be good."

CHAPTER TWELVE

The trip up to Miami is a long one by car, but I like it that way. The harder it is for the idiots to get down to Key West, the fewer of them we'll have roaming Duval Street.

Of course, nowadays they come by air, and by water, and even by bicycle, and there are more of them every year. Soon our small island will sink into the ocean from the weight of so many people. And in a few hundred years, divers will still be poking through the sunken wreckage and bringing up T-shirts and beer mugs.

But for now, the road from Key West to Miami was mostly only one lane each way, and if you timed it right the traffic wasn't too bad. Except that I usually ended up behind a long line of RVs, breathing thick exhaust and plodding along at thirty-five miles an hour. But it was better than the Santa Monica Freeway. And the long trip gave me time to think.

What I mostly thought was that I was on a fool's errand. A dumb, pointless quest to save a maiden from an imaginary dragon. And why? So Anna would sleep at night? Maybe with me?

But Anna was right about one thing. Checking this out wouldn't be that hard for me. At least I had a place to start. If any U.S. law enforcement organization was looking into this, from the Coast Guard to the Cub Scouts, they would be doing it out of Miami. And if anybody in Miami knew anything about it, the Deacon would know, too.

He was called Deacon because he was a lay minister and the only thing he was more serious about was stopping crime. Deacon was a supervisor in the F.D.L.E., the Florida state equivalent of the FBI. The bureaucrats kept trying to promote him out of harm's way, since he had a habit of getting into gunfights. Always justifiable, and he always won. But the new breed of law enforcement administrators preferred quieter law enforcement and tried to maneuver him into a chair in the office.

So far he had dodged it. Deacon had turned down promotions a couple of times so he could stay on the street. His life was a kind of constant struggle, stuck between the bad guys on the street and the suits in the office. He stayed out of the office as much as possible.

I knew Deacon's mobile phone number and as soon as I got into Miami I called him. We arranged to meet in the parking lot of a shopping center on the edge of Liberty City, and I hadn't been there more than ten minutes before he pulled in.

"Hey, buddy," he called out the window of his big blue Chevrolet. He was about 5'9" tall and had a shaved head. One ear was pierced, with a small diamond stud in it. He wore a neat beard and he was the toughest man I had ever met. He looked at me now with the same eyes you see in the old pictures of the great frontier lawmen. Cold blue eyes that have seen everything, eyes that look at life down the barrel of a gun.

I walked over and leaned on his car. "Hi, Deacon."

He shook my hand, looking at me hard while he did. "You don't look good, Billy," he said. "Run into some tough tarpon down there?"

"It's been a rough summer."

"Lot of that going around, buddy. You want me to straighten it all out for you?"

"Can't shoot this one. Just have to live through it to the other side."

"Well then, why're you taking up my time? I got bad guys to catch."

"I've got a little problem some friends asked me to look into," I told him. "It's probably nothing."

"Uh-huh." He hadn't taken his eyes off me yet. "You wouldn't be doing a little investigating without a license, would you?"

"Absolutely."

"Well, good," he said, looking pleased. "God put you here to be a street cop and fight bad guys, same as me. You know that in your heart."

"Maybe so."

"No maybe, son. How long you in town?"

"Just until I get a couple of answers."

"Well, get in, let's see what we can come up with."

I went around to the other side and climbed into the car. There wasn't a lot of room. Deacon had eight radios and two cellular phones crowded into the front seat, plus a stack of forms on three different clipboards.

"They're keeping you busy?" I said with a nod at the heap of hardware.

"I'm heading up a new task force called SCAT," he said. "Street Crime Attack Team. I got to coordinate the troopers, the Sheriff, Metro and my boys. Everybody on a different frequency. No wonder the bad guys are winning." He shook his head. "We know damn well when somebody's done a crime, and we know how to catch 'em, how to stop 'em from doing it again—and the suits won't let us. Instead, they keep coming up with cute new acronyms so they can justify their budgets. When all it would take would be a couple of good street cops with a free hand. But hell, Billy," he said with a sigh, "that's my problem. What's yours?"

I told him and he listened. He was a good listener. He didn't take his eyes off me for even a second, and I don't think he blinked. Just stared straight at me with those gun-fighter's eyes. If I wasn't sure he liked me I would have been ready to confess whatever he wanted confessed. I laid out the three or four facts I had and threw in a couple of guesses.

"That all you got?" he asked me when I was done.

I nodded. "Yeah. It's not much, I know. Like I say, there's probably nothing to it."

"Oh, there's something to it," he said. "No doubt about that."

I looked at Deacon. He was smiling, but he wasn't kidding. "Somebody is killing boat loads of people?"

"Don't look so shocked, buddy. There's a lot of money in refugees."

"If you don't get caught."

"Uh-huh. And most people get caught on this end, when they're unloading. That's the hard part. Nobody stops you loading 'em in back in Haiti. Nobody boards your ship in the Gulf Stream and makes you turn around and take 'em back."

"So if somebody loads them in and then just dumps them—"

"Then they got a low-risk money machine."

"How much money?"

He shook his head. "In Haiti, ten bucks is a big deal, a month's wages. So I don't know how they do it, but those people scrape together two or three thousand dollars for a trip across to America."

"Two or three thousand *each?*"

"That's right. And figure between fifty and two hundred head per trip. It looks like somebody's figured a pretty good way to maximize his profit."

I worked up the numbers and shook my head. It was a lot of money. "All right," I said. "Who's working on it, and what have they got?"

He gave a soundless little cop laugh. "It's not quite that simple, buddy," he said. "I guess you've been a fishing guide so long you forgot how things are."

"Maybe so. How are they?"

"First, you got to understand that there's nothing definite to go on here. Just a pile of bodies that's easy to write off as refugees who drowned trying to come across."

"And nobody is working around the clock to make the connection?"

"Buddy," Deacon said with a tired shake of his head, "Unless a sworn officer actually stubs his toe on the perpetrator while he's committing the crime, ain't nobody ever going to make a connection."

"Except you."

He shrugged. "They keep me in between two very narrow lines, Billy. I can't just put on my cape and fly around looking for wrongs to right."

"So this just goes on."

"If it's happening, it's happening in international waters. Out in the great dark deep. The State won't touch it. Everybody in Tallahassee is pissed off at the Feds because we're going broke paying for all the immigrants, which is a federal problem, but the Feds won't help. So F.D.L.E. can't touch it, Metro doesn't want it, Sheriff says he can't handle it, and Marine Patrol says they're not authorized.

"The Feds won't get involved unless there is a direct threat to U.S. citizens, which they figure at this point won't happen unless more of these guys make it to shore and start taking jobs away from taxpayers. And since there ain't so much as one syllable of public protest on *anything* to do with any immigrant group that isn't Cuban, nobody is being forced into doing anything."

"So everybody knows something's happening," I said.

"They suspect the hell out of it."

"But nobody wants to do anything about it."

He winked. "Too many forms to fill out, buddy. And too many people to file 'em with that don't want to hear about it."

"All right," I said. "What do *you* know?"

"Not a thing. But I'll tell you what I think," he said.

"Tell me."

He held up a finger. "First, we're talking about one boat." Another finger. "Probably one of those old rust-bucket freighters out of the Miami River. And one other thing I guaran-damn-tee you, buddy," he said, holding up his open hand now and closing it into a fist.

"What's that?"

"We've got a file on this guy somewhere. Because what it looks like to me is, he's smuggling refugees, and he's taking their money and loading 'em onto his boat, and then dumping 'em into the ocean, still alive. 'Cause every one of 'em, they died from drowning." He winked. "You didn't hear that from me."

"I didn't hear a thing."

"And somebody who can do that is a cold killer, and you don't come at that from nowhere. You don't just decide one day you're gonna murder five or six hundred people."

"How many?" I couldn't believe the number. It was worse than even Nicky imagined.

Deacon shrugged, but I could tell it bothered him. "Just a guess they've put together, based on some things you don't want to know about."

"So I didn't hear that number from you, either."

"You got that right, buddy."

I thought about it for a minute. Then I shook my head; it wasn't quite tracking. "That's it? Five hundred dead and that's all you've heard about this?"

"Like I say, Billy, I'm kind of in a tight place right now." He looked at his watch. "How'd you like a bite to eat?"

I stared at him. He seemed serious. "I didn't think you got hungry," I said. "When did this start?"

"Started when I found this great little Haitian place a few miles from here," he said. "It's kind of a community center for refugees. Guy who runs it knows everybody in Little Haiti, and everything that's going on," he added with a lot of significance.

"I could use a bite to eat," I said.

CHAPTER THIRTEEN

L'Arbre Vie slouched on a corner in Little Haiti next to a shop with a long line of dried roots in the window. It looked like the whole row of buildings would have fallen down if it hadn't been held up by so much bright yellow and red paint.

Deacon angled the car to the curb in front of the restaurant and as he put it in park, people were already smiling and waving at him.

Deacon shook his head. "No ghetto like this in the world," he said. "You can walk the street at 3 A.M., dead drunk, and like as not they'll give you a cup of coffee and call you a cab."

"They know you here," I said.

"Last year I kind of helped Honore out of a little bind. He's important to the community here, so I guess they all remember me." He chuckled. "Took them some getting used to. You got to realize that most of these people, *cop* means a ton-ton macout. They ain't exactly in any hurry to call 9-1-1 when they got a problem."

He opened the car door. "Let's go see what Honore has on the menu today."

The inside of *L'arbre* should have been dark because there were no windows. But there was so much bright paint on the walls— yellow, lavender, gold, red—that the place seemed lit up brighter than a ballroom.

Along one wall was a mural painted in that unmistakable Haitian style, primitive figures done in a sophisticated way. It showed a huge scene of Haitian life stretching from one wall to the other. In the middle was a giant tree. Its roots went down into a hell with a top-hatted devil, its branches reached up to a pale God, surrounded by a saucer of golden light.

Wrapped around the tree was a snake, and all around were Haitians chopping wood, riding brightly painted buses, making love, dying, cooking and eating, dancing, building houses, fishing, tending animals, playing soccer. The painting took up the whole wall and dominated the room.

"Wow," I said to Deacon.

"Honore did that," he said. "That's where the place gets its name." He nodded at the large tree in the middle. "Tree of Life," he said. "Luh Arbruh Vee-ay."

"Deacon!" a happy voice called from the back. He pronounced it, "Dee-CONE." A tall man, very thin and very black, rushed out of the kitchen and swept down on us.

Deacon took his hand and shook it, looking like he was doing it to hold off a hug. "How's it going, Honore?" he asked.

Honore spread his arms wide. They took up most of the restaurant. "But now you have save my life, beautiful. Of course it is impossible to make any money with things as they are. But—" And he gave a shrug that said oh well, who cares, other things are more important, life is good, come on in, I have my health, and lunch is ready. It was an amazing shrug.

"This is my friend Billy Knight," the Deacon was saying. "He has a couple of questions you might be able to answer."

Honore held up a finger. "No," he smiled. "You will not ask on an empty stomach. Come," he said, and led us to one of the three booths, the one closest to the kitchen.

We sat. People kept appearing at the table and Honore spoke to them in Creole. One or two of them must have been working at the restaurant, because food started to appear very soon, in lots of small dishes, as if we were supposed to try a little of everything on the menu.

While we ate, Deacon and Honore traded news with each other and the parade of people that kept swinging by the booth. And then, almost like there had been some signal I couldn't see, the food stopped coming and so did the people.

"Now," Honore said. "I am happy to answer questions, Bee-lee." It took me a second to realize that *Bee-lee* meant me.

"A friend of mine found a body in the Gulf Stream," I said. "A Haitian refugee."

"The Black Freighter," Honore said.

I looked at Deacon. "I told you he'd know, buddy," Deacon said.

"What's the Black Freighter?" I asked Honore.

"First, it is my time to question. Are you investigating this also, Deacon?"

Deacon shook his head. "I'm sorry, Honore. I'm not allowed to get in on this. Officially, I'm just on my lunch break right now. And Billy is just a private citizen, asking a few questions."

He studied me for a moment. "How much do you know about my country?" he asked me.

"It's half an island. It doesn't have any topsoil. The world's first black republic. Um, Toussaint L'Overture. Papa Doc. Voodoo. I like the music."

"Very good," Honore said, making a face like he'd bitten something sour. "Few people know so much." He waved a long, thin arm. "And yet this is almost nothing."

"Sorry," I said.

"The history of my people is a dictionary of new ways to suffer. We have a genius for it," he said. "This new thing should be no surprise. And even so." He looked away, took a sip from his water glass, folded his hands in front of him. "You mention voodoo, my friend. Do you know what is a *bocor*?"

"No."

"In voodoo, there is good magic and there is bad magic. The good, it is like church, yes? A regular service, with a regular congregation, the rituals and offerings and prayers. This is done by a *papa-loa*. A voodoo priest. Most of the time he will not throw a curse for you for money. Because he worries to keep in, ah, what is the word. In *balance*. He must balance all the things of this world and the next, you see? A curse will upset this balance and the *papa-loa* will not do it. For this you must see a *bocor*. How is it called, a man-witch. A warlock? A sorcerer?"

"Sorcerer works for me," I said.

"Just so. And this man, the *bocor*, he does the dark things for money. Help you steal a man's wife with a love spell. Make your enemy sick. Make a rival to be a zombie. Do not laugh," he said, raising a long bony finger. "I have seen them. It is not a funny thing, not pretty. It is not a thing for your movies, with the arms out, so—" And he did a pretty good imitation of a Hollywood zombie.

"The *bocor* can make a powder," Honore said. "If you eat this powder, or breathe it, or so much as touch it, you are like a dead man but still alive. Then it wears off and you are stupid for a while. He gives you more powder, controls you. You are his slave, like an animal."

"And this guy on the Black Freighter is doing this?" I asked him.

"He is a *bocor*. One of the worst. This we know. If he does this, what might be his name—" Honore shrugged. It was a close cousin to his first shrug, saying thirty or forty different things at once. "No one knows his name, or the name of his ship."

"Then how do you know he's a *bocor*?"

Honore gave me a look of great pity. "Who else could do this thing?" he said. "There are so many who speak of it that one day— pfft—it is a fact and everybody knows it. You may say rumor if you like." The shrug again. "This is another of the small things that separate our worlds. In my world, a rumor reaches a certain moment where it is so persistent that it becomes true. And all the rumors of the Black Freighter say the captain is a *bocor*."

"All right," I said. "Tell me what you know about this guy and his Black Freighter."

"There are many stories," Honore said slowly, as if sorting it out while he spoke. "Some of them—it is how mothers frighten their children to be good, yes? Get a good grade or the Black Freighter comes for you."

"And the rest?"

He smiled. "The rest of the stories say, there is a freighter who takes refugees to America. He takes their money, loads them onto his ship, and no one ever sees them again. He sails away full of people and comes back empty. Perhaps this is just a rumor." He spread his hands to show it was possible, but he didn't look convinced.

"What do you think?"

Honore raised his eyebrows. "Me? I think there is a very bad man, a *bocor*, throwing people into the ocean and taking their money. I think he says, I take you to Miami, to America, but he only takes them half way. Such a one, he would have to enjoy the killing. Perhaps more than the money, who can say. And I think he will go on doing this, until someone stops him, or my country runs out of people who want to come here so much they do not care about the stories of the Black Freighter."

I looked at Deacon. He was pushing a small piece of bread around his plate with a knife. I looked back at Honore. He was looking at me the same way Deacon was looking at the bread.

"All right," I said. "If you were going to look for the Black Freighter, where would you start?"

"Here," Honore said, jabbing his finger down onto the table. The silverware rattled. "Right here, in Miami. He comes here after he dumps the people. He takes back stolen bicycles, old televisions." He shrugged.

"Miami River?" I asked Deacon.

He looked up from his bread. "Be my guess," he said. "A small, independent freighter, that's where he'd have to be."

"You know anything else that might be helpful?" I asked Honore.

He showed two rows of perfect teeth. "Voodoo comes from an old African word," he said. "It means snake."

* * *

Deacon drove me back to the parking lot where I had left my car. The late afternoon shadows were slanting across the tightly packed rows. It made the crummy shopping center look like some romantic old picture.

Deacon nosed into an empty spot. We looked straight ahead. Twenty feet away on the sidewalk a couple of kids came out of a store, stared at Deacon's car, and went back in the store again. One of the eight radios on the front seat crackled. Another one answered it.

"You look into this, I got to tell you, I can't help you."

"Yeah, I figured that."

"They might even send me after you, to stop you from doing anything that might cause them some political embarrassment."

"Are you telling me to go home and forget about this?"

"Hell no, buddy. I'm just telling you the way things are."

"What do you think I should do?"

"That's your problem."

"Yeah, thanks."

"Well how important is this to you? Why are you doing it?"

"I don't know. I don't even know if I am doing it. I just said I'd look into it a little."

"And now you have. You can go back and tell your friends they were right, there's a bad guy in the Gulf Stream doing some murders. Then what?"

I shook my head. I didn't have any idea then what. I wasn't a cop anymore. This wasn't any of my business.

On the other hand, "Not My Job" seemed to be a popular song right now. Nobody wanted this. Nobody wanted to hear it, but somebody was getting away with murder, and they would keep getting away with it, just because they'd found a little crack in the political set-up where nobody wanted to look. And damn it, somebody ought to care.

"This purely bothers the hell out of you, doesn't it?" Deacon said.

"Yeah. It does."

"Not scared of that bad magic?"

"I'll get some holy water."

He was quiet for a minute. Maybe the crack about holy water bothered him. I knew he was serious enough about his religion that he probably gargled with the stuff.

"I don't know what to do," I said finally. "Or even if I should do anything."

"Sure you do. You got a little voice inside you telling you what you should do. I know that, I got the same thing. Now, I can't listen to it for you. But I know it's there, and so do you. And we both know what it's saying." He held up a thumb and forefinger and dropped the thumb, pow. "It's got you. And there's not a damn thing you can do about it, and not a thing I can do to help you. All I can do is bust you if you listen to it." He gave me his best smile, which would have scared the hell out of me if we weren't on the same side. "On the other hand, there's worse things than a few days in the pokey."

"Like being thrown into the Gulf Stream alive and drowning?"

"That's one thing, buddy."

When Deacon had left, I drove around the Miami streets for a while. I found myself down by the Miami River. There's a big shanty town there, maybe thousands of people living in elaborate huts built from packing cases, refrigerator boxes, palm fronds—anything to keep off the rain and the hot Miami sun.

Many of the people living there were Haitian—dangerously thin black people. This was paradise to them. Back home it was impossible to find a box that nice to live in. They were willing to do anything, risk everything to get here. Just to live in a box under the highway. Drink Coca-Cola and send their kids to school.

I drove on, along the river, past a few of the rusty old hulks tied up by the warehouses. In the old days they called them tramp steamers. I wondered what they were called now. Tramp diesels didn't have the same good ring to it.

One of the ships was getting ready to leave. Black smoke trickled from the smoke stack. The deck was piled high with cargo and the ship rode low in the water. Several hundred bicycles were lashed to the outside of the crates on deck. That probably meant they were going to Haiti. There was a very good trade in used bicycles between Miami and Haiti, no questions asked. If your twelve-speed mountain bike vanished from the light post where you had chained it, it probably got re-painted overnight and you could find it on the deck of one of these ships.

Maybe this was the killer ship. The Black Freighter. Maybe they took down a cargo of bicycles and loaded in refugees. Just like the old triangular trade; unload the cargo, collect the cash. Load in the people, collect the cash.

And take the people halfway, dump them in the Gulf Stream. Big savings, less risk. You almost had to admire the cold-blooded efficiency of it. Miami in the 1980s and '90s had perfected this kind of MBA crime, where human life was simply a small marker on the board. If killing somebody was the best way to increase profits, nobody hesitated anymore. People were killed for their car keys. Hell, people were killed for their shoes. Why not for a few thousand dollars?

And the only question was, what the hell should I do about it?

CHAPTER FOURTEEN

The drive from Miami to Key West took almost as long going the other way. There was only one difference. On the way up, I had been kicking myself for taking seriously the brainless idea that somebody was getting away with wholesale murder in the Gulf Stream. On the way back, I was trying to figure out what to do about it.

I wondered how all this had happened. And why it was happening to me. A few weeks ago I was sweating, worrying about how slow business was, wondering when I was going to hit Tiny or make up with Nancy.

Now I was trying on armor, looking for a white charger. And trying to please the princess and Nicky the Wizard. Whoever said life was funny was a sadistic bastard.

It might have been all the driving, the rhythm of the tires on the road and the miles rolling past with the sun going down. But as it got darker I started to feel like I was dreaming. Everything that had happened in the last few weeks pushed back into my mind. It was all gumming up together, turning into one glob of pain and uncertainty.

Anna. The look of her neck and clavicle. Her story of the soldiers coming, the murder of her family.

Nancy. What we had been through, what we had almost been.

The sailboat sliding through the water with Nicky belching on the bow.

The fight with Tiny, which seemed like it had happened to someone else a long time ago.

And pushing out all the other pictures was the image of bodies bobbing in the water, washing up on the beach. And a man with no face far out to sea, counting the money while the voodoo drums rolled.

I didn't know what to do. I felt caught in a nightmare where everything else moves fast, with a purpose, and I was stuck in slow motion wearing lead sneakers. And I couldn't even wake up and pound on the pillow.

It was dark when I got back to Key West. All I wanted to do was go to sleep, stop thinking, let my unconscious brain sort things out. But there was a light showing in my window, and when I pushed my front door open and stepped into the living room, Anna was sitting in my easy chair.

She was wearing a loose white silk shirt and white pants and she looked so beautiful that at first I thought she was another dream image. Except that Nicky was standing in front of her in the center of the room, a beer in each hand, telling her some outrageous something or other, and whatever else he was, Nicky was no dream.

"Billy!" he bellowed, and Anna smiled at me.

"Thanks for waiting up," I said.

"No worries, mate," Nicky said, and he held up one of my beers. "This stuff was going bad so we had to field test it."

"I appreciate it," I said, moving towards the kitchen. "Did any of it survive the field test?"

Nicky looked hurt. "Aw, man, think I'd take your last one?"

"Only if you were thirsty," I said.

He giggled. "Too right. And I'm always thirsty. But I left you one any road."

I opened the refrigerator and took the last beer. There had been a six-pack this morning. Five bottles gone. So I knew Nicky had been here waiting for at least ten minutes.

I took a long pull. I knew they were waiting for me to tell them what I had found out, but I didn't know where to start, how to say it. "It's bad," I said.

"This is why we wait," she said. "So you are not alone with the bad in the night."

I looked at her. It was worth doing. "That's right," I said. "Except it's worse than you thought."

"I *knew* it," Nicky said softly.

"Somebody has killed some people, just dumped them alive into the Gulf Stream and let them drown. As far as I can find out, no American law enforcement agency is looking into it."

"How the bloody hell can they not?" Nicky wanted to know.

"It's in international waters, Nicky. The Australian Coast Guard isn't looking into it either."

"That's eyewash, Billy, and you know it. What's the real reason?"

I shrugged. "It's politics," I said.

"Just so," Anna said softly.

"Bloody savages," Nicky said.

I finished my beer. "They're not bad guys, mostly. They'd just rather not have the hassle. They figure they got enough crime here at home, and they're not allowed to solve those, so why go looking for trouble? It's not really their problem."

"Then who?" Anna demanded, still with a soft, knowing tone. "Who is this problem of?"

"Right," said Nicky. "It's up to us, then."

"The hell it is," I said.

"Mate—"

"No, Nicky, listen to me for a second. This is a very bad guy, whoever he is. He's killed a couple hundred people. What is it you think we can do?"

"Stop him," Nicky said stubbornly.

"Okay, stop him, great. How?" He was quiet and I went on. "Because first you have to find him. We don't even know it's *him*—it could be her. Or them, or it. Where do we look? Rent a helicopter and hover over the Gulf Stream until we see bodies, then follow them back to the source?"

"You know how to find somebody, Billy. You were a cop."

"Sure. You want to know how a cop would do it? Put it out on the wire to all the other cops. Wait for a clue. Hope somebody sees something. Wait some more. Dig through the files and try to find somebody with a past history of similar crimes. Tell the newspapers, set up an anonymous tip line. And then wait, for one of the thousands of other cops or citizens to call with a hint. We can't do any of that."

"All right, Billy."

"And then, let's just suppose a miracle happens and we find him anyway. Then what?"

"What do you mean, then what? We stop him, mate! We make sure he never does it again!"

"How?"

Nicky opened his mouth, then closed it again. He looked like the silence hurt. "I don't know," he mumbled.

"Good. I do know. There's only two ways to stop him. First, we could set him up to get caught by the cops. Have you had any luck getting the cops interested?"

"You know I haven't."

"Well, we can't just grab him, tie him up and hand him over. Because then we're guilty of piracy, kidnapping and who knows what. We'll go to jail and he'll go back to business as usual."

"All right, mate, you made your point. What's the other way to do him?"

"The other way is to kill him."

There was a long silence.

"And if you're not ready in your heart to look him in the eye and kill him dead there's no point in even trying to find him. Which we can't do anyway. Because sure as hell, he'll kill us without blinking."

I felt the pressure of Anna's hand on me. "There is other way," she said. I looked at her. She had been quiet while Nicky and I slugged it out, but she hadn't quit on the idea of justice.

"In this country," she said slowly, carefully, "are the people controlled by the television. If we are making the television interested, then are the police coming so as not to look bad, yes?"

"It's not that easy," I said.

"But what is easy to do with this? Is necessary. You are saying other way is impossible, so not easy is an improve, yes?"

"Fair is fair," Nicky said. "Let's have a go."

"You two still don't get it," I said. "This isn't some kind of Johnny Quest adventure. This is the big game. For keeps."

"I think so too," Anna said. "No one is saying to these dead people, 'Get up, game is over.'"

"We know what we're about, mate," Nicky added.

"No you don't."

"But *you* know," Anna said.

"That's right. And it scares the hell out of me. And it would scare the hell out of you if you understood it."

"So then Nicky and I, we do it without you." She gently closed my jaw with a fingertip. "We will be fine, Billy. You may tell us how to do."

I was back in the dream again, where nothing made sense but it was all whirling around me at a furious speed while I had grown into the floor.

"No," I finally managed.

"Which part no?"

"All of it no." I took a deep breath, wishing I could shut up, but knowing I was going to say it anyway. "You'll wait here while I do it."

Nicky went off like a rocket. "Not alone, mate! Not without me! It's not fair!"

"No, Nicky. This guy is a *bocor*, a voodoo black wizard. He collects body parts and drinks Christian blood. Eats babies. No. No way in hell. You two are out of it."

Nicky gulped, but looked stubborn. "Mate. Billy. Stands to reason, you need me all the more if he's flinging around *palo mayombe*."

"Palo what?"

"*Palo mayombe*. Black magic version of voodoo. What you said, right?" He shook his head. "Very bad stuff. Of course, it explains how he controls the crowds."

"You know about this stuff?"

He looked insulted. "Mate. What is it you think I do all day in me little shop? This stuff is all cake to me. And if you're going up against a *houngan*, you need me to counter him." He winked. "Besides, I got my new weapon, Billy. You'll need back-up."

"If I need you and your weapon, we've already lost." He looked hurt, but I was way past caring. "Here's the deal. I will look into this thing, just skim the surface very quietly. Just to get enough detail so we can turn it over to the TV people, and then hope they put pressure on the cops. But if they do or don't, that's all we do. And then we are all out of it, whatever happens. Because I do not want this guy ever to know who we are. Deal?"

They both looked troubled and poked around at it for a few minutes, saying we had to be sure, but in the end we had reached an uneasy agreement. They would come along and stay in the background, just so they knew that everything possible had been done. And I would not involve them, no matter what, or do anything that might get us close enough to be dangerous. I insisted on that. This was not a crusade, just a quick, clean investigation from a distance and then home again.

It was an important point, and I really thought I might have gotten it across. But of course, I was wrong about a lot of things that rotten August.

CHAPTER FIFTEEN

Considering how much I hated driving between Miami and Key West, I was doing it way too often. And with the weight of what we were about to try, and Nicky singing his awful, tuneless Australian drinking songs in the back seat, it seemed to take a lot longer this time.

Anna didn't say a whole lot. She sat in the front and watched the scenery. If she was disappointed, she didn't let on. Every ten miles or so I would catch her looking at me. She would hold my eye for a moment and then look back out the window. I wondered what it meant.

But nothing lasts forever, no matter how much you don't want it to. We finally hit the Turnpike and all the cars around us accelerated from sixty-five to over eighty like a school of sharks scenting blood. I moved us into the right lane and kept it at a stately seventy. Anna watched the traffic whiz past with gritted teeth. Once, when three cars tried to pass us in the same lane at the same time, I heard her say something under her breath that sounded like, "boga tee." It was probably Ukranian profanity. I wished I knew some. I'd worn out all the English I knew.

I pulled off the Turnpike onto US 1 around Kendall. We drove in relative silence for a few miles and then turned into the parking lot of an anonymous motel in South Miami.

"All right," I said. "Headquarters."

Nicky blinked, looking at the bland, middle class building. "What the hell, mate," he said. "I'm paying. We can go one better."

"It's out of the way," I said. "And it's right on a very busy street. Besides, it has a coffee shop. We could go to one of the fancy joints in the Grove or downtown, but I don't want to attract attention."

"And I don't want to attract roaches," Nicky muttered, but he jumped out of the car anyway and led us inside the lobby to register.

We got two rooms with a connecting door between them. Nicky threw his canvas bag onto the bed in one of them, the smaller room, and went racing off to fill the ice bucket and find some beer.

Anna stood in the middle of the room looking lost. Then she moved slowly over and sat on the edge of the bed. She sat so stiffly that her weight barely made a dent in the bed cover. "Is very funny," she said.

I sat in the chair beside her. "What's that?"

She gave a small huff. "Myself is funny. Because I am having more fears of staying in this room with you than of what we do with the killer."

I sat still. "I don't think it's funny."

"You have not European sense of humor," she said. "In my country would be much laughter for this. The poor girl, afraid of man even when she is very much liking him, and not afraid of the bad killing man. Ha," she said.

I moved carefully onto the bed, leaving a good space between us. I took her hand and just held it.

"How beautiful I now am," she said. "With these, these—how do you call it, snowts?"

"I think you are beautiful," I said. "But I don't know what snowts are."

She blew her nose again. "These are snowts," she said. "From the nose."

"You mean snot," I said.

"Yes, of course, I am saying so. Snowts."

"It's not a real nice word."

"So? What are you calling it then?"

"How about nose tears?"

She looked at me for a long moment, then shook her head. "You are also a poet. This is a beautiful thought, very nice." She held up the soggy tissue. "But I think this is not beautiful. And not tears." She threw it across the room and into the small brass trashcan. "Snowts."

"Whatever you say."

She moved closer to me. "I say, it would be very nice if you will hold me for a few minutes. If you do not object to the snowts."

"Nose tears," I said. "I don't mind." I put my arms around her.

We were still sitting like that, just holding each other and breathing, when Nicky smashed the door open and roared back into the room with a sound like the Spanish Armada breaking up on the cliffs of Dover.

"Hello-hello-hello," he yelled at us. His arms were full of paper bags and before Anna and I could even straighten up he had spread the contents of several of them across the bed.

Nicky had found beer, two six packs of Samuel Adams, and a sixteen ounce bottle of Mountain Dew for Anna. He'd also found a Chinese restaurant, and there were spring rolls with lots of hot Chinese mustard, shrimp fried rice, sweet and sour pork, and kung pao chicken.

"Gung hee fat choy!" Nicky shouted, throwing chop sticks to Anna and then to me.

"It's not New Years, Nicky," I reminded him.

"Hell's peppers, mate, celebration is celebration. Besides," he said, ripping the lid off a container of rice and shoving a good handful into his mouth, "I can't say another bloody word in Chinese. Eat up, love, it's getting cold," he told Anna.

She continued to watch him with something between amusement and horror as he polished off a good half of the food with a kind of suicidal carelessness that left rice stuck to the ceiling above him and small pieces of shrimp fastened to the bedspread.

When we were done eating Nicky belched happily. "Ahhh," he

said. "Hits the old spot, eh? Well then, Billy, what's next, beddy-bye? Do we need an early start?"

"Very early," I said. "How about fifteen minutes?"

He blinked. "What. Fifteen minutes from *now*?"

"That's right."

"Ohhh," he said, and for the first time since this whole thing had started he looked a little uneasy.

"What's the matter? A little worried about going out there into the Miami night?"

"No, no," he said. "It's not that."

"Maybe you think we should wait for daylight to track down a voodoo *bocor*."

"Since you bring it up, Billy—"

"Good," I said, standing up and brushing off a few crumbs of food. "You can stay here with Anna."

"Anna does not stay here," she said.

"Yes, she does."

"We have an agree that I am to come."

"Where I want to go tonight is not dangerous—*if* I go alone. But if I take a beautiful woman—and an astrologer with a loud sense of impulse—it can get dangerous."

She frowned. "What kind of place this is, I am making danger?"

"It's just a joint. A bar for sailors."

"A *bar*?" Nicky bellowed. "Mate, think what you're saying. You're going to a bar—and you're leaving *me*?"

"That's right," I said. "It's a sort of specialized bar. You wouldn't fit in."

"I've never seen the bar where I wouldn't fit in," Nicky said.

"Why should this place be a danger for me?" Anna added.

"A bar's a bar, Billy. Home away from home."

"Do you think I do a sex dance with the juke box, hah?"

I had a full-scale revolt on my hands.

My plan had been to slip quietly into a few of the dives along the river and ask questions. Just one or two innocent questions in each of three places I knew about, so nobody would get suspicious about a whole bunch of significant talk. They were the kind of places that don't appreciate outsiders. I thought I could pass muster; I had the deep-water tan, I knew the dialect, and if it came to swapping knuckles in good clean fun I could hold my own.

It looked like that plan wasn't going to get past The Committee.

"Listen," I said, trying one last time. "We agreed that the reason I'm doing this is because I know how. And one of the things I know is that there is no way in hell I can go into one of these places with you two and not attract attention."

"What's wrong with a little attention, eh?" Nicky demanded. "Best way to find somebody is to let them find you." And he looked really happy with himself for coming up with something that smart.

"Do you really want to be found," I asked carefully, "by someone who's making a lot of money killing people and might not want you to stop him from doing it a while longer?"

Nicky opened his mouth, and then closed it again.

"Although I must say," Anna said solemnly, "one person alone is in more danger. And is very good dus… dusko… How you are calling it when you make to look like something which you are not?"

"Disguise," I said.

"Just so. A disguise. Three people, one of them woman. Who would think of harm from such?"

"She's right, Billy. Can't go in without someone to watch your back, mate."

"My back will be fine. Especially if I'm not worried about watching your backs, too."

But he shook his head. "Sorry. I reckon it's settled."

"No."

"Yes," Anna said.

I held the door for her anyway. Probably it was the cute way she said it, with the accent and everything.

CHAPTER SIXTEEN

The Miami River isn't really a river anymore. It's been turned into a canal that cuts the city in half and then dumps into Biscayne Bay. It has tides and brackish water and it is a kind of second-class port for the smaller freighters.

But of the many things it is, the most important is that it's a strange, self-contained sub-culture. It's a little world of its own along the banks of the large canal. When people in Miami say "Miami River," they usually mean this minor sprawl of marinas and dry docks and bars. It sits a few miles inland from the Atlantic Ocean and several layers of evolution away from the horrors of South Beach.

The residents of this world, known as River Rats, are the real boat people of Miami. These are not guys who take the speedboat out on Sunday after church to see if they can make it to Elliot Key in under ten minutes. They don't spend a lot of time looking at the BOAT US catalogue.

But they are likely to know where you can buy a World War II surplus landing craft, who might have a reconditioned engine for a tanker, or who's been making some extra cash on the run from Colombia.

They range in age from very young to very old, but most of them have that no-age look of men who have always been old but are still spry enough to bend a Buick's bumper with their teeth.

There aren't that many of them, not anymore, and they are at sea whenever they can arrange it. But it's a dying lifestyle, like most of the other interesting ones, and there are fewer berths available every year as the computers take over the ships. So there are always a few dozen River Rats on shore.

Those few only have a couple of places where they hang out. What those places have in common is cheap drinks and a view of the River. My plan had been to slip into some of those places, have a few quiet beers, ask a couple of questions. My modified plan was to lead the parade of Nicky and Anna into a couple of places and try to keep us all from being pounded into the ground.

The first place we went was called The 0. From the outside it looked like it had fallen down a few years ago. Once you saw the inside you were willing to pay for the bulldozers to make sure.

As we pushed through the crooked doorway I felt like we were in a bad Western. A sudden quiet fell over the room when they saw Anna. Even the jukebox stopped and I felt twenty-three hungry eyes on us.

"Christ on a bun," Nicky muttered, looking into the dimness where a dozen battered and scarred faces were looking back.

Then somebody dropped a glass, the music started up, and they all turned away again. They weren't being polite; it was just that anything that wasn't a boat could only hold their interest for so long.

I could see that Nicky and Anna were both re-thinking their attitude of fearless confrontation. But I managed to steer us to a table in the corner without either of them trying to surrender.

Anna's eyes had gotten very big when I opened the door, and walking across the room to the table didn't shrink them at all. Now she sat with her hands clasped on the table in front of her, trying not to see too much.

"Are you sure this is still America?" she whispered to me. "Never have I seen such a place."

"I have," Nicky muttered. "Ever see *Star Wars*?"

"Just don't order a wine spritzer," I said. "Or milk."

"Is beer all right," Nicky asked, "or do I need to eat a broken glass?"

We sat quietly for a while, nursing our drinks. I tried to size up the River Rats in the room without being too obvious, and finally narrowed it down to one.

The guy I picked had been sitting over at the far end of the bar. He looked to be older than most of the others, and everybody who came in nodded to him. Every now and then somebody would go over to him and lean their head in close, talk for a minute, and then walk away.

He was thin and looked to be over six feet tall, though it was hard to be sure with the way he had folded himself onto his stool. He had a worn, deeply tanned face, colorless hair, and wore clothes that looked like they were nice once, but he'd worn them to overhaul the engines one time too many.

In a community like the River, where people come and go, there are usually a couple of people who are the bulletin boards. They stay put and keep track of things. My guy looked like the man who knew everything that was going on and everybody who was doing it.

I waited until he was alone, with only about a half inch left in his glass, and pushed my chair back. "Just stay here and keep quiet," I told Nicky and Anna. They nodded.

I walked over to him at the end of the bar. "Buy you a drink?"

He looked up at me. He didn't look friendly, but he didn't look hostile, either. He was just waiting. If there was a password, I hadn't said it yet.

"Name's Billy," I said. I jerked my head back at my table. "Some friends are looking for a boat."

He nodded.

"Thought you might know where they can find one," I said.

"I'll take a whiskey and water," he told me.

I called the bartender over and got him his drink. He didn't say another word until I had paid and the new glass was in front of him.

Then, he picked up the last of the old drink and tossed it down.

"My name is Bud," he said. "Thanks for the drink."

He didn't put his hand out, so I didn't either. "Bud, I got two people over there looking for a small freighter to hire."

"Uh-huh," he said.

He watched me without making any sign that he knew what I wanted or why I was asking him.

"It would be pretty good money," I said.

"That a fact?" he said.

"I wondered if you knew anybody might be interested."

He still didn't show any emotion beyond barely polite interest. Now he raised one eyebrow, looking at me out of distant blue eyes that weren't saying anything. "Everybody's interested in pretty good money," he said.

"Well, that guy over there," I nodded at Nicky and tried out the story we'd agreed on, "he's a South African. He's looking for a way to get his money out of the country. And, uh—anyway there's a lot of it."

"And he figured that the best way to do that was by investing in an independent maritime cargo hauler," Bud said, eyebrow still up in the air.

"Well, actually I think he's got a pretty specific cargo in mind."

"Oh, uh-huh," he said. "Thinking of making the Colombia run, is he?"

"Something like that," I said.

He blinked at me for a minute. Then he gave his head a half-shake, and he gave me a half smile. It reminded me of an alligator looking at something tender a few minutes after he's already eaten his fill.

"Sonny boy, you're so full of crap it's spilling out your mouth," he said, turning away from me and back to the bar. He lifted his glass over his shoulder in a small toast. "Thanks for the drink."

Strike One. "Listen, Bud—"

"I am listening," he said without turning around. "I appreciate creativity, Billy, and I know you're not going to let me down."

"We're not cops," I said.

He turned and gave me another half smile. "Oh, I'm sure of that. You by yourself might be, but no cop in the world would walk into a joint like this dragging along beauty and the beast over there." He nodded towards Anna and Nicky. "So like I say, I'm really looking forward to hearing your story. As long as we both admit it's a story and don't get hung up trying to pretend that either one of us believes you even for a Detroit minute."

There comes a time in the life of any lie when the paint peels off and you either tell the truth or make up a brand new lie and start all over. Bud was telling me that this lie was there.

"All right, Bud," I said. "But sometimes the truth sounds pretty stupid."

He smiled again, real amusement this time. "That's how we know it's the truth," he said.

I had to decide how much to tell him, and decide right now. Part of being a cop is reading people. I'd always been good at it when I wore the badge.

So while I knew Bud might have a stake in either saying nothing or, worse, letting somebody know we were asking questions, I didn't think he would. He looked hard as nails, sure, but he also looked straight.

I decided to go with my gut.

"What do you know about the Black Freighter?" I said.

A couple of things ran across Bud's face. He clamped down on them pretty fast, but before he did I saw the first expression on his face that he hadn't put there on purpose. It was so fast it was hard to read, but I caught it and it told me I was right. He knew, and he didn't like it.

"What do you want with *that*?" he said in a suddenly flat voice.

"We want to stop it," I said.

He cocked his head a quarter of an inch to one side. "You said you weren't cops."

"That's right."

He moved his lips in and out and squinted. "Reporters?"

"Nope."

He looked at me for a long moment, flicked his eyes over to Anna and Nicky, then looked at me again. He shook his head and picked up his glass. "I don't get it," he said finally, taking a long pull on his drink.

"I'm not sure I do, either," I said. "We're just trying to find out enough to give somebody a starting place on digging in and stopping it."

He looked at me with complete disbelief. "Concerned citizens?"

"Yeah, that's right. Sorry it sounds like that."

He drained his glass and put it down on the bar. Somebody had gouged a chunk out of the bar there and the tumbler stuck in the pothole, tilted at a crazy angle. "I'll take another drink," Bud said.

I got him his drink. But he didn't take a sip from it, just stared at the ice cubes. "I came here in 1959," he finally said. "You probably weren't even born."

"Probably not."

He jerked his head at the huge dinosaur of a jukebox over in the corner. "There was Pat Boone and The Crewcuts on that thing first time I came in here. Most of the guys in here were veterans, got used to the sea during the war. Just looking to stay on the water, do a job, make a few bucks."

Now he took a drink, draining off about half of his whiskey and water. "Started to change around 1965. New kind of cash cargo coming in."

"Dope."

"Dope," he agreed. "Changed everything." He sighed heavily and finished the drink, letting the glass hang from his hand, tilted so that one ice cube hung just inside the rim. "Changed... Everything," he repeated, drawing out the vowels. "Used to be a pretty damn good life. Not curing cancer, maybe, but you could feel good about what you did. And then drugs started creeping in, until you never knew when you might have some stuck in your hold, hidden in something else. You accept it, you go along because either you can't be sure or hell, everybody else is doing it, making that amazing money, why not. And once you've gone one step down that road, there's no going back."

He sighed again and looked in his glass, but it was still empty.

"Things have just gone from bad to worse since then. Maybe I should have seen something like this coming, the way things have just been turning bad, a little worse every year. Hijacking, piracy's coming back, murder so common it doesn't even make the papers anymore."

He wound down and just stared at the floor for a minute. I didn't want to interrupt him, but I didn't want him to stop talking either. "Let me get you another drink," I offered.

"Hell, I don't need another drink, I'll start crying." He looked up at me with guarded intelligence. I'd seen him put down three drinks, and who knows how many before that, but there was no sign of the drinking in his eyes. "What do *you* know about the Black Freighter?" he said, turning it right back on me.

"I don't even know if it's real," I told him.

"Then why in hell are you knocking around looking for it? Hellfire, boy, you have any idea at all what you might be sticking your nose into?"

"I was hoping you might tell me."

"I'll tell you this, I hope you swim mighty good." He raised his glass halfway to his mouth, realized it was empty and put it down on the bar. "Listen, sonny, the professionals don't want to touch this thing, that tell you anything?"

"It tells me it's complicated."

"Complicated. That's very good, complicated. Sure, it's as complicated as a thump on the head. Complicated as quick death." He turned away, slid his glass down the bar and nodded at the bartender for another. "Go home, sonny boy. It's dark out there and full of monsters."

I know the sound of a door slamming when I hear it. I also know a few ways to pry them back open. I could try to scare Bud, maybe grab him and lift him straight into the air and shake him a little. That didn't seem like a good idea, since I was surrounded by his friends, and they were all guys who thought losing a tooth in a fight was like putting a quarter into a jukebox; a small price to pay for so much fun. Besides, I wasn't sure this guy would scare.

So I tried something that wasn't quite as subtle. "Sure, Bud. I understand. You don't want to get involved, that's fine. If I was retired I'd probably be a little scared, too."

He sighed and shook his head without turning around. "That's very funny, Billy. Kick him again, he's still moving." The bartender put a new drink in front of Bud and he swirled it once. The ice cubes rattled. "A little scared doesn't cover it. This is major league terror, and if you don't understand that, you're sticking your head in the lion's mouth with your eyes closed."

"My eyes are open, Bud."

He spun around and looked at me. "You think so, don't you? You think you're tough enough, got all the moves and know all the tricks. You think you're ready for this, but let me tell you something, sonny boy. You're not this tough. You're not ready for this."

"Maybe I'm not, Bud. Maybe nobody is. Is that your decision?"

He looked at me hard, just looked. Then he slumped back onto the bar, leaning on one elbow. "How much money you got, Billy?" he finally asked me.

"How much do you need?"

He turned and looked at me with a little bit of anger on his face. "I don't need a thing. But I have a friend I want you to meet, and he needs money or he won't talk." He gave me a very small smile. "His name is Otoniel. He used to think he was a hard case."

"What does he think now?"

Bud shook his head. "He doesn't think at all. Something scared the shit out of him."

"The Black Freighter?"

He shrugged. "Oto was making a lot of dough recently, too much for a normal run. Then he started getting nightmares. Got the shakes so bad he had to stay on shore. Now he drinks so he can sleep. And this was a guy who liked to hurt people."

"He was working on the Black Freighter?"

Bud shook his head. He didn't mean no, he just meant the question was out of place. "Why don't you ask him yourself?" He turned back to the bar, cradling his drink. "Be here tomorrow night. Bring him maybe a hundred bucks." He sipped. "Don't come too late or he'll be passed out already."

CHAPTER SEVENTEEN

"What else did he say? He must have said something else."

Nicky was frantic, practically clawing at me for details. I had refused to say anything in the bar, except, "Let's go." Nicky and Anna were so intimidated by the place that they had followed quietly.

But Nicky has always been one of those terrier-like people, filled with frenzied energy clawing to get out. And when we got to the car, he couldn't hold it in any longer.

"Come on, mate, this is inhuman! What'd he say? Where are we going? Give it up, there's a boy!"

"I know you're upset," I told him calmly. "All that work on your South African accent, and you didn't get to use it."

"It's a grayte eksent, too," he said, shifting slightly from his usual super-charged Australian.

"What is now happening? Are you giving out?" Anna said, speaking for the first time since we'd gone into the place.

"Giving *up*, love," Nicky corrected her. "Can't be, lookit 'im, he's too happy-lookin'. So what's up? Come on, eh? Who was that man?"

"His name was Bud," I said, taking some pity on him, but not too much. I started the car. Nicky scrabbled at the seat belt, too excited to fasten it.

"Oh, well, we know his name, great, problem solved," Nicky

moaned. He finally snapped his seat belt shut. "For the love of God, what the bloody fucking hell did you and *Bud* talk about?"

"Bud knows somebody who maybe can tell us something," I said. "For a price. We're supposed to meet him here tomorrow night."

"How much is price?" Anna asked.

"He thought $100 would do it."

"This is very much money for maybe," she said. "Does he tell the truth, or does he want money only?"

"I won't know until I talk to him," I said. I filled them in on the details; the tough sailor named Otoniel who made too much money and now was drinking too much.

"I got the idea from Bud that something scared the hell out of this guy. And I think the fact that it scares Oto scares the hell out of Bud."

"And so what is it we are now doing with this tough man?" Anna wanted to know.

I shook my head. "We'll talk to him. Find out what he knows. If he knows anything."

"You think this *Bud* fella might be having a skite?"

I looked at Nicky. His brow was knotted together. He was clearly looking for all the angles and not sure what they might look like if he saw them.

Every now and then Nicky forgets what country he's in. Or maybe he figures Australian is, or should be, universal speech, like Esperanto. Whatever it was, he would slide out some strange turn of speech and expect me to answer him.

"What does that mean?"

He looked at me, blinked. "Eh?"

"What's a *skite?*"

"Aw, come on."

"That's not American. It's not even English."

"Pull the other one."

"Really."

"You're having me on."

"Scout's honor."

"Having a *skite*, you know. It's, it's… Look," he finally said. "Here's the thing. Do you trust this Bud fella?"

It was odd, but I hadn't really thought about that yet. I thought I knew what he wanted. He wanted to keep his position in the River community, but even more he wanted to see this thing stopped. He couldn't stop it himself, and he couldn't rat out anybody, but he couldn't allow it to go on without changing his picture of who he was, changing it in a big bad way. If I could take care of it for him, that would be all right with him.

"Yeah," I said. "I trust him. At least as far as getting the guy there tomorrow night, and not setting us up to get whacked on the head."

"Oh. All right," Nicky said, and from the way he said it I knew he had been worried more about getting ripped off for the hundred bucks than he had been about getting killed.

We drove the rest of the way back to the motel in silence. I think Nicky was starting to realize what he was into. It was no longer truth, justice and the American way. It had turned into something very real and very scary.

At the motel, Nicky went into his room and turned the TV on and started making telephone calls. I don't know who he talked to. He had his whole New Age support network. I'd never met most of them. Judging from the one or two I had met, that was a blessing.

I kicked my shoes off and lay back on the bed, trying to figure out how to keep us all safe tomorrow night.

I had to watch three backs. For that matter, the fronts weren't all that secure. Nicky didn't have a clue how to handle anything we might run into. He still thought carrying a gun was protection.

As for Anna, I couldn't be sure what she knew. She had escaped from an inhuman war zone. She had seen things and gone through things that put her outside my experience. Maybe she was being quiet because she realized what we might be facing. And maybe she just didn't have anything to say.

A lot could go wrong tomorrow night. There were too many variables, too many different ways it could turn sour. Somebody who's talking to you for money can't be trusted. Sometimes they figure out they can get more money by playing double. And sometimes they figure they're so tough they'll just take your money for nothing, or lever more cash out of you, or—

The silence got a little deeper and I looked up. Anna had closed and locked the interconnecting door between Nicky's room and ours.

She was standing with one hand on the door, watching me. As I looked she turned her head away quickly and ran one hand through her short blond hair. It occurred to me that this was the first time I'd seen her look nervous, unsure of herself. Like so many very physical people she almost always had a strong sense of confidence.

That was gone now, and she looked strange without it. She met my eyes again and took one step towards me. "Billy—" she said with a small catch in her voice.

I sat up.

She took another step towards me.

"Billy," she said again. She half-raised a hand. It was shaking. She stepped to the bed on unsteady feet. The hand went to her throat and toyed with a button on her shirt. She tried to say something else but it wouldn't come out.

I stood up and put an arm on her shoulder. "Relax," I said. I sat her down on the bed and sat beside her. Her muscles tightened and stood out like she was an anatomy drawing. "Anna," I said. "You don't have to make yourself do anything you don't want to do."

She unbuttoned the top button of her shirt. "But I want to," she said.

"And I want you to," I said with a mouth that was suddenly very dry. "But if you do this before you're ready it won't be right. You'll regret it, and sooner or later so will I."

She undid another button. "But how can I know when I am ready," she said. "Perhaps only by doing am I then ready."

It would have been hard enough to follow her slightly twisted English under the best conditions. But sitting on the edge of a bed in a cheap hotel with my heart pounding hard enough to wake the neighbors and all my concentration on the next button, I really had to work at understanding her. She got another button undone before I figured out what she had said.

"Anna, listen," I said.

She undid one more button and put her lips on my ear. "I do listen," she whispered.

Her breath slipped over my neck and onto my face and shoulder and it felt like a live wire dragging across my skin. I could feel all the little hairs on my arms stand up and all the blood rushed from my brain straight down.

I put my arm around her and held her close. Her arms went around me, too, and we fell gently backwards on the bed. Her shirt came open. She had nothing on under it and I could feel her nipples rising, hardening as they rubbed against me. I slid a hand across them and Anna gasped softly.

Anna shrugged her shirt off the rest of the way and unbuttoned mine. She put her hands inside, on my chest, and rubbed them up, across my shoulders, pushing the shirt aside until it whispered off and fell next to hers.

She locked her hands behind my neck and pulled herself forward until our foreheads touched and our eyes were so close that when she blinked I felt the movement of her eyelashes. Then she rubbed her breasts sideways across my chest and pressed them against me hard enough to bruise me.

I ran my hands along the incredible satin smoothness of Anna's back and up onto her shoulders. Her hands paused and she shivered. She pressed her face against my neck and shoulder and I could feel her breath coming faster. I moved my hands lightly up her spine and then down again, sliding one hand under the waistband of her jeans and onto the ripe swell of her bottom.

And as I did she caught her breath, stiffened, and pushed slightly away from me.

"No," she said, in a half-strangled voice.

I paused. I could feel the muscles in her lower back tighten.

She gasped. It was not the sound of pleasure. "Please, no,"

she said again.

I took a very deep breath and let it out. "All right," I said. I lifted my hands away from her and dropped them down onto the bed. "Okay."

For a long moment she didn't move at all. Then I heard her breath catch again and felt a tear run across my shoulder. "I am sorry," she said. "I am not as ready as I am thinking to be."

"That's all right," I said, putting a hand back on her shoulder, her bare, smooth shoulder. "It's all right."

CHAPTER EIGHTEEN

"I'm not going unless I go alone," I told them both for maybe the sixty-third time. Anna had accepted it. She sat quietly on the bed looking worried. Since she had seen the bar and the River Rats inside she didn't want to go back.

But Nicky was another story.

"It's my money," Nicky said.

"It's my life. And I'm not tossing it away for your ego."

"Go piss down your leg. Ego is going into this solo with no back-up. You need me there, mate."

"Anything I can't handle is going to be way too much for you."

"Piss down your leg," he repeated. "What is there to handle? Go to a bar and talk to a drunk. Think I can't do that a damn sight better'n you? Eh?"

"There's more to it than that. I have to be ready for something to go wrong."

"Exactly my point, mate. And you need me there if it does."

"Nicky—"

"I can handle this. I'm in touch with my warrior-self. Look at my aura."

I looked at Nicky, a full five feet of Australian New Age deadliness. I couldn't actually see his aura but maybe he was surrounded by a bright glowing war-like haze that would terrify and intimidate anybody who tried to hurt him. Anything was possible.

But if I couldn't see his warrior-self aura it seemed like a safe bet that there were other people who couldn't see it either. And if one of them decided to stick a knife down Nicky's throat, just for the hell of it, that would be a big distraction for me.

"You asked me to do this because I know how to do it," I said. "This is part of what I know."

"Eyewash," he said stubbornly.

I reached for the bedside pen and notepad, "I need you here. You're my last back-up. If something goes bad, if I don't come back or call you by 2 A.M., that means I'm in trouble and I need help."

"Pull the other one."

"I mean it. If it goes wrong I'll need a hole card. You're it."

"Seriously?" He was beginning to doubt a little.

"Seriously. I need you here, out of reach of whatever might happen. Just in case."

"I'll come for you, Billy," he said in a voice I was sure he'd picked up from Australian late night television.

"No, you won't," I said, writing out a telephone number and tearing off the page. "What you'll do is call this number." I handed him the slip of paper with the number written on it. Nicky raised an eyebrow. "It's a man named Deacon," I said. "He's a very good cop."

Nicky looked doubtful. "Are you having me on, mate? Make a phone call? That's it? Besides, 'the last back-up' sounds like a Bruce Willis movie."

"Anything that can take me out can take you out, too."

"Don't be so fuckin' certain."

"This way, if I'm still alive, I've got a chance. The Deacon will know what to do."

"And I don't?"

"This is shits," Anna said. She had been watching us like we were a tennis match. Now she stood up and put a hand on Nicky's shoulder. "We are doing this as Billy says. Please."

The look on her face would have melted marble. Nicky still wasn't completely convinced, but he accepted it. He smoothed the paper a few times and then folded it and stuck it in his pocket. "All right, then," he said. "If that's what it takes."

"That's it," I said. I took a deep breath and let it out through my teeth. For some reason I was feeling a lot tenser about this than I should have. Because it really was pretty simple. Like Nicky had said: go to a bar and talk to a drunk. Nothing to it.

Except that when Anna had shivered and looked at me, all the hair had stood up on the back of my neck. And now all my instincts were saying that it would get ugly, had already gotten ugly, and I was walking into a snake pit. I was stepping off into darkness with no idea what might be under my feet. I didn't like the feeling.

I shook it off. "Listen," I said, wanting to believe what I was saying. "We're making too much out of this. It's not a big deal, I just want to play it safe."

"Oh, yeah," Nicky said, slightly bitter. "With a last backup. That ought to do."

"Nicky, I'm just going to ask a few questions and come back. I'll be gone a couple of hours, no big deal."

"Fine, Billy. I'm sure I couldn't possibly ask the bastard any questions."

"Nicky—"

"Go on, Billy. Get out. You're a right proper bastard when you want."

I shook it off and turned to Anna. I put an arm around her and pulled her close. "You're safe here," I said. "And I'll be back soon."

She tilted her face up and looked into my eyes. I thought she was going to say something, but instead she pulled my face down onto hers and gave me a long, searching kiss. "Be careful," she said.

It was about twenty minutes of driving to get back to The O. The Miami traffic didn't do much to shake off my uneasy feelings, but at least it gave me some real danger to concentrate on.

Every city has a style. You see it in the way people look at strangers on the street, you can hear it on the local talk radio shows, you can read it in the local papers. Cities have their own flavors, and I had just gotten a taste of Miami's.

When I first came to Miami it had been like the kind of woman who is beautiful without any awareness of it, without consciously using that beauty on you. There was a freshness in the city, the hint that anything might be possible but whatever came would be good.

Now the city's beauty was coarser. There was too much makeup, too much soiled arrogance in the good looks. The lovely woman had picked up the hostility of the relentlessly small-time, trying to prove herself major league. Miami had become a part-time hooker, the kind who calls her tricks "dates" and thinks of the money as loans from her many boyfriends. Under the mask of beauty and freshness, the smell of decay had already taken over. Every year the people are a little more sour; they drive like they're trying to get revenge for something they don't remember. Everybody on the streets is a target for the kind of petty meanness that makes you want to stand on the hood of your car and shoot out the street lights.

Still, South Beach is very nice, isn't it? That is, if you can find a place to park, keep to well-lighted areas, and stay lucky.

I got to The O about fifteen minutes before the time I had agreed to meet Bud and his pal Oto. The inside of the bar looked like it had been sprayed in plastic to preserve it from last night. Nothing had changed. The same bartender stood behind the slanted, pitted bar. The same tough crowd slouched in the same positions at the same tables.

There was only one small difference tonight. Down at the far end of the bar, Bud's stool was empty.

No big deal; there was time yet. I settled at the bar with a glass of beer, facing the rest of the room, keeping one eye on the door and one eye on everything else.

I finished the beer. It wasn't the kind of place where you get up and dance to the jukebox, so I ordered another one. Bud was late. I looked around the room. Nobody looked back. I nursed my beer, taking tiny sips with a few minutes in between.

I finished my second beer and ordered another one. A few more and it wouldn't matter if Bud came or not. I was living the high life.

There were a lot of reasons why Bud might not show up. It was possible that his drunk buddy was too drunk to navigate. Maybe his car wouldn't start. He could have a 24-hour flu. And maybe PBS was showing *Downton Abbey* and he didn't want to miss it.

Whatever the reason, after I'd had three beers I was pretty sure Bud was not coming tonight. I could play it safe and drink another beer, but then I might have to call Nicky to come down in a cab and drive me home.

I pushed away from the bar and headed out into the night. We hadn't said anything about it, but I was willing to bet that Bud would show up tomorrow night. He might not have Oto with him, but he'd be back. This was his place.

When I got back to the hotel room, Anna and Nicky were sitting on opposite sides of the room, Anna on the bed and Nicky in the straight-backed chair at the little desk. They were just sitting, doing nothing. A stack of empty beer bottles was ranged around Nicky. As I opened the door their heads swiveled in unison to look at me.

And the nicest thing I had seen in a long time was the way Anna's face lit up when she saw me. She jumped up and came to me, getting her arms around me before Nicky had the chance to do more than bellow, "Billy!"

I walked Anna back across the room and we sat down on the bed. "Well, mate," Nicky said. "Was there any change?"

Maybe it was the three beers I'd had, but I didn't get what he meant. "Change in what?"

He shook his head. "Change from the hundred dollars. Was there any left, or did he take the whole lot?"

I hadn't even thought about Nicky's money until now. I pried it out of my pocket and flipped it across the room to him. "It's all there," I said.

"Outstanding," Nicky said. "Did he talk?"

"He didn't talk. He didn't show up."

"Not at all?"

"Not even partly," I said. "I drank a few beers and heard *Achy Breaky Heart* seven times. That's it."

Nicky frowned. Anna frowned. It looked better on her.

"And so?" Anna finally said.

"I don't know," I said. "I guess I go back there tomorrow night and try again."

"It's a classic bargaining technique," Nicky said. "Straight out of Sun Tzu. Keep 'em off-balance. Hold fast. Don't go over a hundred dollars, no matter what."

I looked at Nicky. He was serious. "You're getting awfully attached to that money."

"Aw, come on, it's a hundred dollars."

"The money is nothing," Anna said. "Important is why does this Bud not come tonight?"

"I'm telling you why," Nicky said. "He's pumping up the price."

"I don't think so," I said. "My reading of Bud might be wrong, but I don't think he'd work that way."

"Just wait, mate. You'll see."

"Maybe so. We'll know tomorrow night. Until then—" I shrugged.

"So we are only waiting now, and nothing more as this?" Anna asked.

"That's it," I told her.

CHAPTER NINETEEN

The next day was long. The day before we had been waiting, tense, expecting something to happen and thinking that one way or another we would have an answer that night. That hadn't happened and there was no way to know if anything at all would happen tonight. We didn't know whether to be nervous or disappointed so we were a little of both.

So there was waiting, and politeness all around to hide the frazzled nerves, and the routine of meals. And soon it was night again and I was repeating my good-byes to Anna.

She held me for a minute, and then looked up at me, and then put her head on my chest.

"What?" I asked her.

"Is most of nothing," she said. "Only—"

"Only what?"

She looked up again. "Last night I am having this bad feeling and nothing is happening. So tonight I am having it even more so, and so perhaps even more nothing will happens. Only I am afraid of something to happens when I am not yet being so much a woman for you."

I kissed her on the forehead. "You are being plenty a woman for me," I said. "And nothing will happens. I'll be back in a few hours." And I left her there in the hotel room, before she could say anything more.

Nothing had changed in the Miami traffic, and nothing was different in The O, either. I took my stool at the bar and worked my way through a glass of beer. I had just started on my second when the door opened and two cops pushed their way in.

When I had come in the other night with Nicky and Anna the place had gotten quiet. The cops got the opposite reaction. Everybody talked just a little louder, putting a lot of work into being innocent.

The cops stopped inside the door and looked around for a few seconds. The O wouldn't be on anybody's regular beat. They wouldn't come into a place like this unless they were making a collar. I wondered who it was.

I didn't wonder long. The taller cop, a thin black guy with a mustache, nudged his partner, an older Hispanic man, and they both moved towards the bar.

Towards me.

"Could you please stand up and place both hands on the bar, sir?" the taller one said. According to his nametag, he was DENNIS. His partner, LOPEZ, stayed a few steps to the side to cover me in case I pulled a LAWS rocket from my beer glass.

"What's the problem?" I asked him.

"Put both your hands on the bar," Dennis repeated.

"Sure," I said. I put both my hands on the bar. They both looked serious about this and there was plenty of time to clear up whatever the misunderstanding was.

Dennis patted me down. He took my pocketknife, a large stainless steel Buck knife Betty Fleming had given me for Christmas. I turned my head. Lopez was talking to the bartender, who was nodding at me.

"I don't know shit," I heard the bartender say. "Whyntcha ask him. He knows sumtin, tell ya that."

"Are you going to tell me what this is about?" I asked Dennis.

"We'd just like to ask you a few questions," he said, putting my knife carefully into a plastic bag. That didn't look too good. Bagging the knife meant he thought it might be evidence of something. That meant the questions they wanted to ask me might be a little bit sharp.

"Am I charged with something?" I asked him.

"We're just going to ask a few questions," he repeated. He twisted my arms behind me and snapped on the handcuffs. I let him. Arguing with two highly trained, heavily armed guys is a bad idea.

I kept telling myself that after they stuck me in the back seat of their car. Riding with your hands behind you isn't a lot of fun. Especially in an enclosed space with the windows rolled up where somebody had been very sick not too long ago. It smelled like their diet of muscatel and road kill hadn't agreed with them and the cheap disinfectant hadn't done more than add to the stink. Police work is so romantic. All the TV cop shows say so.

Luckily the ride wasn't too long. But the wait on the other end was. They stuck me in a small holding cell that smelled familiar. Whoever had been riding in the back seat of the cops' car before me had come here with some friends. They'd had a contest; who can cover the most floor space with a single vomit. From the smell, I'd say it had been a three-way tie.

I sat in the holding cell for a couple of hours before they came to get me. I guess they had to think out the questions. Judging by the two detectives who were waiting for me, they should have taken a little more time.

The uniforms took me to a small room filled with a table and a few chairs. An ashtray smoldered in the middle of the table. Down at the far end a guy smoldered in a chair. He had a rumpled silk suit with a thin tie, black, Pat Riley hair and a thin mustache. His feet, in tasseled loafers, were on the table. He glared at me when they ushered me into the room.

His partner was a fat guy with a really bad haircut and a broken nose that looked more like an animal's snout than a human's nose. With his jowls and baggy suit he looked like Porky Pig's mean cousin having a bad hair day. He nodded at the chair directly opposite him. "Have a seat, William," he said. His partner cleared his throat with a sound like a dog growling. Great. I was being grilled by

Porky and the Wolf.

I sat.

"They treat you okay?"

"Sure. Except they forgot to tell me what this is about," I said.

Porky nodded. He just watched me with a half-pleasant smile. His partner continued to glare at me. A couple of minutes went by like this. I knew the technique. I was supposed to get uncomfortable with the two of them staring at me. It would break down my defenses and make me want to please them by admitting I had done it.

It's surprising how often that routine works. That's why cops use it. The only problem was that I didn't know what I had done. I could give them a kind of general confession and let them slap it on where they wanted it, but I had the feeling they might try to make it stick. I decided to play it straight.

"Listen," I said. "I'll be glad to cooperate with whatever you got going here, but first you have to let me know why I'm here. As far as I know I didn't see anything or do anything interesting in the last few days."

"Sure," snarled the Wolf. "Nothing at all. Innocent as a baby. It's fucking amazing how everybody we talk to is innocent as a fucking baby."

"Lorenzo," Porky said to him.

Lorenzo slapped the table. "He pisses me *off*. Look at him! He thinks we're just stupid spic cops, ha? Is that what you think, *pendejo?*"

"All right, Lorenzo," Porky said, giving me a weary smile that said, *See what I put up with?*

I felt honored. I was actually getting the Mr. Hard and Mr. Soft Routine. Cops have used that routine since Cain killed Abel. I was surprised to see it in a place as sophisticated as Miami. Maybe they'd seen *Miami Vice* too many times.

"We have a problem, William," Porky said.

"Yeah, you do. You're grilling the wrong guy."

He ignored me. "Our problem is this. We think maybe you know a few things we want you to talk about. If we could just clear this up quick, Lorenzo could go home." He leaned his head towards his partner with a small smile. "He gets cranky when he's up this late."

"This guy thinks he's tough." Lorenzo slammed his chair back and stood up. "Is that what you think? You're too tough for a couple of *puercos gusanos?*"

"Sit down, Lorenzo," Porky said.

"He's pissing me *off!*" Lorenzo said, but he sat down.

"What about it, William?" Porky said, giving his head a sympathetic shake. "Can you help me out here?"

"I'll be glad to," I said. "First, tell me what you think I did, then read me rights, then ask me a couple of real questions. That way we can settle this and Lorenzo can go home. Does that help at all?"

Lorenzo slammed his hand down again and said something in rapid Spanish with no consonants. Porky raised a hand to calm him down and said something back. Then he smiled at me.

"All right," he said. "Let's play this your way. When was the last time you saw Arthur Nagle?"

I stared at him. The question told me they had a body somewhere, but it didn't tell me anything else. I'd never heard the name in my life. "As far as I know," I said, "I've never seen Arthur Nagle."

"You lying sack of shit," Lorenzo said.

"Lorenzo," Porky warned him.

"We got a dozen witnesses, fuckbag, so just drop that shit right there."

"That's enough, Lorenzo."

"That fucking bartender said you were—"

"¡*Cállate!*" barked out Porky, and this time he meant it. Lorenzo looked at him with surprise.

"I wasn't going to say anything," Lorenzo said, looking hurt.

"You already have," Porky told him.

And he had. I knew why I was here.

The only bartender I had seen in the last few weeks was the one at The O. So he had called in and told them to come get me. They had come pretty fast, and that told me that Arthur Nagle was dead. And the fact that it was the bartender that dropped the dime on me told me one other thing, too: I knew who Arthur Nagle was.

Bud.

Bud was dead.

It was a damned good excuse for not showing up to meet me.

"Do you have an alias for Nagle?" I asked Porky.

He glanced down at the file in front of him. "His friends called him Bud," Porky admitted.

"Okay," I said. "I knew him."

"No shit," Lorenzo snarled.

"Some shit," I said. "Most if it coming from you."

Lorenzo stood up again. He thought he was going to come down and swing at me, but Porky held up a hand. "*Siéntense*, for Christ's sake," he said. "You got it coming." Lorenzo sat down and Porky swung his busted snout back to me. "What was the nature of your association with Nagle?"

"I met him in the bar, The O," I said. "We talked, had a few drinks."

"And when was the last time you saw him?"

"Two nights ago, in The O. That was also the first time I saw him."

Porky and Lorenzo exchanged a look, then Porky came back to me. "So you meet the guy in a bar, never seen him before, and just start talking, is that it?"

"Yeah. It happens."

"And what did you talk about?"

"He said he was going to go look for a friend of his."

"Did his friend have a name?"

"I don't know the last name. First name was Otoniel, called Oto."

Lorenzo was on his feet again. "You son of a bitch—!" he yelled at me.

"Lorenzo!" Porky yelled.

"The son of a bitch did them both! He's fucking with us!"

Porky stood up and in two quick steps he was on Lorenzo. He grabbed his partner by the shoulders and whirred out some rapid Spanish. Lorenzo rattled back, pointing at me and looking like he wanted to spit. Porky had to hold him back from jumping at me.

I barely noticed. I was too busy re-shuffling everything in my mind.

I had been taking it for granted that Oto had killed Bud; maybe for money, maybe because Bud was talking about things Oto didn't want to talk about, maybe just because scary guys turn into scary drunks.

But if Oto was dead, too, then somebody had killed them both. It just couldn't happen any other way. There's such a thing as too much coincidence, too many bodies, even in Miami.

And there was only one person who might have had a strong enough reason to kill two guys who didn't do anything more than hang out in a bar and talk. I didn't know his name, but I knew who he was.

He was from The Black Freighter. If he wasn't the captain, the captain had sent him. He had found out that somebody was asking Oto questions and he had stopped it quickly, brutally, finally. Just exactly the way he did his business out in the Gulf Stream.

I wanted to think that this was different, that killing two American citizens in the heart of a major American city was not the same as killing Haitian citizens in the middle of the ocean. But I knew better. People get away with murder. Cops are overworked and a low profile death doesn't get the attention it needs. When Porky and Lorenzo were convinced that I didn't do it, this case would probably slip to the bottom of their pile. They'd already spent a whole shift on it, and that was too much time not to have any result.

They weren't going to catch this killer. It had to be me, and I wasn't going to do it by sitting in jail.

It was time to play my trump card.

I looked up. Porky had calmed Lorenzo down without using a club and he was settling back into his chair.

"You were telling us about Otoniel," Porky said with his patented tired smile.

"I'm sorry," I said. "I must have looked pretty good for this and you were hoping you got lucky. But I didn't do Nagle, and I didn't do Otoniel."

Porky nodded. "Okay, William," he said.

"Yeah, I know, it's tough to swallow. But maybe I can come up with something that will help you believe it."

"We'd like to hear that, William," he said.

I tried hard not to smile as I said, "Do either of you guys know The Deacon?"

CHAPTER TWENTY

It was close to two hours before The Deacon came to get me. Part of that time was spent persuading Porky that I really had Deacon's private number and that he would want to know that I was in jail.

The rest of the time, as I soon found out, The Deacon spent trying to calm down his wife.

"Angel had a shit-fit," he told me. "She wanted me to leave you here."

"I thought she liked me."

"She did. But she's Cuban. She believes that anybody who's in jail after midnight, when she's trying to sleep, is guilty of *something.*" He winked. "She might go easier on you if you got married again."

The Deacon walked me through the paperwork and out to his car with amazing speed. It made me very happy to see that a little old-fashioned string-pulling still worked, even in The New Miami. The look on Porky's face when he saw The Deacon come in was as close to hero-worship as you'll ever see from a full-grown cop with a nose like a pig's.

The paper-shufflers up front were just as eager to please. It didn't have anything to do with Deacon's rank. He was a supervisor, which was not high enough to make anybody jump through a hoop. It was partly his reputation. Everybody knew The Deacon, and what they knew about him made them very anxious to make him happy.

But he had something more. When he walked into a room, people stopped talking and looked up, even before they knew who he was. Several of the cops unconsciously dropped their hands near their holsters before they registered Deacon's badge, hung on his jacket pocket.

He had me out in near-record time and led me outside with one hand on my elbow.

"How do you rate our jails?" he asked pleasantly as we walked to his car.

"The ventilation isn't good," I said. "But I thought they'd be more crowded."

"Got lonely, did you?" He chuckled. "Boy, you broke some hearts in there. They thought they'd finally solved one. That's why they kept you isolated. They were breaking you down."

"It probably would have worked," I admitted, "If only I'd been guilty and had an IQ of less than 70."

"Franco and Lorenzo aren't bad," he said. "Just sort of basic. They've been working the River too long."

"What do they have?"

Deacon shook his head. "Two bodies found together. You were seen talking to one of them, the older one."

"Bud Nagle," I said.

"And the next night he turns up killed."

"How?"

Deacon chuckled. It was never a sound that brought a smile to my face. It was even colder now. "Hard to say, buddy. The coroner isn't done yet, but they just can't seem to figure whether they were crushed first and then bled dry, or the other way around."

"Crushed?"

"Until their eyeballs absolutely popped out of their heads," Deacon said. "Three cops on the scene threw up, which is a new record for one Miami crime scene." He shook his head. "Still no guess as to how it happened. I haven't seen the file. But they were crushed. Big cable, maybe. Whatever it was, it wrapped around and squoze 'em so hard there wasn't anything left inside 'em."

"Bad way to go," I said.

"You know a good one?"

We got to his car. It was parked cop-in-a-hurry style, angled in with one wheel on the sidewalk. I leaned on the roof while Deacon unlocked. There was a bare hint of a sunrise starting to show in the sky.

I was tired. Not just from staying up all night, either. This whole thing had been dumb and dirty and this trip had never seemed more pointless than it did right now.

Deacon popped open the passenger door of his metallic blue Chevy. I had to push some of the electronic clutter over a few inches in order to fit onto the seat. "Is one of these things a telephone?" I asked him.

"Two of 'em," he said. He reached over and picked one up. "Try this one."

"Thanks." I took it from him and dialed the motel. They had one of those automatic switching things where an obnoxious recorded voice tells you to punch in the room number. I did. It rang a long time. Nobody answered.

Anna had probably stepped out. Maybe to get something to eat. That was probably all it was. And Nicky was in the other room and couldn't hear the phone ringing over the TV. There was nothing to worry about. Nothing at all.

I let it ring a little longer. I thought about all the time I had been in jail, and talking to the two detectives. I thought about somebody who had killed Bud and Otoniel at the smallest hint of a question. Crushed and bled dry.

I put down the phone.

"Deacon," I said, "can you make this thing go fast?"

He put his foot down before I even finished speaking. The car jumped ahead. "That's one of the things I'm best at," he said.

There wasn't much traffic at this hour. Deacon slid his big car through what little there was. One guy kept up with us for a while, just for practice, I guess. Then he saw the blue light on the dashboard and dropped back.

We were at the motel in five minutes and I was out of the car before it stopped moving. I ran up the stairs, fumbling for a room key.

I didn't need it. The door was open about two inches. A blast of cold air from inside hit me and went right through me, chilling me to the bone.

I pushed the door open.

The first thing that hit me was how neat and empty the room looked. It felt dead, the way only an empty motel room can. There was no sign that anything at all had happened; no broken ashtrays, no overturned chairs, no license plate numbers scrawled on the wall in blood.

I pushed the door further open. It hit some resistance. I stopped pushing and slid through, looking to see what it was.

It was Nicky.

He was stretched on the floor behind the door. One arm was spread out in front of him, the other folded under his body. A bruise ran across the side of his face, another on his throat.

I went down onto one knee and felt for a pulse. It was there, slow and steady. I heard something behind me and looked up. Deacon was there with a radio in one hand, already calling it in.

"He's alive," I said.

I went quickly through the room, the bathroom, the connecting door to Nicky's room, the bathroom in there. I knew what I would find, and I found it.

Nothing.

Anna was gone.

I went back into the other room with a dead lump forming in me. It felt like something huge and hot was sinking down my throat to my feet.

Deacon was bent over Nicky, the radio wedged between his shoulder and ear. He looked up at me. "I think we got lucky," he said. "This one isn't too bad."

"Not so lucky," I said. "There's one missing."

He looked at me for a long beat and then said a word I didn't think he knew. "Give me a description," he said.

I told Deacon what she looked like. Each detail hurt me. I could see her so clearly, almost feel the smoothness of her skin. Some small scent of her remained in the room.

An ambulance came. I stood in the shadows made by the blinking light and watched as they got Nicky inside. They moved him quickly, without seeming to hurry. I guess they had a lot of practice. It was less than three minutes before they slammed the doors and took off for Jackson Memorial Hospital.

I rode along behind with Deacon. We didn't say much; he tried to cheer me up by complaining about the paperwork I was causing him, but when I didn't say anything back he fell quiet.

They wouldn't let me see Nicky at the hospital. It was against policy. They shuttled me off to a waiting room that smelled only a little better than the jail cell I'd been in a few hours earlier. They said it might take some time.

I spent the time doing some thinking. With all that was going on between my ears it wasn't easy. It was like trying to hear somebody whispering in a room full of people shrieking at the top of their lungs.

Anna. God knows what was happening to her, but it wouldn't be good. I had to find her. I had to get her back from them, before it was too late. She'd come so far from what had happened to her, and now this.

I had to find her.

But to figure out how to get Anna back, I had to know why they—or he—had taken her. The three main reasons I came up with were that she'd been taken as a warning, as punishment, or for profit.

If they took her for profit they would get in touch with me. So I didn't need to think about that one yet.

If they took her to say, *watch what you do; We have your girl and we can hurt her if you try to hurt us*, then she was alive and well and all I had to do was find her before that changed.

But if they took her as punishment, to show the world what

would happen to anybody dumb enough to mess with them—

I didn't want to think about it. Anna had been through hell one time already. This time wouldn't have the same happy ending.

It was possible that she was already dead, or so mutilated that death would be a blessing. I tried to shove that out of my mind. I tried to make myself believe that it made more sense for them to keep her alive so they had a hold on me, a way to keep me off them.

It all came down to the same thing anyway. I had to find her as fast as I could.

I blinked and found that there was a large blonde woman in a white coat standing in front of me, looking at me expectantly.

"I'm sorry," I said. "Did you say something?"

She shook her head. "Only a couple of paragraphs. It's your friend."

I felt a sick lurch in my gut. I'd watched this scene as a cop too many times. And now I was playing a big part in it, as the guy who let it happen. "Nicky? Is he—?"

The woman looked amused. "He's fine, if the intern doesn't kill him. He'd like to see you."

"Nicky? Nicky's awake?"

She smiled. "Apparently he regained consciousness in the ambulance. He's got quite a hard head."

I followed her down a hall to the room where they had Nicky. He was in a hospital gown and propped up on a couple of pillows. A young intern, a pale guy with straw-colored hair and a bad complexion, was seated on the edge of the bed, taking his pulse.

I realized Nicky was taking the intern's pulse. He had a grip on the guy's arm and was probing with the stiffened fingers of his left hand.

"—here, and *here*. No, *here*, mate. There's seven levels of the pulse. You got to listen for it. Listen with the *inner* ear. The Chinese have been at this for 3,000 years, and they—" He looked up and saw me. "Billy!" he shouted, sounding only a little hoarse, and not at all weak. "Tell these wonks to give me back my clothes."

The intern wonk had jumped to his feet looking guilty. He

cleared his throat and looked at the large blonde woman. "Ahem. Actually," he said, "we'd like to keep you overnight for observation."

Nicky made a rude noise and the intern looked indignant, turning to me for moral support. "He sustained quite a severe shock to the side of the skull and I can't rule out the possibility of a concussion, and even a small leak in the blood vessels of the brain that could—"

Nicky made a farting sound again. "Pull the other one," he said. "I'm fit as a fiddle. Think I wouldn't know if I was about to pop off?"

The intern frowned. A light flush came to his cheeks. "Actually, it's possible that a problem wouldn't show itself for quite some time. That's why we keep people. For observation."

"Aw, mate, I've just been telling you. The *third* level of pulse would show it. I've got no concussion, no cerebral hematoma, nothing." He threw off the sheet. "Where's me pants, there's a good lad."

The intern shrugged and clenched his fists. "We can't let you leave," he said.

"You can't stop me," Nicky told him cheerfully. "I don't actually need the pants."

"This is against medical advice."

"Not mine."

The blonde woman cleared her throat like she was trying hard not to laugh. The intern took a couple of deep breaths and flushed a darker red. Nicky reached back and started to untie his hospital gown.

"All right," the intern said, "just a minute." He dashed over to a cupboard and came back with Nicky's clothes. "You really shouldn't," he said.

Nicky winked at him. "No worries," he said. "If I die, I can't sue, eh?"

The blonde woman pulled a curtain around the bed and in a few seconds Nicky burst out through the screen, buttoning his pants. "All right, Billy, off we go," he said, rushing out the door and into the hall. He turned in the hall, looking both ways and waiting for me to catch up. "Where have they got Anna? How is she?"

The door closed behind me. I looked at him. He didn't have any idea. He was cheerful, confident and ready to go, like a small dog about to go for a walk.

I couldn't say it. I shook my head.

"What," he said. "What does that mean? How bad is it? Come on, Billy, I need to know."

"She's gone," I said. "They took her."

Nicky turned pale green, as if all the blood in him had suddenly poured down into his feet. "Aw, no," he said softly. He looked for a place to sit down. There wasn't any. He leaned against the wall, looking old and beat up.

Beyond him, at the far end of the hall, I saw The Deacon coming towards us with his easy, gun-fighter's walk.

"They tell me you think you're leaving," Deacon said to Nicky as he came up to us.

Nicky turned to look at him.

"What's that?"

"This is The Deacon," I explained. "The man I told you about. The number I gave you."

"The copper?"

"That's right," Deacon said. "And I have a few copper questions to ask you."

CHAPTER TWENTY-ONE

The Deacon generally worked out of the front seat of his car, but he had a small office that he never used. It was in the regional F.D.L.E. headquarters, near the airport. It had a window, a desk with a telephone and computer, and two metal folding chairs.

I'd been a cop in L.A. for seven years, and I'd gotten to know a couple of the movie people out there. One of them once told me that you could tell how important somebody was by their office. A corner office with lots of windows, a potted plant, art on the wall and a couch meant this was a major player, somebody really important.

The rating system was so clear, my friend said he could tell at a glance where somebody ranked, even by what kind of plants they had. "Anybody can have a ficus," he told me.

Deacon didn't even have a ficus. It didn't seem to bother him. He led us into the office with his name on the door like somebody going into a strange room. He looked around once, as if trying to figure out where everything was, and then settled uncertainly into the chair behind the desk. "Sit down," he said, waving vaguely at the folding chairs.

I gave Nicky the chair directly across from Deacon and sat with my arm wedged against the wall. I felt sick, empty, tired. I closed my eyes. Too many hours had gone by since Anna had been grabbed. It was already too late, and I wasn't doing anything. I hadn't done anything right yet.

"Okay," Deacon poked with his pointer fingers at the keyboard. His dark triangular eyebrows were wrinkled down and his tongue was shoved out the side of his mouth.

He punched in a final command, shook his head, and looked at Nicky. "Now, son, I'd like to get a description of the guy that clobbered you."

Nicky shook his head. The Deacon just looked at him.

"Aw, look, I dunno," Nicky said. "I barely saw him, it was so fast—I dunno what I can tell you."

"Anything at all might help," Deacon said.

Nicky frowned. "He was a black fella, I know that. But—" Nicky looked over at me. "I'm sorry. But I didn't even get the door open and he was upside my noggin. And I'm on the floor, on my side, and that's it. Lights out."

"Sometimes it helps," said the Deacon, "if you close your eyes and try to see it all in slow motion."

Nicky looked up at him, surprised. He blinked. "Of course," he said. "I'm a silly shit. Self-hypnosis."

"What's that?" Deacon asked him.

"Self-hypnosis. I can put myself into a trance, right? Do it all the time, for channeling and that."

"Nicky," I said. I didn't want him going off on one of his Spiritual Odysseys right now and channeling the spirit of a 12th century Tibetan monk.

But he was already into it, leaning back in the chair, pointing his chin at the ceiling, blowing his breath out and sucking it back in again.

I looked at Deacon. He raised one of those eyebrows at me and I shook my head. We both stared at Nicky.

His face looked subtly different. Some of the lines on it had smoothed out and he seemed—I don't know—more serious or something. Not his usual elf-self.

"Okay," he said. His voice was breathy, but clear.

Deacon shrugged. "How does this work. Somebody knocks at

the door, is that it?"

"Who can this be?" he says, and I feel ice cubes along my spine. It's Anna's voice.

"Must be Billy," he says in his own voice.

"And you go to the door," Deacon says.

Nicky laughs, a high-pitched cackle. "He's forgot his key!" he says, and then changing to Anna's voice again, "Nicky, no! Wait!"

Nicky turned in his chair, a quarter-turn to where Anna is. "Eh?" he says, and frowns.

"You open the door," Deacon suggests.

"Oh... Yeah," he says, in his slow, breathy voice. "I... open the door. I'm half-looking at Anna. She's rising up off the chair. And something... Uh," he says.

"What is it?" Deacon asks.

"He... *hit* me."

"Who did?"

"The guy. The guy at the door. He grabs my throat, really tight. Christ, he's a strong one. And he smacks me on the head... Ah, fuck..."

"Can you see him, Nicky? What does he look like?"

"He's black. Seems too thin to be that strong. And fast. Christ on a bun, he moves faster than... anything."

"Describe the guy who hits you, Nicky."

Nicky frowned. "Pencil..." he said.

Deacon shoved a pencil and a legal pad across the desk and without looking, Nicky grabbed them up. Eyes still closed, he began to sketch quickly.

I watched as a face began to take shape. It was lean and triangular, running from a wide forehead across slightly slanted eyes, a strong, wide nose, down to a sharp chin. High cheekbones stood out, and so did the bones around the deep-set eyes.

The face was handsome, even pretty, without being even a little bit attractive. "Guy's about thirty-five, thirty-six," Nicky said, eyes still closed. "About five foot ten, 165 pounds. Moves like a fucking snake. Oh," he said, sounding surprised.

"What is it?" Deacon asked.

"The snake. He's got a snake tattooed on his arm, left arm, just above the wrist." Nicky frowned, shivered all over, and opened his eyes. "How'd I do?"

"How the hell would I know?" Deacon said, staring at the picture. He reached over and picked it up. "What am I supposed to do with this?"

Nicky looked offended. "You're supposed to *use* it," he said.

Deacon shook his head, looked at me. "Billy?"

"I think the description is probably pretty good," I said.

"A snake tattoo?" Deacon said. "I'm supposed to put out a BOLO for a guy with a snake tattoo because Captain Marvel here saw it in his magic trance?"

"You have something better?" I asked him.

He shook his head again. "I got nothing, buddy."

"He's had Anna for twelve hours," I said.

Deacon looked at the picture again, then at Nicky, then at me. "I'll put this out," he said. "And then you and me are going snooping."

He turned back to the computer and typed in the description. When he was done he punched a final button extra hard and a printer whirred behind him. "All right," he said. "I'll put that out as a BOLO. Now let's us do the *real* work." He crammed himself in behind the desk again and leaned on an elbow. "We're figuring this is connected to these two murders," he said. "Nagle and—what's the other guy?"

"Oto," I said. "I don't remember his last name."

"Don't matter," he said, turning back to the computer. "I'll have it all up here in a second." He slowly punched at the keyboard, looking more like he was sparring than typing. The printer whirred again and he pulled out a page.

"Otoniel Varela," he read in the syllable-by-syllable way cops from the South use on Hispanic names. "Age thirty-four, occupation merchant seaman. Currently unemployed."

"Currently dead," I said. "If we can find out the last couple of boats he worked, one of them will be the Black Freighter."

"You think that's where she is?"

I shrugged. It took all my energy. "It's all I can come up with. It's a start, anyway."

He started whacking away at the keyboard again. "Shouldn't be a problem. I can call up the records from the Union rolls, and..." He trailed off, lost in trying to work the computer. "Bingo," he said after a long moment of silence. "The *Maria Chinea*, about six months ago. Been on shore since then."

"Before that?"

Deacon frowned. "Little bit confused here. He's down for a couple of them at the same time, and then it shows he didn't take either one. Then before that, about two years on the *Petit Fleur.* "

"It's one of those two, *Maria* something or *Petit Fleur.* It has to be."

"I'm with you on that, buddy. But which one?"

I shook my head. "Can't say. It could have worked out that he worked the *Fleur*, got fed up, and went through a couple of jobs fast. Or it could have been the *Maria.* But one of them is the Black Freighter. It has to be."

"Don't want to jump on the *Petit Fleur*, just 'cause it's a Haitian name," he said.

"Why not?" Nicky blurted. "Man's a voodoo priest, stands to reason."

Deacon shook his head. "These old freighters go back and forth all over the Caribbean. Might change hands a dozen times."

"But the name," Nicky insisted.

"It's bad luck to change a boat's name, Nicky," I said.

"Oh."

"Check 'em both," I told Deacon.

"Uh-huh," he said, and began pecking at the keyboard again. "Let's us just see what we can find..."

Deacon hammered at the computer for about five minutes, muttering softly to himself and a couple of times to me, saying things like, "Hang on, buddy."

Finally he slapped the keyboard and the printer started to whirr again. Deacon leaned back, looking satisfied. "Well," he said.

"You found something?"

"Yes I did, Billy. I surely did find something." He grabbed the paper from the printer. "Gervasio Lopez is the master of the *Maria Chinea*. He has stayed at our fine hotel in Raiford on two occasions. Once for drug smuggling, once for manslaughter." He looked up. "That one was a plea bargain down from Murder One. Apparently he's in with the Cali syndicate. They can buy some pretty good legal help."

"He sounds like a drug smuggler. We're looking for a witch doctor," I said.

Deacon held up a finger. "Now don't go jumping to any conclusions, Billy. A lot of the Colombian syndicate guys do a kind of black magic version of *santeria*. Human sacrifice and everything. Remember that thing in Mexico a few years back?"

"Matamoros," I said. I remembered.

"That's it. They thought eating human body parts would make 'em rich and keep them from being arrested. This Lopez could be another one."

"What about the other ship?"

Deacon glanced at the printout. "Patrice du Sinueux. Known as Cappy." Deacon frowned. "Funny. We got some detail on this guy but no arrest record. And so no picture." He ran a finger down the page. "Okay. That explains it. He was a mid-level guy in the *ton-ton macoute*. Guess that would be with Baby Doc Duvalier. Got in some trouble, tried to claim political asylum here in the U.S."

"What kind of trouble?"

Deacon frowned. "Doesn't say here, but it's a good rule of thumb that if you're running from that crowd you're a good guy."

What Deacon said made sense. All we had heard from Honore about the Black Freighter had said its captain was a voodoo *houngan*. But Honore was Haitian. He would put things in those terms. And *palo mayombe*, the dark side of Santeria, was similar enough to voodoo that somebody who knew about one of them would recognize the other.

So although a small voice in the dark of my head was telling me the Haitian captain ran the Black Freighter, my head said it made more sense to go for the convicted felon, rather than a man who had apparently tried to escape from the *ton-ton macoute*.

"All right," I said to Deacon. "I vote for Lopez."

Deacon nodded. "Me too. I just hope we're right, Billy," he said, reaching for the telephone. "Let me call my buddy in Customs."

CHAPTER TWENTY-TWO

The *Maria Chinea* had probably been a nice ship once—maybe fifty years ago. Now it was a bucket of rust held together by the greasy cables around its deck cargo. There was a thick smell of old fish dipped in diesel clinging to the deck.

The mate was on deck when we got there, smoking a cigar that looked like it had been launched about the same time as the ship. He was a tanned, creased guy in his fifties, dirty and unshaved, with a face like a disappointed gorilla. As our car pulled up he stood, knocked the coal off the end of his cigar, and stuck the battered old thing in his shirt pocket.

Ray Hall got out first. He was Deacon's friend in Customs, an out-sized good ol' boy who had played tackle for the Gators and come home to South Florida to fight crime.

Whatever else people may say about the Good Ol' Boy Network, if you're inside it, it works for you. And Deacon was definitely inside it. Ray had been happy to pull a couple of spot inspections for his ol' buddy Deacon. Customs does them all the time anyhow, randomly picking ships from a master list of everything in the harbor. Having Deacon suggest a couple of ships was no problem.

Ray had looked a little dubious about bringing us along, but when Deacon explained why he had shrugged it off. "Just you all try to look the part," he'd said.

"What part, mate?" Nicky asked him.

Ray looked thoughtful when he heard Nicky's accent. "We take other law enforcement personnel along with us all the time? So nobody's gonna give two tick's off a dog's ass if I got a couple more with me. Just you look serious, like you know a lot more than you're saying, and maybe I can make them fools think you're from Australian Customs, come to learn how to do it right."

Ray led the way up the gangway and we followed, Nicky stretching his face into the grim look of a man who's learning to stop beer smuggling.

The mate stood waiting for us at the top, blocking our way onto the ship, arms folded, a look of passive hostility on his face.

"Customs," Ray told him, showing his ID. "We need to see your paperwork and check your holds."

The mate didn't budge. "*¿Qué?*" he said.

Ray switched to perfect Spanish, with no accent I could catch, and repeated himself. The mate stared at him for a minute, then shrugged and turned away to get the papers.

When he disappeared into the superstructure, Ray turned back to us. "I'll keep him busy," he said. "Y'all go ahead and poke around. Just don't get too messy." And he wandered after the mate.

We searched the ship. From the mate's attitude of half-dead hostility I was already sure it was the wrong one but we searched anyway. We went through the holds, the moldy living area, the engine room. A small, ferret-like guy with no shirt sat on a folding chair in the engine room. He looked up at us when we came in, but he didn't move and he didn't say a word.

Other than that there was no trace of life on board, aside from a few rats, and some things that were growing on the walls in the galley.

No sign of Anna. No sign of anyplace where they might have tucked her away.

We met up with Ray in the wheelhouse. He was flipping through a large stack of papers, firing questions at the mate in rapid Spanish. Ray looked up when we came in; Deacon shook his head slightly, and Ray rifled once through the papers and then handed them back to the mate.

"All right," Ray said. "Anything else?"

Deacon raised an eyebrow at me.

"Ask him if he remembers a guy named Otoniel Varela," I said. "He worked on board a while back."

The mate had lifted his head up when I said Oto's name. As Ray asked him the question he was already nodding. Before he answered the mate spat out the wheelhouse door. Then he raced through a couple of minutes of furious talking mixed with hand signals, grunts and groans, and at one point a long, shrill scream.

He talked fast and without consonants and although I speak a little Spanish, I couldn't follow it. My ears were used to the slower, more careful, Mexican Spanish and the Caribbean variety left me far behind.

But one word I could pick out, because he used it several times, and even moaned it once right after the scream, was "*sueño.*" Dream.

And right around the scream, the mate moaned something that sounded like, "las looooozes," which I puzzled over for a while and couldn't get.

When the mate had finished, Ray nodded and handed back the papers. "*Bueno,*" he said, and then added something almost as fast as the mate's speech. Then he turned for the door and we followed, down the stairs, across the deck and down the gangway. By the time we got to the car, the mate was already sitting again, staring at his cigar.

"Quite a story," Ray said as we settled into the car. He was behind the wheel with Deacon beside him and Nicky and I were in the back.

"He remembered Oto," I said.

"Be a job of work to forget that boy," he said. "I don't know why you're interested in Oto, but Oto like to be some major shit for somebody pretty soon."

"Too late," I said. "He's dead."

"Uh-huh. Well that ought to help the sleep problem."

"The what?" Deacon asked.

Ray shook his head. "Your Oto worked the boat here maybe six months ago. The mate—his name's Garcia, by the way. Providencio Garcia."

"Old Providencio says Oto had a sleep problem," Deacon said.

"Yep. Says he didn't like Oto's looks when he showed up. Sort of wild looking, one side of his face unshaved, big rings under his eyes. Smelled like a bordello floor on Sunday morning. Providencio says he would have turned Oto away if he could, but his papers were all right and with the Unions and all he had to take him on.

"Anyhow, first week out Oto kept the other hands awake all night with his moaning and kicking all night long. And he was drinking, screwing up on the job. Not a real popular guy. And one night he wakes up screaming."

"What was he screaming?" I asked.

Ray smiled. "Las luces!"

I suddenly got it. *Luces*, not *loozes*. "The lights?"

"Yeah. That's what Providencio says."

"Did he say what that means?"

Ray shrugged. "Says that Oto woke up in a real bad sweat and grabbed for his bottle. Swigged about half of it down. One of the other hands said something to him and Oto just kept drinking. Tried to take the bottle away and Oto broke the guy's arm. Two other guys jumped in. Oto puts 'em both down, one with a concussion, the other a busted up kneecap. He goes crazy, starts breaking things up.

"So they fetched Providencio. He talks Oto down a bit, Oto sits back down with the bottle. Takes a big slug, most of the rest of the bottle. Providencio tries to get the bottle away from Oto. Oto won't let go. Starts babbling, *saltan en el agua, todo el mundo saltan en el agua.*"

"What's that?" Nicky demanded.

Ray gave him a half shrug and a small smile. "They all jump in the water," he said.

"Oh," said Nicky, frowning like he could make sense of it.

Ray went on. "Anyway, Providencio tells him that don't make any sense, they're all on the ship, they're gonna be okay, and everybody'd like to get some sleep. Oto says yes, he can make you sleep, too, he's a *bocor*, he has the powder."

"Bingo," Deacon said softly.

"Providencio says maybe old Oto ought to take some of that powder, because he's keeping everybody up," Ray went on. "And Oto gets even more worked up, says they don't even need the powder 'cause they got the lights. He starts laughing, shoutin' out, '*¡Crean que estan en Miami! ¡Pero es solamente las luces! ¡Todo el mundo saltan en el agua!* And after a couple of minutes of that, he falls over, dead drunk asleep.

"Short-handed like that, three guys too busted up to work, and one too drunk-crazy to find his ass with both hands, it was all they could do to get in to port. Old Providencio couldn't wait to get Oto on shore and off his ship."

I ran over it in my mind. Oto had taken out three sailors at once, guys who tended to be pretty tough. Oto was tougher. But not tough enough for whatever it was he'd gotten into—like murdering refugees, maybe? But how?

Saltan en el agua. ¡Crean que estan en Miami! ¡Pero es solamente las luces! It didn't make much sense; most likely it was just drunken ravings. *They think they are in Miami. But it's only the lights. Everybody jumps in the water.*

It meant nothing to me. But that last sentence, the one he had repeated. *Everybody jumps in the water.* Why would they jump in the water? Because of the lights? What lights? What kind of lights made everybody jump in the water?

I shook it off. None of this mattered. All that mattered right now was finding Anna. "Let's get to the next one," I said.

Deacon looked at me with sympathy. That made me feel even worse. "Sure thing, buddy," he said. "That would be the *Petit Fleur*," he said to Ray.

Ray picked a clipboard off the dashboard and flipped through a sheaf of papers. "Okay. Just up the way a piece," he said, and started the car.

We drove in silence for a couple of minutes until Ray pulled the car over beside an empty slip.

"Let me check on this," he said, lifting his cell phone and calling. "Probably got the slip number wrong."

Ray turned away and spoke rapidly. But even before he clicked off I knew. This was the right slip. The right ship had been in it. Anna had been on board.

And now it was gone.

Ray looked tired, beat. "Guess we should have checked this one first," he said. "*Petit Fleur* cleared Customs and left for Haiti about ninety minutes ago."

CHAPTER TWENTY-THREE

I'm not sure how long we sat there. It probably wasn't very long, but it felt like a couple of hours. My mind was far away, out over the ocean, trying to get to a small freighter. It couldn't be that far out. Not more than ten miles. If it was on land, I could run it down in an hour or two.

But it wasn't on land. It was on the ocean. There were no roads, no paths, nothing to follow and nothing to run on.

And no way to get out there. No way to find the freighter even if I did get out there.

As my mind circled around the same thing for the thousandth time, I felt the silence in the car. I looked around. They were all looking at me.

Ray put an arm across the back of the seat. "Well," he said weakly. "I guess I just fucked up." He looked away, out over the water. "I'm sorry, Billy."

"Not your fault," The Deacon said. "Let's get back."

"Can you get a chopper?" I asked Deacon.

"Son, I know this is rough on you. But we have no actual proof that a crime has been committed—"

"You know damn well—"

"Now, hear me out, buddy. I'm talking proof in the legal sense, which you and I know's got nothing to do with what really happened.

But a chopper is going to cost the department thousands of dollars. And from a budgeting standpoint they're going to need that kind of proof—not just that she's out there, but enough proof to get a conviction, before they commit to that kind of money."

"For God's sake." I felt like the world was unraveling.

"I will ask them. I will call in every favor I got laying around out there. But I don't want you thinking this is gonna solve the problem, because smart money says it won't."

"She's out there. You know she is."

"Yes, I do know. But it's not my chopper."

Ray put the car in gear.

Instead of calling it in, Deacon thought he'd have a better chance asking for the helicopter face to face. But even at high speed it was twenty minutes before we got back to Deacon's office. Figure a speed of around ten knots. Maybe a little less. The ship would be another three or four miles away.

Nicky and I sat in Deacon's office while he ran up and down the hall trying to find the right string to pull. Nicky was unnaturally quiet. Maybe he was blaming himself. He'd opened the door and let Hell in. I guessed he was telling himself he hadn't been strong enough, or quick enough, or man enough. I wished I could blame him, too. Anger would have been a lot better than the dead misery I was feeling.

Deacon was back in twenty minutes. Another three or four miles. I didn't need to ask how it had gone. It was right there on his face.

"I'm sorry, buddy," he said.

I stood up. "I need a boat," I said.

"It's going to be the same answer," he told me. "They're just not convinced down there. Say it's too complicated, what with no clear and compelling evidence of a crime, international waters screwing up the jurisdiction—I'm sorry, buddy," he said again. "But they'd rather let this one slip away than ruffle feathers in Tallahassee."

"Get me out of here," I told him, and I started for the door. "Take me back to my car." I would find a boat. I didn't know where, and I was sure it would be too late, but I'd do it.

Nicky followed me out the door, looking grim and indignant, and Deacon came behind.

As we drove back to my car I tried to think of all the options. It was pretty easy. There weren't any. Rent a boat? Not the boat I needed, with the big fuel tanks and the kind of speed and equipment to catch the freighter. Steal a boat? And get caught, flung back in jail, seal Anna's fate for sure?

I looked out the window. It was still Miami out there. Beautiful, angry, uncaring Miami. Paradise lost. There were no boats waiting on the street corners. I couldn't go into that mall we were passing and put a boat on my credit card. And I couldn't—

"Stop the car," I said.

Deacon nosed into the curb and stepped on the brake, turning to me with a raised eyebrow.

"The mall," I said. I closed my eyes and tried not to breathe too hard. For the first time in hours I could feel my heart turning over, the blood moving through me, into my hands, all the way down into my toes.

"I see it, buddy," Deacon said patiently.

"Pearl's," I said. I closed my eyes. "Fast, Deacon. As fast as you can go. Get me to Star Island."

There's a guard gate on the bridge to Star Island, but if you flash a badge and ask the way to the Pearl's house they don't give you any trouble. They direct you to circle around to the right, look for a big place with a massive iron gate and a huge wrought-iron modern sculpture in front.

We found it quickly, easily. Deacon showed his badge again, to the guard on the Pearl's front gate. He was a big guy with a crew cut and a dead face. He examined it carefully, asked us our business, and listened politely while Deacon said we just wanted to see Richard Pearl for a few minutes. Then he stepped back and spoke into a radio he had unclipped from his belt.

In less than two minutes we were waved through the gate, around the big circular driveway, and up to the house.

A stocky woman was waiting in the door. She had grey hair, a silk dress, and enough jewelry hanging off her to pay off the national debt.

"What's he done this time," she demanded.

"Is Richard Pearl here?" Deacon asked her politely as we climbed out of the car.

"I'm his step-mother. What did he do?"

Deacon glanced at me, then back at the woman. "As far as I know, ma'am, he hasn't done a thing. We have an emergency we think he might be able to help out on."

"An emergency."

"That's right, ma'am. Is he here?"

The crossed her arms and tapped her foot. She looked at Nicky, looked at me, then back at Nicky again, like she wasn't sure she'd seen it right the first time. Then she looked at Deacon. He looked back at her.

"Wait here," she said, and disappeared back into the house. The big dark wood door slammed shut with a very solid sound. Barbarians and commoners, stay out.

Waiting is always hard. Waiting when I knew that every six minutes took Anna another mile away was almost impossible. In about five minutes Mrs. Pearl was back. She opened the front door and glared out at us.

"I spoke to my husband's attorney," she said.

"Yes, ma'am," Deacon said politely.

"He wants to know if you have a warrant."

"Who's your attorney, ma'am?"

"Steven Dade," she said, as if everybody knew who that was. And I guess everybody did, in South Florida.

Deacon smiled. He reached into his pocket and handed her a business card. "Tell your attorney my name," he said. "Tell him Richard is in no way implicated in any crime whatsoever. We simply want to ask for his expert opinion."

She snorted. "Expert. Richie? Expert on tanning, maybe."

"And boats," I said.

She swung her head to me. "Oh," she said. She blinked. She looked down at the business card. "Well. I suppose so." She blinked again, then slammed the door.

She was back much quicker this time. She stepped shyly out into the sun, as if she was afraid it might melt her clothes.

"Are you really The Deacon?" she asked him.

"That's what my friends call me," he said cheerfully.

Mrs. Pearl licked her lips and put a hand behind her, feeling for the door. "He says you owe him a two-pound grouper filet."

"Yes, ma'am, that I do. Can we see Richard?"

She hesitated for a second, but she couldn't think of any other reason to stall us. "He's out back," she said. "On the dock."

"Thank you, ma'am," Deacon said, but I was already moving, circling off the front steps and around the side of the house. I ran across the acre of lawn toward the dock, which was attached to a boathouse. Savage roaring sounds came from the end of the dock. It pretty well matched the way I felt. I ran out the length of the dock to where a long black racing boat was tied up.

The engine hatch stood wide open. A pair of legs stuck out, splotched with grease. "Rick," I called.

The engine roared, then fluttered to a throaty growl. I called again. "Hey, Rick."

The legs kicked, flopped for a grip, and Rick pulled himself out of the engine. He blinked a couple of times, shading his eyes with a hand, and finally focused on me.

"Hey!" he said. "Billy! Whoa, great, what's up?"

"You said if I ever needed a favor, just ask," I said.

"Uh, well, yeah," he said, climbing unsteadily to his feet. "What, uh, what do you need?"

"Your boat," I said. "I need to borrow your boat."

He stood blinking at me for a minute. Nicky came out the dock and stood beside me, then Deacon. Rick looked at the two of them, then at me.

"Uh," he said. "Can you tell me about it?"

CHAPTER TWENTY-FOUR

Rick's boathouse had a large workbench in it, covered with metal filings, dried globs of fiberglass and paint, old oil, and small machine parts. A large fluorescent strip light hung over the table and a rack of power tools stood beside it.

A chest-high metal filing cabinet with eight thin drawers took up one corner and Rick slid open a drawer and took out a stack of charts. He spread them out on the table.

"Okay," he said. "I made this run two, three years ago. You're bucking current on the way down, and probably wind, if there is any. This time of year the weather can turn on you pretty quick, too. And if you don't pick him up before dark, you're kinda screwed."

"You won't pick him up by dark even if you got Joshua stopping the sun for you," Deacon said, leaning in to look at the chart. "That's a big ocean out there, buddy, and a mighty small boat."

"I'll find him," I said.

"We know where he's headed," Nicky objected. "He's going to Haiti. He's on a straight line between here and Haiti."

Deacon shook his head. "Even if he stays on it, that straight line can be ten, twenty miles wide. Visibility in any kind of sea is going to be a mile or two at best." He raised his head and gave me a look that might have knocked me over if I wasn't leaning on the table. "And there ain't anyway *any* kind of guarantee that he's going to Haiti."

"He's going to Haiti."

"He's *got* to be," Nicky insisted. "Where else?"

"Anywhere else," Deacon said. "He's grabbed the girl and he's running. No reason he should run right where we can find him."

"Plenty of reason," I said. "He's safe there, and anyway he's not running."

"I don't care if you call it advancing to the rear," Deacon said. "He's running."

"No, listen," I said, and he paused and cocked an eyebrow at me. "Nobody's done anything to try and stop him so far. He's killed a couple of hundred people, and we know he's watching his back trail, and we can guess that he's got antennas out in a lot of directions. But everything tells him he's safe, nobody's after him."

"Except us," Nicky said.

"Except us. And so far we haven't been very scary. So he's watching but he's not worried. And I think he wants me to catch up with him."

Deacon spat at the large metal trashcan. "Spare me the psychological profile, buddy. The killer wants to be caught so he can be punished? That's a load of bull and you know it. This guy don't want to be caught."

"That's not what I'm saying."

Deacon spread his arms wide. "Well then what are you saying? Because whatever it is, it don't make sense so far, and we got a bad guy getting away."

"I can find him."

"Wishful thinking. You're going to get out there in the Stream and run out of gas, or capsize, or get run down by a tanker, and we'll lose you, too."

"It's Anna's only chance."

"You're so sure he's going to Haiti, why not fly there and be waiting on the dock?"

I shook my head. "He'll be expecting that. He'll be ready, or Anna will already be over the side. Anna's best chance is if I get to him before he gets to Haiti. And my best chance is to board him at sea, when he's not expecting it."

"You're not the U.S. damn Marines, Billy. You're not Rambo."

"Deacon," I said. "I'm doing this."

"It's piracy. He can have you hung for piracy."

"Who are you now, Deacon?" I said, meeting that icy stare.

"What does that mean?"

I leaned a knuckle on the workbench and moved my face a few inches from his. "It means I know you must have heard those words before. From your superiors, when they're chewing you out for something you did when you knew it was right but it broke some rules. You ready to sit behind a desk and say that stuff to other guys now, Deacon? Turn in your white hat for a grey suit? Or are you still one of the good guys?"

He didn't blink. He just kept looking at me. His expression didn't change. It was like looking down the barrels of two big Colt Peacemakers. "All right," he said at last. "All right." He frowned at his knuckles. "Just jealous, I guess."

Rick cleared his throat. We looked at him and he blushed again. "Uh," he said. "I mean, as far as the *how* part goes. I got radar. But if there's a good-sized sea it might not pick up anything unless you're close enough to see it anyway. It's mostly for weather. Can't really see anything too low."

I nodded and looked back at Deacon. "You better show me the boat."

* * *

The Gulf Stream in late August can change quickly. It can be smooth and flat and flowing along at five knots and then suddenly, with no warning, the weather blows up and you're fighting for your life. And just as suddenly the squall passes and you come out of a thick wall of water into moonlight, peace, and the calm, steady flow of the Stream again. Because it is always there, always moving at its unchanging pace.

I kept telling myself that last part. The Stream was calm out there, not too far away, just on the other side of this squall. But I had been in a cocoon of rain for the last fifteen minutes. The storm had swept across the flat empty water at me just as the sun went down. Just when I was almost out of hope and thinking things couldn't be any worse. And of course, they could. They always could, especially lately. And now they were.

I had been scanning the horizon so hard my eyes hurt, glaring at the fuel gauge and trying to make it stop moving towards the big red E at the left side. And suddenly I was inside rain so thick I had to turn my head to the side to breathe. The sunset vanished. The ocean was gone. I was all alone. I might as well have been in a very wet closet.

As my world shrank to a couple of inches around me, I throttled back and started thinking. I pushed the ugly unwelcome thoughts away but they kept coming back.

I remembered a girl I had found once, a few years back when I was still a working cop. She was fifteen. An outlaw motorcycle gang had her for six days. By the time they threw her out there was no one left inside. She had been doped and raped almost non-stop for the whole six days. She couldn't identify a single one of her attackers. She couldn't even identify herself.

I had to find Anna. I had to find Patrice and his Black Freighter. They were out here with me, had to be.

But I couldn't find them. I had been running on a zigzag course through the corridor where they had to be, and they weren't there. It was the Caribbean counterpart of a big game trail, the route all the freighters took between Florida and Haiti. It was a narrow band of water, only a few miles wide. There was no other way to go. They had to be in it somewhere.

But they weren't. I had passed plenty of traffic, each time running Rick's fine fast boat up to the stern to read the name, each time dropping back again, disappointed.

Now I was running low on fuel, time and hope.

Hopeless. It had been a stupid idea to begin with, but the only idea I could come up with. From the start it had depended on speed, close figuring, and luck. The squall took away the speed, the close figuring could easily be wrong, and the only luck I'd had was that so far I hadn't rammed anything in the rain.

Maybe this guy, this Patrice du Sinueux, really was a sorcerer. Maybe he could make his ship invisible.

Or maybe he was making me blind. If so, he was doing it to the radar, too. The screen was backlit and if I bent over I could just make it out. It had showed nothing for the last forty-five minutes and now, in the middle of the squall—

I blinked and tried to wipe the rain from my eyes. Then I wiped the radar screen and looked at it again.

Something was there.

It was about the right size and shape for a freighter and, if I was reading the radar right, it was about five miles away.

A gust of rain hit my face, driving harder than the storm around it. That must mean it was blowing out. Any moment now I was going to come out of it, I was sure, but until I did there was nothing I could do but throttle back and watch the radar.

Then the squall went up another notch and the rain was so thick I couldn't see the bow of the boat and the wind drove the rain into my face hard enough that it felt like gravel. I hunkered down and squinted. It seemed to blow even harder, and go on for several minutes, and then it stopped.

Just like that, like turning off a switch, the rain stopped. There was one last sigh of wind and the boat ran out into a clear, moonlit night on the gulf stream. Ahead of me, just in the line of sight, were the lights of a freighter moving south.

I pushed the throttle forward. The boat jumped ahead, rattling my spine. I aimed for a spot well behind the lights. I wanted to come up in its wake. The water was calmer there, but more important, if it was the Black Freighter—or any freighter—they wouldn't be watching backwards. The watch would be scanning the horizon forward. And from what I knew about freighters, they wouldn't be doing that very carefully.

Rick's boat ate up the distance. It was the fastest boat I'd ever been on and the feeling of speed and power was almost dream-like. It took less than five minutes to hit the wake of the freighter, about a half mile back. I turned the boat south, moving even faster in the smoother water where the freighter had just pushed through, and sped up to the ship's stern.

I throttled back. The turbulence increased close to the ship. I moved as close as I could, making constant small adjustments on the throttle and the wheel. I could just see the lettering on the stern, but couldn't make out what it said. I moved my boat to the side, hoping some gleam off the water would light it up; no luck.

I moved close again. I couldn't risk shining a light on it. Somebody on board might see it and there would go my surprise. So I got in as close as I could get without losing control of the boat. The constant whirlpool of backwash from the prop made it tough to control the boat without smacking the freighter's steel hull. I tried to look up at the lettering and down at the water at the same time. I was getting a neck cramp, but not much more.

I had to risk a small light. There was no other way. In a clamp beside the wheel Rick had mounted a spotlight, the kind that can pick out rock formations on the moon. There were no smaller flashlights on board as far as I knew. I looked to the bow of the boat, trying to gauge the backwash, and I had an idea.

I pointed the boat directly at the freighter's stern. I eased up as close as I could get and flicked the bow running lights on and off as quickly as I could.

The light made an eerie red glow that ran up the ship's stern. It was just enough to read the letters.

Petit Fleur.

This was it.

CHAPTER TWENTY-FIVE

Securing a small boat to a moving ship at sea is not easy. I didn't have time to do it right—any moment now somebody might lean out over the stern to spit and see me. But I was hoping to sneak Anna away without too much noise, and the boat was my only escape route, even if it was almost out of gas.

But there was no way to tie it off at the freighter's waterline. I would have to tie it from on deck. That increased the angle dangerously, but that's all there was.

There was also no way to get up the stern without making a certain amount of noise. I would just have to risk it. I'd come prepared with some things from Rick's shed, including a small folding grappling hook and 100 feet of nylon rope. I had meant it to be a last resort, in case there was no other way up. It would be dangerous and uncertain, and I would be vulnerable for a long minute while I hung from the rope.

I threw the grappling hook up and waited. A small clunk; then, no sound. Nobody yelled "Hey," or "Oye," or "mon dieu." So I slid up the line hand over hand. It was even harder than I'd thought. The freighter was pitching one way at its own speed. Rick's boat was pitching must faster. With each end of the rope going at a different rate I felt like a yo-yo until I finally pulled myself up to where I could grab the rail of the freighter and ease onto the deck with the bowline of Rick's boat clamped in my teeth.

As I climbed up onto the deck I lost about two yards of skin on a large, shiny cleat. I decided I could risk a few quiet words, and said them. The bleeding wasn't too bad, and I rubbed the spot for a moment. What the hell was a cleat doing there, anyway? I tied Rick's boat off to the cleat and limped into the cover of a packing crate.

I looked along the deck. It was open here, stacked in a few places with crates of deck cargo and tangles of bicycles. There was no sign of anything living.

Far ahead, maybe sixty feet away, the superstructure stuck up, wheelhouse on top. I thought I could see a shape in there behind the glass, but whether it was human I couldn't say.

I decide to assume it was. That was safer. I moved forward a step and stumbled. I had ducked behind a large chunk of strangely shaped plywood. Whatever it was, the thing had two pontoons on its bottom. I looked it over. It was a jagged, angular shape, ten feet high and maybe twenty feet long. A handful of wires ran down it into a large waterproof battery case bolted to the top of the pontoons. I ran a finger along one of the wires. It led to a Christmas tree light bulb that poked through the plywood. I crouched beside the thing. A long nylon cable was secured to a ring welded to the pontoons. It was probably supposed to be towed or moored.

I moved on, doing my creepy-crawly along the deck, trying to think like a shadow, sliding from one hiding place to the next. In a few minutes I had worked my way across the deck to the stairs that ran up to the wheelhouse.

Now the fun started. I had to get up the stairs and inside without being seen. If I could do that, I could probably persuade the guy at the wheel to take a nap for a while. Then I could find Anna quickly and quietly and get away.

I thought about making him tell me where Anna was, but decided it was too risky. The best plan was to take him out fast. Then I could move through the ship easily. I didn't worry about hurting an innocent man or any of that softheaded crap. If he was on board this ship he was not innocent.

I thought about the rest of the crew. At this hour it was slack time on board. The crew would be sleeping, playing cards, relaxing. Not worrying about a flat-fishing guide sneaking around the ship with murder in his heart.

I looked carefully up and down the deck from my hiding place behind a crate. Nothing moved, nobody leaned against the rail.

The stairs were brightly lit, but they ran up the side at a steep enough angle that the man at the wheel couldn't see them without leaving his place. So all I had to do was glide up the steps and whip open the door—and hope the door wasn't locked or bolted.

I took a deep breath and used a trick I had learned in the Rangers. I gave myself a mental countdown —5, 4, 3, 2, 1, *go!*— and I was across the small patch of deck and up the stairs.

I grabbed at the handle and hit the door with my shoulder in one motion and was in the wheelhouse and on top of the guy steering before he could do more than turn a few inches and gape at me.

I slammed the heel of my hand into his temple and he slid to the floor. Perfect. No fuss, no muss, no bother. All according to plan.

Except that I hadn't planned on the second man behind me.

He had been slouching down on a bench against the back wall, probably just hanging out and shooting the breeze. Out of the corner of my eye I saw him straighten up, then jump to his feet, and he was on my back before the first guy hit the floor.

He was strong as well as quick. He got an arm around my throat and I was seeing stars in just a few seconds.

No matter how much you study martial arts and dirty fighting, there just aren't that many good counters to a choke hold from the rear. The best one is to keep your opponent from getting behind you.

I had missed that one. He was behind me, and he had a knee in my back and he was pulling hard enough to make my neck creak. I tried to knock him loose with my elbows, but he put enough distance between us and I couldn't reach.

My throat felt raw and I could hear my heart pounding, even over the sound of the two of us scuffling. I needed air but there was none coming in.

I tried to run him backwards into the wall, but he braced a foot against the bench he'd been sitting on and just pulled back harder.

But to do that he had to take the knee out of my back. I was close enough now and I slammed an elbow in to his kidneys and heard him grunt. But the bastard held on.

The world was getting dim and blurry and seemed far away. I knew I didn't have a lot of time before he turned my lights out. There was only one thing I hadn't tried yet.

Moving as quickly as I could, I dropped to one knee. He dropped with me, but he had to bend over from the waist to do it. That gave me enough room and I turned, whipping a leg at his ankles and sweeping him off his feet.

He held on, which was a pretty good trick, but now he was on his back and holding the back of my neck. I took in a deep breath. It sounded like an old man dying and it felt like sandpaper going in but it was the sweetest breath I'd ever taken.

I took just a half second to enjoy it but that was too long. My friend on the floor dropped his arm from my neck and kicked at my face. I didn't block the kick completely, but I managed to slip it off my face and onto the side of my head.

Good, Billy, I thought as stars exploded in my head. *Very good. Protect that handsome profile at all costs.*

I managed to shake it off in time to see the second kick coming, and this one I knocked to the side with both hands. Then I lunged over it and grabbed at his throat with my left hand. When he blocked that I brought my right hand around and slammed it into his face.

His muscles went slack for just a second, but it was enough. I hit him again, a text book right to the point of his jaw, and he went completely limp.

I gave him a ten count with my fist cocked. Then I raised his eyelid and looked.

Nobody home. That's really tough to fake. If somebody touches your eyes and you're in there, you flinch. You can't help it.

He didn't flinch, and his eyes were rolled back into his head. He was out.

I stood up and moved over to check the first body.

He had a pulse, slow and steady, and his eyes were empty.

I looked around the room for something to keep them quiet. There were no coils of rope, no rawhide lanyards—nothing. These guys were barely nautical at all.

I wondered if one of them was Patrice du Sinueux, the voodoo *houngan* himself. Maybe I should kick them each a couple of times, just to be sure. Nothing major; just break a couple of ribs, loosen a few teeth.

It occurred to me that I could check it easily enough. Nicky had said he had a tattoo of a snake on his arm. I bent down beside first one unconscious man, then the other. No snake tattoo. Not on either one of them. That made it a little easier to leave them lying there, instead of pitching them over the side.

I stood up. I didn't have a whole lot of time. Sooner or later somebody would find my two friends, and it was safer to bet on sooner. I needed to tie them up quickly and get on with searching the ship.

I gave the room a quick inspection. In a drawer of the chart table I found a roll of electrical tape. It would have to do.

I got both men onto their stomachs with their mouths taped shut. I used the rest of the tape on their wrists, binding them behind their backs, and then taping their ankles together.

I also went through their pockets quickly. They each had a large folding knife on their belts. I took both and threw them out the door and into the water.

The man at the wheel had a small automatic pistol in his pocket. I checked it over quickly. It was a Rossi .380, a respectable weapon. There were rust patches along the barrel and a greasy feeling of too much gun oil on the grips. I wiped it on his shirt and stuck it in my belt.

The rest of the stuff in their pockets was uninteresting: money, cough drops; the man from the bench had a large ring of keys and a blackjack. The wheelman had a few polaroid pictures of naked women, tied up and begging for mercy. I could make out a background with a couple of ringbolts, a mop hanging, and a shelf next to a rusting porthole. It looked like the shots had been taken on board a ship, probably this one.

It was nice to get a reminder of who these guys were and why I was here. These were not simple, honest merchant seamen. They were concentration camp guards, sadistic killers who enjoyed throwing people by the dozens into the ocean to die.

The world has come a long way since the Nazis, we tell ourselves with little pats on the back. Sure. Tell it to the Khmer Rouge. Mention it in Bosnia and wait for the laugh. The fact is, there have always been and always will be plenty of work for the kind of guy who likes to hurt people. Many governments recognize that and quietly round them up for official work. Other people, like these two, prefer to operate in the private sector, where they could torture somebody without a lot of red tape.

The pictures showed that this guy was pretty good at his work. Had spent a lot of time getting it right. Even thought about it in his off time. He'd go far. Maybe I could help send him there.

I dropped the pictures and wiped my hands on my pants. I felt unclean. I wished I'd hit him harder.

I stood and looked out over the wheel. The squall I had come through was gone without a trace, like it never had been at all. There was a moon now and the reflected light rippled on the water of the Gulf Stream.

According to the compass we were headed south-southeast, straight down the corridor to Haiti. I put the wheel over, just a few points. I wanted the ship to swing back towards Miami—but so slowly that no one on board would feel it swing.

If I managed to get Anna and get away, I would still call the Coast Guard as soon as I was clear of the freighter. The closer the ship was to US coastal waters, the better.

And if things went bad and I didn't make it, it wouldn't hurt to have the sweat start when they found themselves off Miami again, instead of Port-au-Prince. I would check through the ship quickly and then come back and re-set the course.

I stood and counted to thirty as the ship turned maybe two degrees east. Good. It would take at least five minutes to turn 180 degrees. That was too slow for anybody to feel it turning. I locked on the auto-steering and moved out the door and onto the stairs.

The deck was quiet in the moonlight. Nothing moved across it and there was no sound except for the slap of the water against the hull, and the hum of the wind in the ropes holding the deck cargo in place. I watched for a moment to be sure, then went down the stairs and to the door leading down into the ship.

I searched the top level quickly and found nothing. The crew areas were deserted. I guessed they must all be down below, leaving only the two men of the watch up in the wheelhouse. Still, it was spooky to find everything deserted.

The last door was locked. It might have been a storeroom—but it also might be where they were keeping Anna. I put an ear to the door. I didn't hear anything, but that didn't mean much.

I leaned my weight against the door. There was no give to it. Maybe I could bust it open—and maybe I would just break an arm trying. And in any case just trying would make enough noise to bring the entire crew on a dead run.

I stood there for a minute trying to think. I wasn't doing very well at this. I realized my heart was pounding and my stomach still felt full of sand. I'd had this feeling of hopeless dread since I'd started out and it wasn't going away. And if I kept making simple, stupid mistakes—

I remembered the big key ring on the man in the wheelhouse and called myself a handful of bad names. I should have brought it. Of course they would have Anna locked up.

I took a deep breath and turned around. I went carefully back outside and up the stairs. I opened the wheelhouse door and stopped in the doorway with no breath.

I had left the two sailors unconscious and securely taped only five minutes ago.

Now they were gone.

The wheelhouse was empty.

CHAPTER TWENTY-SIX

A lot of things went through my mind in the half second before reflexes took over. Then I was inside the door, crouching out of sight with the greasy little gun in my hand.

I followed the gun all around the room with my eyes. Nothing moved. Nothing was out of place. There was no way anybody else could be hidden anywhere in the room.

I spun around to cover the door. I counted to one hundred and nothing happened. I duck-walked quietly to the doorway and looked out.

There was still no sign of life anywhere on deck. Nothing moved, nothing had changed.

Somewhere below I heard a muffled thump. I held my breath. And then, as if to make sure I didn't miss it, the sound came again, *THUMP*.

Then quiet.

The seconds stretched into minutes and nothing else happened. My knees were aching from staying in a crouch for so long. My tongue was stuck to the roof of my mouth and I was panting in breath through clenched teeth, but nothing happened.

I don't know how long I stayed like that. It must have been several minutes. All my muscles had knotted, my shirt was soaked with sweat and my throat was almost closed from the dryness in my mouth. My heart had settled into a steady pulse of 175. I was close to the point where I would scream just from waiting for something to happen. And then it happened.

The drums started.

At first it was no more than a faint vibration in the deck. I thought it might even be soft footsteps and I flexed my fingers on the pistol, getting ready.

But the volume grew slowly, steadily, and soon it was a soft throbbing; urgent but patient, so overwhelming that I felt my heartbeat start to keep time with the drums.

BOOM-ba-de-THUMP-ity-BOOM-ba-de—

A little louder, a little more urgent. The hair on the back of my neck stood straight out. I still couldn't tell where the sound was coming from. It was everywhere without being centered in any one spot. It seemed to be in the steel of the deck. I could feel it in the soles of my feet as much as I heard it.

BOOM-ba-de-THUMP-ity-BOOM-ba-de—

I have faced junkies with knives, cold killers with guns, drunks with broken beer bottles in their hands, and I had not felt as helpless as I did listening to those drums. For a gun or a knife there is a direct threat and a way to deal with it. You can plan a response or an attack.

None of my instructors in the Rangers or at the L.A.P.D. Academy had ever had anything to say about how to deal with voodoo drums. You can't put a restraining hold on a sound. You can't punch it or kick it or slap handcuffs onto it.

But it is just as aggressive, just as dangerous, as much a threat to your health and sanity as a stiff hand to the solar plexus. Because it gets inside you and tells you to *do* something, anything, just get up and do it and make the drums stop.

Which was exactly the wrong thing, the stupid thing, to do. When you have no idea how many enemies you're facing or how they're armed, or even what they intend to do, you find a secure spot with cover and elevation and stay there. A place like the wheelhouse, where I was now. I could see anybody who tried to approach me from any direction and probably shoot them before they shot me. I was fine where I was. Couldn't be better.

No matter what the sound made me want to do, I was not going to charge down the stairs and try to find the drums, make them stop, do something stupid. I was going to stay right where I was and make them come to me. That was my best chance. No doubt about it. Forget the damn drums.

So I took a deep breath, looked carefully around the deck, and started down the stairs with the gun ready.

I moved across the deck in a crouch, as quiet and smooth and ready as I could be.

The drums were louder now. Not faster, but more persistent, overwhelming the other sounds of wind and water. I could hear three separate drums, blending together, keeping one rhythm, but playing with it around the edges. The sound pressed itself on me, blotted out everything else. I couldn't think, could hardly swallow. The rhythm was taking over everything. I felt like I was breathing drums.

BOOM-ba-de-TRUMP-ity-BOOM-ba-de—

There were several large outdoor loudspeakers on the deck. I hadn't noticed them before. Maybe because they hadn't been blasting out voodoo drums before. A pair of them were bolted to the top of the wheelhouse. As I saw them the volume seemed to go up another notch, and the rhythm got more demanding.

BOOM-ba-de-THUMP-ity-BOOM-ba-de—

I slid behind a crate. Were they watching me? Trying to startle me into something? Because it might work. It *was* working. I scanned the deck again and moved quickly across the open space to the door.

The door below wasn't latched. It slid open without sound. Not that I could have heard anything over the drums. I stepped into a darkened hallway and moved quickly to one side of the doorway, then dropped to a knee, closing the door behind me. A doorway makes a great frame for a target, especially when you are backlit by moonlight. I was being stupid, yes, but cautiously stupid.

My eyes adjusted to the darkness. The hallway was empty. There was one faint light shining, coming from under a closed door at the far end of the hall.

They were herding me. There was no question about it. The drums had come out of the silence to make me move and there was only one place to go. Now there was only one spot of light and in the darkness of the hall it seemed to me that the drums were coming from there, from somewhere in that faint bar of light, and it pulled me forward like a candle pulls a moth.

Even knowing that, knowing that somebody wanted me to do just what I was doing, I did it anyway.

Part of it was that I couldn't stop myself. I had to get to the drums, make them stop, get that crazy rhythm out of my head.

But the other part was what Deacon would have called Rambo pride. I wanted to face this son of a bitch and say all right. You want me? You got me. And then I wanted to get my fingers around his throat and squeeze until his evil God damned eyes popped out.

I had never met this Patrice du Sinueux, never seen him face to face. And I had never wanted so badly to kill somebody.

It looked like I was going to get my chance. The idea of sneaking quietly onto the freighter, grabbing Anna, and sneaking away, was gone. It had died when the drums started. Or earlier, when the two guys in the wheelhouse had vanished.

Now it was face to face. Step into the monster's lair and slay the dragon, or end up as just another pile of bones outside the cave.

I straightened to a crouch and moved down the hall toward the light.

Even here in the interior of the ship the sound of the drums was overwhelming. The road company of *Chorus Line* could be coming up behind me wearing their tap shoes, and I wouldn't have heard them.

BOOM-ba-de-THUMP-ity-BOOM-ba-de—

I took my time moving along the hall. I paused carefully at each door, watching for any kind of set-up. But the hallway was empty, except for me and my invisible herdsman.

I could feel the sweat on my palm around the pistol's grip. I stood still for a moment, just two steps away from the lighted door, and wiped my hands on my pants. I took a deep breath and

JEFF LINDSAY

tried to concentrate.

This was it. Behind that door was the big spider, and I had come here to squash him. I'd thought I could tiptoe past his web and take away one of his bugs. He'd let me know that wasn't possible.

Of course, there might be no one there. Maybe they were all down in the hold, playing the drums and drinking rum and this was all my imagination working overtime.

But I didn't think so. I was mortally sure that I would open the door and come face to face with Patrice du Sinueux. That's what he wanted. He had driven me down here to this meeting as surely as if he'd taken me by the hand and led me.

I was going to open that door and come face to face with a truly evil man, and I was going to kill him. That was the only way now.

I took another deep breath, held the gun ready, and kicked open the door.

The drums stopped.

A man sat behind the desk in a circle of light. Just one man. There was no one else in the room, just him and me and he was sitting, unarmed. He was either stupid or so confident in his magic he didn't think he'd need any help.

He was a light-skinned black man, with a slender build and close-cropped hair. His hands were resting in front of him on the desk. They were clean, strong-looking, manicured, and the fingers were much too long.

A deck of oversized cards stood on the desk at his elbow and as I entered he was stroking it with the fingertips of one hand.

Behind him was a steel coat rack. A black silk top hat was perched on top. A pair of white gloves was thrown over one branch and an elegant black cane hung from another.

And wound around the rack was the biggest snake I have ever seen.

It was twenty feet long and it was thicker around the middle than my leg. It had a pale yellow color with soft grey markings and a huge, wedge-shaped head that it lifted at me, its tongue flicking in and out.

The man at the desk moved. He opened a drawer of the desk. My eyes and my gun snapped over to cover him. He looked up at me and smiled. His eyes were a startling light green and they locked onto mine.

"*Bon soir*, Billy," he said in a voice like the silk of the hat. He waved one of those long elegant hands. "Come in. Sit."

"Let me see your hands," I said.

He took his hand out of the desk, with mocking slowness. He was holding a small saucer and a razor blade. "This will not harm you," he said, sounding like somebody I couldn't see was tickling him.

I couldn't think of much to say to that. I watched him as he placed the saucer on the desk and, as he began to speak, calmly slashed his arm and begin to drip blood into the saucer.

"I have raised Bebe from the egg," he said, nodding at the snake. "I have given him a special taste." He looked up. His blood was dripping into the saucer and the snake was starting to uncoil towards him. He smiled, a pleasant smile. "For blood. He likes human blood." He shook his head happily. "Very unnatural. His kind, they do not normally like the human blood. It was very hard to teach him, but well worth it. He has been a great help in my work."

He pursed his lips and whistled, a soft trill of a whistle that was strangely intimate.

The snake wound down from the coat rack and onto Cappy's shoulder. He whistled again. The snake moved its huge flat head down to the saucer and began to drink.

"To him, he knows it means he will soon be fed, you see? And I have trained him to take the blood and then—" He gave me a beautiful smile. "—then he wrap himself where I say and squeeze. Very helpful with the sacrifices. For Papa Legba." He laughed, then shrugged. "A parlor trick, yes. But it is very impressive, to the peasants in particular."

"Your snake killed the old man. And the sailor, Oto," I said, trying to keep my eyes on him. But it was almost impossible not to watch the snake.

"Two in one night," he said with great satisfaction. "I was not sure he could do it. But he did," he crooned to the snake. "Ey, Bebe?"

"Put the snake away," I said.

He raised an eyebrow. "He will not hurt you," he said. "He is not hungry, not for two, three more days." The last *s* trailed off into a long, soft hiss.

"Put him back," I said again.

He shrugged. It was a dark version of Honore's shrug, saying of course, what's the point, only because I want to, you're a coward and a fool, I'll get you anyway. And with one slow hand he guided the big snake back onto the coat rack and then slapped a bandage onto the razor cut.

"And so?" he said. "Now I am helpless, without my Bebe. So now what will you have me do?"

It's not possible to get across the insult and menace he managed to put into those words. But as he spoke, smiling and leaning back in his chair, the hairs stood up on my neck and without thinking I took a step towards him, leveling the gun at a spot between his eyes.

He made no move to defend himself, pretending not to notice my gun, as if he believed that I would never dare to shoot him, or that bullets wouldn't hurt him.

I hoped to surprise him. I moved right up to the desk, the gun aimed at the center of his forehead. I couldn't miss at this range. But I also couldn't shoot him when he was just sitting there, smiling. And not before he answered at least one question.

"Where is she," I said, in a voice that sounded crude and raw next to his sleek French accent.

He raised an eyebrow and tapped his fingertips together. "She has not been harmed," he said. "I am saving her for something very special."

"So am I," I said.

He laughed, three light, musical syllables. "You will be— disappointed."

"You will be dead," I said, taking the last step to the front of the desk. The barrel of the gun was only about eighteen inches from his forehead now but he still gave no sign that he had even noticed it.

Instead, he reached for a can of soda at his elbow on the desk. I could see the snake tattoo on his forearm. He picked up the can. A brightly colored drinking straw poked out the top. I didn't recognize the label on the can, but as he brought the straw to his lips something else filtered in through my rage and tension.

There was no sweat on the outside of the can, no circle of water on the desk where it had been sitting. We were in the tropics and this man was drinking room-temperature soda.

Or—

I was already moving sideways as he whipped the straw out of the can and blew. He was fast, so very fast, and I felt myself doddering clumsily to the side as he pointed the straw at me.

A cloud of powder came out of the straw. Most of it missed me as I lunged to the side, but I felt a light stinging on the side of my face, an unpleasant odor in my nostrils, and an instant numbness spreading from my cheek into the rest of my face.

"Good night, Billy," he said in his delicate laughing voice.

I straightened and looked at him as I felt all the power drain out of my body and then I—

CHAPTER TWENTY-SEVEN

The fireworks were endless this year even though it was too dark to see them. They exploded without light over and over in reds and greens and yellows. The wooly blackness was hung with the swirls and patterns of the millions of dark bursting rockets and below them I sank toward the ground that was falling away from me just a little bit faster.

And now the rockets burst into bones, whole skeletons forming in the sky, red viscera dangling from the ribs. And still slowly falling, I became one of the skeletons as I fell out of my flesh in a dark red burst.

My bones rattled and burned with a cool green glow, the luminescent green of rot. I felt my skeleton begin to dance without me and I was afraid.

One coil of the darkness wrapped itself around a passing skeleton and became The Snake. At first I thought it was dancing, too. But then I saw that it was making the bones move to its own pattern and the mouth on the skull was opening and closing slowly, saying, "Help me." And I felt The Snake coil on my bones, moving me to its bone dance.

My mouth was opening and closing to the same rhythm, but I couldn't hear the words. I could hear nothing but the pounding clash of the falling bones and the laughter of the snake.

And I fell and danced and cried for a time longer than there are words to tell.

And after this unbearable long time I finally smashed into the earth and shattered into cool darkness.

• • •

There was rhythm. I could not move but at last I could hear and there were drums and I could feel and there was pain.

All of me burned with a terrible fire and the pain in my head was like a living thing trying to eat its way out but I could not move even a little to try to ease the pain.

I was as dull and stupid as it was possible to be and I could not understand where I was or what was happening or why my whole body felt like it was rotting off my bones, melting away in terrible heat.

But slowly—oh, so slowly—I came back. Just a little bit at a time, but I came back. First there was awareness. I was. That was enough for a while.

And then from nowhere two words popped in: Billy Knight. Those words meant something. I let them echo in my head. Billy Knight. Billy Knight. Billy Knight. I said them too often and they lost all meaning again. It scared me.

I was just scared for a long time. Nothing more. There was no room in me for anything more complicated.

After a while the fear pushed that thought back into my head. Billy Knight. I knew what that meant. Billy Knight.

That was me.

I was Billy Knight.

I could feel my brain move up another level, a little faster, as the thought took hold. Okay. I had a name. That was good. Now on to the tougher questions. Where was I? I couldn't see anything. I couldn't hear much except drums. I gave up. Where I was seemed too hard.

Why did everything hurt? I was pretty sure it wasn't supposed to feel like this, like my whole body was smoldering in a slow fire. I could almost remember a time when it didn't feel like that.

A few more brain cells came online and I remembered something else. Oh, right. If you're being burned, move away from the fire. That thought made me happy for a few minutes. I knew what to do.

I went up another level. Good; you know what to do, move away from the fire. So do it.

And I tried.

I could remember the idea of moving. I could almost remember the *feeling* of movement. But the mechanics of it were beyond me. How did that work? How did you move? Move? Move— Movemovemovemovemove—

I said the word too many times and again it lost meaning. It was just a sound, mooooow.

The fear ran over me again with sharp little rat's feet. What was going on? What in God's name was happening?

Why couldn't I move?

I was almost sure it shouldn't be like this. This wasn't natural, wasn't right. I was supposed to move. I was supposed to feel good and know who I was. This just wasn't right.

It wasn't right. It hadn't been like this before.

Before what?

I thought. That was beyond me. I didn't know before what, but that idea of *before* seemed to have a lot of other ideas hanging off it. The pain, the not moving, that was *now*. Something else was *before*.

There was something I was supposed to do, something I had to do, and now I would not do it and something terrible would happen. Something worse than me being dead. I could not remember what any of it was, but I remembered that it was all up to me and I had failed. I was dead.

I felt something cool roll across my face. A tear. That meant something. I bit down hard in my mind so I wouldn't repeat the word too many times and lose the meaning.

Tear.

I was crying.

But—

If I was dead, I couldn't cry. Could I? I thought hard for a minute, as hard as I could, and managed to sweat out an answer: no. When you're dead you can't cry.

I was crying. So:

I wasn't dead.

I wasn't dead.

I did not know what I was that I should feel like I was dead but I could not be dead because of the tear. I was alive.

It was another eternity before I went past that thought. Just the idea of being alive set off a soundless, motionless party in my mind and I celebrated for a very long time. And then more grey cells woke up and I thought, hang on. When you're alive you're supposed to be able to move and see and speak and know where you are. I can't. Why not?

Something was wrong. Something had happened. I tried hard to think what and I couldn't. It was hard to think through all the pain, the burning across my skin and the pounding in my head. And those damned drums. How could I think at all with those damned drums rattling away like that?

Drums?

Were there supposed to be drums?

I listened for a while. Drums were not normal. But I had heard them before. Not long ago, too. I had heard drums and then something had happened. Something bad. Had the drums made me like this?

I thought hard for a while. It came back to me slowly: No, the drums had not made me like this. Drums could not do that. But something that went *with* the drums had.

For a time that was enough. I was satisfied. Something that went with the drums was not good. Now I knew.

I came back to that question eventually. What had happened to me? If not the drums, what? What was the bad thing connected to the drums?

I worked on that. Nothing came to me. I drifted for a while, listening to the drums.

There was a new sound. A door opening. The drums got louder for a moment. I heard scuffling, heavy breathing, a sharp *SMACK* sound, a thump.

The feet moved closer to me and I felt a new pain blossom in my side, about the size and shape of a foot. A voice hissed something in a language I did not know. The foot kicked me again. The voice laughed.

"You've bloody killed him!" said a different voice. "You fucking bastards!" I knew the voice. I was sure I'd heard it before, but—

"Not dead. Zom-BEE!," the first voice said, sounding very happy. "Your friend is a zom-BEE!" And it laughed.

I almost didn't even hear the feet moving away, the door opening and closing, the lock clicking home. Because I had begun to remember and it all came pouring back over me, cascading across my mind in a terrible flood.

I remembered. I knew what had happened to me and what the drums meant. I knew where I was.

I was on the Black Freighter.

CHAPTER TWENTY-EIGHT

"Christ. Oh hell, mate, what've they done?"

I felt a hand touch me, shake me, slap my face. Although the voice was in my ear the hand felt far away. It was as though he was talking to me and touching somebody else.

"Bloody fucking Christ," Nicky said. I heard a soft fumbling sound and then he was forcing something small and cold between my lips. I felt a few drops of something bitter roll slowly across my tongue and into my throat. Then I felt Nicky lift my hand into the air and feel for a pulse.

"We'll be all right," he said, as if he was trying to convince himself. "Long as they haven't given you the second powder. That first dose just puts you out, mate. The second, that's what makes you a right proper zombie. We'll be all right."

I wanted to talk back, make some small joke about my condition. I couldn't. I tried to move just a little bit to let him know I was alive. I couldn't. I tried as hard as I know how to speak, to say I couldn't move, and I couldn't. I think I managed to twitch one corner of my mouth.

"Gotcha," Nicky muttered, but whether he had seen my mouth twitch or just found my pulse, I don't know.

And then, as strange as anything that had happened to me so far, Nicky dropped my arm, picked up my foot, and started to take off my shoe.

So they got to him, too, I thought. They've pushed him over the edge. Poor Nicky. He was never strong enough for this, never meant to stand up under this kind of treatment. Of course he's cracked, poor guy.

He had my shoe off now and I felt his thumbs digging in around my toes, and just above my arch and below my big toe, at the large pad on the bottom of the foot.

And if I needed any more proof that Nicky had slipped quietly out of his tree, he started to hum at me. At first it was just sounds, "EEeeh," and "Aaah." He would hold to one note and sing it for a full breath as he poked at my feet.

And then the sound changed and he was humming, "All You Need Is Love."

It didn't make sense. I was in mortal danger and paralyzed and my friend was poking at my feet while singing The Beatles' greatest hits. The weirdness of the whole thing suddenly made me want to laugh out loud. A huge bubble of hysterical laughter built up inside me, tried to explode.

"Uh," I said, very softly.

"Right," said Nicky cheerfully, "We'll have you dancing in no time," and he swung into "Penny Lane."

I had said something. My mouth had opened—only a little, sure, but sound had come out.

And Nicky had been expecting it.

It didn't even begin to make sense. Which one of us was really crazy?

Did he know what had happened to me—and how to fix it? It seemed impossible. But Nicky was rubbing my feet briskly, poking at the same two or three spots on both feet, and humming at full blast—now it was "Good Day Sunshine." And as he did—as a *result* of what he did?—I felt a slow flush spread outward from my heart and climb from the base of my spine up to the top of my skull.

I pulled in a deep breath. It felt better than anything else I could remember.

"Ee-hah," Nicky said softly.

More deep breaths. The flush spread outward to my toes, my fingers. I wiggled my index finger and felt like the world was starting all over again. And finally, after "When I'm 64," with the first notes of "Mother Nature's Child," my right eye opened.

"G'day, mate," said Nicky. He didn't stop rubbing my feet.

The other eye struggled open. It was like trying to lift a Dodge van, but I finally got it open. For a minute there were two Nickys rubbing four feet. Terrifying. I felt his thumbs dig in at a different spot, on my two middle toes. Gradually the Nickys on the right and the left swam together and there was one Nicky with two feet in his hands.

"Nuh," I said, trying to say "Nicky." But "Nuh" was all I could manage.

"I know, mate, I know," Nicky said cheerfully. "It'll come, never fear."

Two fingers moved now. The thumb joined them. I wiggled them at my face. Hello, Billy. Welcome back. We missed you.

I remembered the terrible burning and the bone dreams and with great effort and a lot of fear, started scanning what I could see of my body. It seemed okay. I couldn't see all of me; my neck wouldn't move. But what I could see looked all right.

I was alive. Everything seemed to have gotten faster and brighter while I was away, but I was back. I felt a terrible thirst and my head was pounding with a pain that made all other head aches I'd ever had seem funny, but under the circumstances I didn't mind. Maybe I was going to be okay.

My whole hand moved now, and I rolled my head to the side. It felt wonderful, even when the head movement made my headache flare up higher. I looked at the grey steel wall. The rust specks were beautiful, the grey paint seemed lush and colorful.

I turned my head the other way. I was laid out on the floor in a small storeroom. There was a row of hanging mops and brooms, some buckets, and a shelf of cleaning supplies, all packed in with nautical efficiency. One dim light bulb hung from the middle of the ceiling, and a small porthole was rusted and bolted shut on the far end of the wall.

There was also a little more space than you might expect to find in a place where a ship's cleaning supplies were kept. There were several spools of chain and rope hanging from spindles. and something looked familiar about the wall over there but I couldn't say what. I frowned, trying to remember. I looked at the wall again. I had seen it before, but when? Something was different, missing, in that part over by the ringbolts fastened to the wall—

I remembered. The pictures I had taken from the sailor in the wheelhouse, of women begging. The women had been fastened to those ringbolts. Slowly, painfully, I came back to life. It was a long and awful trip. One small piece of me at a time would wake up and sluggishly, awkwardly, start to talk to the other parts. Nicky kept rubbing my feet, kept singing, and eventually rolled me over and rubbed my back, too.

I didn't object. I didn't have the strength yet. But as soon as I could form a thought and make my mouth work I asked him to please stop singing for the love of God.

He looked hurt, but he stopped, only mid-way through "In My Life."

In the background, now that Nicky was quiet, the drums were overwhelming. I could hear other noises over them, sounding like a really wild fraternity party at the end of spring term.

Finally I sat up. For a few minutes I just sat there. I felt stupid and stiff, as if I had been stitched together from mismatched parts and there must be little bolts in the sides of my neck.

Nicky watched me, beaming, and hopping on one foot like a kid who has to go to the bathroom. When I finally tried to stand he was there to catch me if I needed it.

I almost did. The roaring and pounding in my ears nearly drowned out the sound of the drums. After a few lifetimes of standing and enjoying the pain I sat back down again.

I took a couple of deep breaths and managed not to throw up. Then, when the world steadied again, I looked up at Nicky.

"How?" I said. It was very tough to put thoughts together. "How you… here?"

"You put us through the wringer, you did," Nicky said, dropping to the floor next to me. "We didn't hear from you. Didn't have a clue if you were out of fuel and drifting, or maybe eaten by sharks. Not a fucking clue, mate."

"How long?"

"I waited three days, Billy. Three awful fucking days. Going right off my nut. Finally Deacon called a mate of his in Port Au Prince. Fella calls back and says *Petit Fleur* is in port. Has a racing boat in tow. So now we know he's got you, too.

"I caught the first plane. Spent a day nosing around, buying a few things."

"What?"

He chuckled. "*Things*, Billy. Things I couldn't get through customs, or couldn't get in the States. Some special medicines, like what I fed you. Some other stuff." He leaned close and whispered, "Guns, Billy. World's greatest gun market out there. I've got three of 'em stashed on this ship. Good ones. If we can get out of this room we'll be all right yet."

I grunted. The thought I wanted to tell him was too long and hard to put into words, but there was a heavy accent on how stupid it had been to buy guns in a place like Port Au Prince. It wasn't much brighter to think that having one in his hand was going to make everything all right.

But that was Nicky. New Age gunslinger. Guru with a gun. In his mind a pistol was a magic charm to ward off evil. He'd spent hundreds of hours firing at targets, practicing his quick draw, changing magazines as fast as he could.

I'd tried to tell him it wasn't the same as hearing that unique flat ripping sound of a bullet just missing your head, and trying to fire back without wetting your pants. He'd never quite believed it could be all that different.

And now, unless I could remember how to work my feet, he was going to get us into a shooting match with a bunch of guys who killed for fun and profit.

I shook my legs. They were still numb, but a little better. With time I might make it.

"They caught you," I said to Nicky. Good, Billy; almost a full sentence.

"They did that," Nicky admitted. "I slipped on board right after they cleared all the cargo off. Looked around a bit, stashed a couple of bundles. Three small backpacks, Billy. Food, water, weapon. So if they find one, I got a back-up." He looked so proud of himself; so damned clever, sneaking around stashing guns and granola, out-foxing the enemy.

He went on. "I watched 'em start to load on people. Another full day. I was up on top, in the big life raft up there. Couldn't move around, look for you. People everywhere." He shrugged. "I waited. Figured they had to blink sometime, eh? Then I could sneak round about, have a peek, see if I could find you.

"Well, it got night, and just as things slowed down a bit, the boat starts up and heads off to sea. And I figure all right, Nick-lad, time to earn your keep. I slip out of the life raft and down the stairs."

He paused and I turned to look at him. I could hear my neck creak from the effort and a pain shot straight up my spine and out my eyeballs, but I looked.

Nicky was looking at his toes. He kicked his feet, left, right, left. "Shit-peppers. They grabbed me before I got three steps down. Dragged me in to see Cappy. The fella with the snake tattoo. He knew me right off. Thought it was pretty funny, us sneaking aboard one at a time. 'Now I 'ave you all,' he says in that horrible silky froggish accent he's got.

"And then he raises up that eyebrow of his and wants to know, is anybody else of our merry little gang going to come a-calling? And I figger if I say yes, lots more, he'll think I'm bluffing. So I say no, that's the lot. And he looks at me a good long time, smiles, and says, 'Bon.'

"Then he has his boys bounce me around a little and asks me again. And I say all right, there's one more boatload, they're waiting in the Gulf Stream. And I can't tell if he believes me or not, but they bounce me around a little more and then they throw me down here."

"And here we are, mate. Here we are."

He sounded almost happy about that. I managed to grunt, "Anna—"

He was a quiet for a moment. "Billy—I don't know, mate. I—tried to look for her, but… I don't know, mate."

I closed my eyes and let the sound of the drums rolls over me, mixing with the pounding of my headache. I couldn't make my brain work fast enough to be sure but it seemed like Cappy had had Anna almost a week. I had to find her, had to get my stupid brain and wooden body together and find her. It was impossible that she was all right, but I had to know.

Which meant I had to get on deck into the middle of what sounded like a cannibal's dinner party, get past a gang of pet killers, and face the Man With The Snake. Simple enough.

But first I had to remember how to walk.

CHAPTER TWENTY-NINE

It took some more time to get my legs back. The party overhead didn't slow down. If anything it got louder and wilder. By the time I had walked back and forth for a few minutes and felt ready to go, it had gone way beyond wild frat party. Now it sounded like after hours at the Republican convention.

I still felt slow, stupid and stiff, but it wasn't going to get any better anytime soon. "All right," I told Nicky.

"Right," he said. "What's the plan?"

I looked at him. He was all eager and confident, looking like he didn't have a doubt in the world that we would waltz up on deck, clean up the rascals and sail away into the sunset.

"It sounds like everybody is on deck, so I'm going to search below-decks," I said. "Try to find Anna."

Nicky nodded. "Then we'll split up," he said. "I'll go for that pack I stashed, so we've got some artillery to back us up."

I wanted to tell him he had seen too much American TV. A gun doesn't always save the day. He didn't have a clue, and I could barely function, and we were about to take on a crew of killers on their home turf. And he was convinced that a gun would even things out. If I only had enough gripping strength I would have grabbed him and shaken him.

But what the hell. If he realized how bad things were, he might experience aura meltdown. So if looking for his gun kept him from jumping into the ocean screaming, maybe it was a good thing. It was all right if one of us had hope.

In any case, I wanted him out of the way. I was going to kill Cappy, no matter what it took, and I didn't want him there for something he might not be able to handle. Let him look for his gun. It was better than looking at murder.

"Go," I said. "I'll find Anna."

"Where do we meet?" he asked.

"At the wheelhouse," I said.

"Gotcha," he said. "Luck, mate," and he turned away. A second later he turned back. "Door's locked."

We got the door open in about five minutes, using a screwdriver we found with the cleaning supplies, and then Nicky shook my hand and disappeared in the darkness.

I wondered if I would see him again. I wondered if either of us would ever see Key West again. And when I stumbled as I took my own first step into the darkness, I wondered if I would make my legs work anytime soon.

I hung onto the screwdriver. It was big and flat bladed and the weight was re-assuring. I felt my way along the passageway to the office where I had met Cappy.

There was no light showing this time. I listened carefully at the door and heard nothing. I bent over the knob with the screwdriver. It took me a couple of minutes, fumbling around in the dark with what still felt like somebody else's fingers, but I got the door open and slipped inside.

The room was empty. I pushed the door closed again and felt for the desk light I had seen the last time I was in here. I found it; the snake was gone—the whole coat rack was gone.

I found a large key ring in the desk and stuck it in my pocket. There was a lot of other stuff in there that might have been interesting another time—ledgers and other business stuff, and a lot of things that looked like charms, magic powders, and small vials of liquids.

It might have made Nicky very happy. I didn't really feel like getting too close to any of it. I left it and turned out the light.

I slid back into the passageway and went from door to door. I listened for a minute at each one before trying the keys. It seemed like I was working through the entire key ring each time, but I did get all the doors open eventually. The screwdriver might have been quicker.

All the rooms were empty. I found crew quarters, cargo holds, the galley, machine shop, engine room—everything you would expect on a small freighter in the Caribbean, and not a sign of life anywhere. One of the holds was loaded down with cheap-looking luggage, bundles of clothing, paper bags filled with food. The kind of stuff Haitian refugees might carry into a new life.

But that was it. If Anna was on board this ship, she was somewhere above decks.

Either she was at the party or she was already over the rail, and it was hard to figure which was worse. In any case, it meant the same thing to me. I had to go up on deck and check.

The noise up there hadn't let up at all. As I got closer I wondered why Cappy would put on a party like that for a crowd of people he intended to kill.

Maybe he really believed the dark voodoo stuff, and he was making a sacrifice to whatever evil spirits he worshipped. And maybe he enjoyed toying with them; go on, have a drink, by the way—you're dead.

It didn't seem likely to be any normal motive, whatever it was. It didn't really matter a hell of a lot. I took a deep breath, stepped through the door and out onto the deck.

It took a minute for my eyes to adjust. Or more accurately, for my eyes to convince my brain they were telling the truth.

I was looking at a scene from hell. It was like one of those medieval paintings where everybody is half-naked and committing every possible sin, from drinking to what my grandmother used to call cavorting.

There were about a hundred people on deck. I counted only four that had to be Cappy's crew. They stood at the edge of the crowd, holding cattle prods and making funny comments on the dancers.

The madly dancing rest were all over the deck, going crazy under the thundering umbrella of the drums. Some of them were spinning wildly in circles, with each other or alone. Some stood in place and stared at something nobody else could see. A few were having sex, others drank from rum bottles, and a few simply ran or danced around the whole crowd mouthing furious syllables that didn't seem to belong to any human language. Most of them just seemed to be dancing to the sound of the drums, which rose over the whole scene like the sound track to a movie about eternal damnation.

At the far end of the deck, in an open space, four posts held a canopy about twelve feet off the deck. The posts were painted to look like they were wrapped with vines. Under the canopy an altar was set up. Rising up above and behind the altar was another post. A thick vine coiled around the post. As I watched, the vine moved; it was the python, hanging above the whole scene like a pale demon god.

The altar was piled high with baskets of fruit and other foods, and bottles of rum, cigars and pictures of saints.

And one other thing: Anna.

She was lying in the center of the altar. From this distance I couldn't tell if she was dressed in a white robe or just draped in a sheet, but she was there, all in white, and her face was as pale and bloodless as the cloth that covered her.

She did not move, not even a twitch, in spite of the horrible carnival going on around her, and she looked as dead as a person can look.

As I stood there feeling like I'd been pole-axed, Cappy stepped up to the altar, raised a conch shell to his lips, and blew a trumpet blast on it.

He lifted the shell high over his head and shouted, "Ay bobo!" The crowd went crazy. They repeated the cry, "Ay bobo!" whirled faster, shivered harder. Two of them fell to the deck and lay there, twitching and bucking.

Cappy shouted a few sentences in what must have been Creole. Then he pointed the shell and shouted triumphantly. The crowd swayed, then ran to the rail and looked where he pointed.

I looked, too. From where I stood I could just make out the skyline of Miami, its lights and skyscrapers standing out against the dark sky, no more than half a mile away.

It didn't seem possible. If Nicky's timetable was right, we should be in the middle of the Gulf Stream. And even Cappy wouldn't hold a voodoo service with 100 illegal aliens this close to the Port of Miami.

But there it was. The skyline was there, and the crowd recognized it as easily as I did. It was their dream. Some of them had been saving up and dodging death for ten years to see those lights.

And now Cappy had brought them here. He shouted something again, blew the conch shell, and shouted, "Ay bobo!" and the people began to crowd over to the rail.

The crewmen with cattle prods were waiting for them. Each person who came to the rail was searched, everything removed from his or her pockets. Then the guards "helped" them over and into the water.

And still the crowd pushed to get there, to jump in and swim the short distance to a new life.

I had thought the scene before was hellish. This was worse. They were pouring over the side and into the water in family groups, in handholding twos and threes, mothers holding children and jumping.

And for those few who hung back, unsure or unwilling, there were Cappy's crew to encourage them forward with cattle prods.

A small piece of the puzzle clicked into place. I had wondered how a small crew could force such a large crowd into the water. It was a simple and, in its ugly way, elegant solution: don't force them. Make them *want* to go over the side.

But how could we be this close to Miami? Unless—

I leaned out as far as I could and looked at the skyline dead astern. Something was not quite right about it. Something about the lights—

I got it pretty quickly, which might mean I was recovering. The lights of Miami's skyline are many colors, many shapes and sizes. These lights were all the same size and shape.

The last piece clicked into place.

I remembered the strange chunk of plywood on pontoons I had stumbled over. I remembered the rings on it, like it had been meant to be towed, and the batteries.

And I remembered what the mate on the *Chinea* had said: "They all jump in the water. They think they're in Miami…"

Nicky's estimate of time was right. We were still in the middle of the Gulf Stream. But we were towing a plywood silhouette of Miami, hung with cheap Christmas lights. And the people, a little unbalanced from a few hours of drinking and dancing, were going over the rail. They thought they were swimming the half mile to freedom. Instead they were dropping into the big deep.

They see the lights. And everybody jumps in the water.

Cappy blew a final long blast on his conch shell. He put it down and picked up something else; a knife. Looking serious, even solemn, he raised the knife high over his head.

And turned to Anna.

I jumped forward. I heard a kind of dumb animal howl and realized it was me. The fifty feet between Cappy and me seemed like nightmare distance. I moved forward with lead feet and the distance stayed the same.

Most of the crowd, still on deck, whirled around in my way. A man jumped on my back, yammering syllables that sounded like, "Ya-laylee loto lulu!" I threw him off. A woman leaped at my face with a maniac smile and poured rum on my head. I pushed her away. Two happy men grabbed my arms and tried to pull me into a ring of dancers. I yanked my arms free and stumbled forward, leaning on the ship's gunwale for a second to get my balance.

But one of the crew had spotted me. He ran forward, holding his cattle prod like a baseball bat. He swung for the fences. I was not quite quick enough to duck. I caught it on my arm and felt the force and the shock travel all the way up the arm and through my whole body.

For a second I couldn't move at all. The crewman raised the prod for another swing at my head and I stumbled at him. I didn't have full use of my arms, so I rammed him with my shoulder. He fell back, into the gunwale, and I scooped him up and over, into the ocean.

I ran for Anna, trying to shake the feeling back into my arm. I got some back, and it wasn't good. The spot where I had blocked the cattle prod felt broken.

Well, if I lived I could get a cast.

The crowd spun past. I stumbled, shoved and battered my way through to the altar.

I was close enough now to pick out details; the patterns carved on the wooden bowls around Anna, a bad spot on one of the mangoes. I could see that Anna was still alive. The bad news—

Cappy had slashed Anna's arm at the bicep, where a doctor takes a blood sample. The blood was running into a silver bowl and the snake was slowly untwining itself from the tree above the altar and moving down toward the bowl, toward Anna, tongue flickering.

And Cappy himself had turned to wait for me, smiling, the sacrificial knife hanging loosely by his side.

He looked so cool, so superior, and so damned happy. And I felt like I was cobbled together out of backyard mud by clumsy six-year olds. Everything hurt. Anything that worked was slow, filled with sludge and rust. I couldn't keep a clear idea of what to do, except that I had to save Anna and smash Cappy, flatten his head, crush his skull—

I rushed him. I lowered my shoulder to crash into him and he flicked up the tip of the knife, still smiling. I almost ran right onto the knife; at the last second the message got through to my brain and I twisted aside, skidding to a stop beside the altar, facing him from a few feet away.

He moved. Maybe it was my sluggishness, but I couldn't react. I had never before seen anything move so fast. I felt a coldness along my good arm, and then wetness, and he was standing there smiling again. My arm was bleeding where he had lightly slashed with the knife.

Before I could do anything but stare he did it again. I managed to stumble half a step back this time, but he had opened up a new cut on my forearm.

Cappy stood watching me, relaxed and hardly breathing. He looked like he was having fun, like a kid with a new toy who knows it will be broken soon, but for now he's having a blast.

When you are fighting someone that much faster than you, the textbook says you find your edge. Are you stronger? Tougher? Longer reach? More skillful? Then you try to trap your opponent in a position where his speed will not help.

It was a great theory. But I was having a hard time finding my edge. He was astonishingly fast; he had a knife, a snake, and a couple of thugs on call. I was half-dead with a broken arm, and a long way from home.

And Cappy was not giving me much time to ponder. He snaked the knife in again and found the side of my face this time. I jerked back. The knife might have taken out my eye if I had not. As it was, I now had my own dueling scar.

I was just about out of time and options. If I just stood there, Cappy would cut me to ribbons and the snake would crush Anna. And if I rushed him, he would skewer me and feed me to his snake.

He moved again. The knife went for my eyes and I got my arm in the way. I felt the point go in at the bicep and glance off bone. I twisted a little and the knife came out of Cappy's hand and slapped to the deck. Without waiting for either one of us to go for the knife, I drove my shoulder into him.

I caught him high and he leaned backwards. A dim reflex from high school football got my legs churning and I pushed him into the altar. I heard the breath whoosh out of him and brought my broken arm around to hit him with an elbow into the face. It hit him hard, but it might have hurt me more.

I kept leaning, pushing him into the solid altar, not giving him a chance to recover, pick up the knife, get that smile back on his face.

His fist came forward, holding a mango from one of the offering bowls. It smacked me hard on the side of the head and I felt something trickle down onto my neck, whether blood or mango juice, I couldn't say.

There was a ringing in my ears to go with all the other aches and pains. It didn't matter. I had him now. If I could keep him pinned to the altar, his speed wouldn't help him and he couldn't get to the knife. I could live through a couple more mangoes. I couldn't use my fists, but that didn't matter, either. There are other ways.

I hit him with another elbow, this time with my knifed arm. He grunted and leaned backwards as I brought the other elbow forward. It missed him. He groped behind him for something, but I was too close to see what it was. I brought my knee up and caught him just below the belt, then hammered my head forward into his solar plexus.

I felt a rib crack. If I could keep this up for just a few more hard blows, he would be down.

I didn't get the chance. He brought his hand forward, the one that had been groping behind him on the altar.

He wasn't holding a knife, or a gun, or a baseball bat, or even another mango. I would rather have seen any of those things than what I saw him pull forward and drop onto me.

The snake.

And as Cappy gave his peculiar trilling whistle, the snake whipped a coil around me and tightened.

The pain was enough to cut through all the numbness. It was fire where the knife had gone in, and dull agony on the broken arm.

I tried to move, but it was like being drugged again. I was helpless. My arms might have been sewn to my sides. The snake tightened again, and the world went a few shades darker. I could hear a rib snap, feel the sharp pain of it in my side. For the first time that night, the sound of the drums faded just a little, covered by the pounding of blood in my ears.

I couldn't breathe. The snake seemed to get heavier, forcing me down to one knee.

Cappy followed me down, his face just a few inches from mine, watching me with his soft, relaxed smile back in place. And as I watched him, the life being squeezed out of me, my breath gone, my vision dimming, that smile was all I could see. Like the Cheshire cat, Cappy faded and all I could see was the white of his teeth.

I did not want to die looking at that smile. Reaching for all my last reserves, I got back to my feet. It took almost the last of all I had, and as I stood there almost blind and deaf from the snake's constriction, Cappy took it away from me. He moved into my field of vision again. I saw his lips pursed and I heard faintly the whistle he made for his snake.

The snake squeezed harder. My upper arms were crushed against my chest and I heard more ribs breaking.

My knees buckled again. I leaned on the altar, close to Anna's face. It was so pale and beautiful. It was a pretty good choice for the last thing I would see. It summed up my failures as well as the pleasures of life.

I'm sorry, Anna, I thought. I died trying.

She did not answer. The snake squeezed. I looked Anna over one last time, thinking about what might have been. Already I could feel a kind of distance from all that silly human stuff. All the agonizing and self-torture.

We could talk it over soon enough. Anna would follow me into the black unknown. The bowl beside her was nearly full of her blood. It wouldn't be very long now. Too bad.

The blood.

The bowl of blood.

No matter how far gone you are, how completely you have already accepted the idea of death, there is always a tiny voice in the background yelling at you to for God's sake get us out of here. And as I looked at the bowl of Anna's blood the thing stood on its tiptoes and yodeled for all it was worth.

Pick up the blood. The snake likes blood.

Ah, said the part of me that had already quit. But I can't really move. So it's useless, you see?

Try. Wiggle your fingers.

All right, but what's the point? Look, they wiggle, so what?

So pick up the bowl of blood. Pick it up now!

My right arm was free from just below the elbow down, outside the snake's coils. It hurt like hell, but I could just do it. I picked up the bowl of blood.

Okay; now what?

The snake moved its head past my face, tongue flicking. I had its attention and for a moment it wasn't squeezing quite so hard. That huge flat head moved past mine and waved down to the bowl. It dipped into the blood.

Cappy moved close, purring to the snake, coaxing it back to duty. He put one hand out for the bowl and one on the snake's head.

Now! screamed my annoying little voice.

I threw the bowl. It wasn't much of a throw, more like a flip using just my wrist, but it worked. It hit Cappy in the chest and the blood soaked him.

Cappy looked at himself, annoyed. The snake looked at him, too. And slowly, very deliberately, it moved off me and onto Cappy.

He scolded it. He wheedled. But the scent of blood was too strong. The snake slid onto his shoulders and threw a couple of gentle coils around Cappy, relaxing, exploring the blood.

I leaned on the altar, panting, watching. The most wonderful feeling I had ever had was the air moving into my lungs. Breathing took everything I had. If Cappy wanted to kill me with his bare hands now, I could not raise a finger to stop him.

I watched, wondering what I would do when Cappy had the snake back under control again. And it seemed like he did. He turned toward me, the snake wrapped around him, weaving its head at me again. I had bought a little time, a couple of beautiful breaths, no more.

Cappy stepped towards me, the snake coiled around him, head raised alertly. And somewhere far away I heard a small flat sound that didn't fit with the background of the drums. The snake jerked, convulsively squeezed. Cappy's eyes bulged and his hands went to the coils around his neck.

I looked for the sound. I saw nothing anywhere on deck but the last of the party, a final group, mostly children, moving toward the rail and looking over at the skyline of Miami so close.

The last two guards were running towards me at full speed. Too bad. I had almost made it, but there was nothing I could do to stop them. I could barely move.

The flat popping sound came again, twice, three times.

The closest guard pitched forward onto his face without slowing down and slid another six feet before ramming headfirst into the altar. The man behind clutched his stomach and crumpled to his knees, then fell over and lay still.

I looked far away, up to the top of the wheelhouse. Something moved. A small form stood there in classic pistol shooting stance, both arms out in front.

Nicky had found his gun.

He waved at me and I blinked back. Closer at hand I heard a gurgling. I looked.

Cappy had gotten one hand between the snake and his throat. It wasn't helping. Nicky's shot had taken the snake in the head and it was in its death throes, squeezing with everything it had, loosening for a half second, squeezing again. Each time it squeezed, it forced Cappy's knuckles deeper into his throat. Each time, Cappy got a little weaker.

He dropped to one knee. He was not smiling anymore. I saw his lips move, trying to whistle, but he didn't have enough air. The snake squeezed, there was a delicate crunching sound, and Cappy fell over. The snake still thrashed around, squeezing convulsively, and I did not want to get too close to check for a pulse. But Cappy's eyes were already glazing.

He was dead.

I turned to Anna. As I fumbled to stop the bleeding, Nicky ran up beside me.

"I thought you were dead," he said.

"I still might be," I said. "Help me with Anna."

He ripped a large chunk of the white gown she was wrapped in and made a pad of it, winding another strip around to hold it in place. I watched him work. There was strange mad light in his eyes, like he wasn't sure what to do but wanted to do it at top speed.

"You saved my life." I nodded at Anna. "Both our lives."

He looked up at me, eyes burning. "It was good shooting., eh? Real fucking great, wasn't I?"

"The best I ever saw. Thanks."

He looked at Cappy. He looked at the two guards, one motionless and one still struggling with the hole in his guts. Nicky pulled the pistol from his waistband and looked at it for a minute. Then he threw it as hard as he could, over the rail and into the deep waters of the Gulf Stream.

"Filthy fucking thing," he said.

CHAPTER THIRTY

They took me to Jackson Memorial Hospital, I guess because it was an airlift. Or maybe they weren't sure I could pay for all the work I was going to take, and Jackson is where they take you if you can't pay. I didn't look like the kind of guy who pays cash for a new Bentley. Or even a pair of tube socks. My clothes were battered, ripped and stained with blood. So was I.

I was going to take a lot of work. They all agreed on that. The X-ray technician clucked and shook her head and hurried away to get the doctor. The doctor hissed and called for a couple more doctors. The three doctors went into a huddle over the X-rays and kept looking at me sideways.

It came down to five broken ribs and a broken arm, with a whole lot of assorted tissue damage and subdural hematoma over two-thirds of my body. One lung was punctured, they were very optimistic about the liver damage and the tendons in my arm, but there was a toxic residue in my blood none of them could figure out—except for one intern from Jamaica who didn't say anything, but made an extra wide circle around my bed when he had to go past.

They wouldn't let me go with Anna and I couldn't move that far by myself. So Nicky went with her and shuttled back and forth with progress reports: she's lost a lot of blood but seems okay; they can't identify the sedative she's been given but it seems like some kind of organic compound; and finally that she had opened an eye for a couple of seconds.

I drifted in and out of sleep with the painkillers they dripped into me. I woke up when they taped my ribs and again when they put the cast on my arm. I slept through most of the stitches.

And then much later I woke up again knowing I was not alone. The painkillers had lost their edge and I felt like I'd been through a threshing machine. A circle of cold eyes stared down at me, not doctors.

Two of them wore Coast Guard uniforms. The others were wearing the kind of suits you wear if you're a politician and you think you're going to make the six o'clock news.

There must have been something really strong in my IV after all. I had the damnedest time figuring out what they were saying, until finally it occurred to me that I was being grilled. A couple of the suits were from INS, and the rest were local and federal law enforcement.

They were on me like hyenas onto bad meat. I saw Deacon at the back of the pack, leaning against the wall and cleaning his fingernails with a large buck knife.

I tried to concentrate on what the hyenas were saying, but they all had a speech they had to make, and they couldn't decide who was more important, so it was tough going for a while.

It seemed to come down to this: they were considering charging me with a number of things, including piracy, murder, felonious assault, hijacking, and fifty-nine separate violations of INS code. That was the first time I'd heard the number of Haitians they'd managed to save. The longer they talked, the lower that number seemed.

In the end they stood around and took turns making threats, and when I didn't say anything they looked at each other for a minute and then left, assuring me I hadn't heard the end of it and it was a very serious matter.

Then they were gone and only Deacon was left. He put away the buck knife and gave me a short smile. "How you feeling, buddy?" he said.

"My left toe feels great," I told him. "Thanks for coming to my hanging."

"A real pleasure. Haven't seen that many agencies show that much cooperation my whole career. Inspiring. You got a real talent." He moved over and stood close the bed. "They sent them back, you know. The people they fished out of the water."

"Back to Haiti?"

He nodded. "That's right. Priority mail, on the first cutter that got to the scene."

I closed my eyes. I wasn't dumb enough to expect a parade and instant citizenship for the refugees, but it seemed like I'd been through an awful lot just to keep things the same. I said so.

"Life isn't perfect, Billy. And alive is better than dead any old time. Most of 'em probably try again."

"That's very encouraging," I said.

"Well, hell, buddy. You got the bad guy, and that's a big step forward."

"Hard to feel good about that," I said.

He winked. "That's what makes you one of the white hats," he said.

A nurse came charging in and started clucking at Deacon. He waited for her without saying anything. She checked my dressing, my pulse, my temperature, and gave me a new IV bag with what I truly hoped was more painkillers.

Then she glared at Deacon and said, "He needs rest."

Deacon smiled at her. "Yes, ma'am. He'll get it."

They had a staring match for just a second, then the nurse shook her head and went racing out again.

I let my eyes fall closed again. "What do you think will happen with all that other stuff?"

"The piracy charges, all of that?" He made a sound that was either clearing his throat or a dry chuckle. "Hard to say. Guess we could get you an eye patch and a peg leg. But I have this gut feeling that somehow a pretty good local reporter is going to get a hold of this story and shake it 'til all the bugs drop off. There'll be a lot of noise for a while, but in the end there'll just be too damned much public pressure to do anything. They're not going to name a bridge after you, but they won't dare file charges, either. They're mighty damn scared of looking bad."

I could feel myself drifting off again, and I guess I looked it. Deacon leaned a little closer.

"One last word on the subject," he said.

I managed to get one eye open. "Just one word?" I asked.

He nodded. "Proud," he said. He tapped the side of my face with his open hand, and then he was gone.

CHAPTER THIRTY-ONE

It was a too-bright day in September with no trace of autumn in the air when they wheeled me out the front door of Jackson Memorial Hospital. They made me stay in the wheelchair until I was out the front door—hospital regulations—and I didn't fight them. I was too grouchy, groggy, and grungy to fight anything.

Nicky danced beside me the whole way out like a leprechaun on speed. He led me down to my car. It stood at the curb—

—with Anna in the front seat.

She was looking straight ahead when I saw her. The sunlight coming through the windshield lit her, made her near-perfect profile stand out like it was carved in marble. She looked like the girl who pets the unicorn. She was so pale and pure and clean that I almost couldn't believe she was real.

As I got into the back seat of the car she turned to me with a funny smile and reached to touch my hand, then blushed.

I wanted to say something. But then Nicky jumped into the driver's seat, laughing and burbling like a demented elf.

"Right! Off we go, then! Buckle up, Billy. Can't have you bouncing through the windscreen. Hee hee!" Anna turned around to face the front.

The ride home was long and strange. We went through prolonged spells where nobody could say anything, and then suddenly everybody had something stupid to say at the same time.

Maybe it was my pain pills. They had given me some pretty strong stuff and I kept drifting in and out of focus. The world had an extra edge of brightness to it, and time was doing funny things. We made it from Florida City to Key Largo in the blink of an eye, but crossing the Seven Mile Bridge took a lifetime and a half, the rails going past like they had always been there and would never end. And every time I looked at Anna—which was a lot—she was staring out the window, watching the flat blue of the water below.

And so in a cloud of anxiety, fake jolliness, and anesthesia, we rolled into Key West as the sun was about an hour from closing in on the horizon. Nicky and Anna helped me into my house, one on each side, and into bed. They got me propped up, with a large plastic cup filled with ice water and a straw on the table beside me, and promises of chicken soup.

Nicky bounced away to his house to get a pot of the stuff ready for me, and I was finally alone with Anna.

She stood beside the bed, clenching and unclenching her hands, looking at everything but me. I wondered if the sight of me so banged up was bothering her. Maybe it brought back bad memories, or she felt guilty, since she might think it was her that got me into this.

"Hey," I said, holding out my hand, trying to get her to relax just a little. I touched her arm; she jumped like she'd been shocked. She settled down with a small smile and took my hand in hers. "What's wrong?"

"Ah," she said. "Surprisement. Too much of think."

"What kind of think?"

She was very quiet for a long time,. Finally she shook her head slowly. "Is very much the ball of roach," she said, and I didn't have any idea what she was talking about. She made a knotted, confused gesture with her hand. "Like so."

"Worms?" I asked her. "A ball of worms?"

"Yes, worms. As I say," she said. She pulled her hand away and I let her. "There is so much, and it is all exactly nothing."

"That's just the way I feel," I said.

She looked at me, then shook her head. "When you are better, then I say these things," she said.

"Anna," I said. "There is a small spot on my right leg with no pain. You're making it hurt. You're raising my blood pressure, and that cancels out my pain medication. If you have something to say, say it fast before I pop a blood vessel. Otherwise, just sit still for a few minutes and look perfect for me." And I collapsed back into my pillows, feeling the pulse throb in all my broken bones.

Anna sat on the edge of the bed and took my hand again. "All these times you are in hospital," she said. "I am thinking you will die. I am watching you, sitting beside you even at this bad time when there is the electronic noise and all the doctors run in."

"Thanks," I said. "It helped me to feel you there."

"Piff," she said. "You are saying politeness. I am trying to say true. Billy—" She paused and put my hand carefully onto the bed.

"Yes," I said.

"All this time when I think you will die, I think also it is my fault, that I have killed you."

"That's a load of—"

"Please," she said. "I know what this is loads of. I know this *now*. But then in the hospital I do *not* know. Watching your life go *blip bleep* on the machines. And is my fault. That you do this for *me* because of you have these feelings for me. And I say myself, how am I feeling of this man? Am I feeling him love—or just guiltiness only?"

"Oh," I said. For the first time I got an idea where she was going. I didn't want to go there.

"And as more I think, as more I do not know," she said. She lifted up my hand again, turned it over. "And as more I do not know, so much I am thinking how important it is to know this."

"Yes," I said, "it's important to know this."

"And so I think when you are coming home again, I will know. And I do not know still. And I must." She looked up at me. Her eyes were bluer than anything I'd ever seen before, bluer than the water from the Seven Mile Bridge, bluer than any sky had ever been. "All this things we are now going through, this evil things on the boat, this cannot be the thing to make us be together, yes? Only evil comes from evil. What is bringing us together, it must be from good. It must be here—" She touched her heart. "—and here." She touched her forehead. "Because else, because if we allow the evil to make us together, this is another kind of evil which we cannot so easy go away from."

"It didn't seem that easy to me," I said. She ignored me.

"Because is not looking to be evil, is two nice people together only, and so there is no way out."

"Anna," I said.

"There must always be a way out. I am knowing this since so big. Is not the freedom without. And without freedom is not the love.

"I must know first," she said. "First I must know."

She turned my hand over again, running the finger of her other hand along the lines on my palm. "And so I am feeling bad again. Because you are so much broken for this. For me. And I am saying thank you, very nice, please leave me alone now. This is the way to behave of a shit."

"No."

"Piff," she said again. "Again you say polite. Let me be the shit, is more the better." She smiled. It was only about half-mast, but it was the nicest thing I'd seen since I'd opened my eyes.

"All right," I said. "You are the shit."

"Good," she said. "Now we are saying the true. And now say me the true of how you feel." She put a hand on my chest. "In here."

I looked at her eyes, those autumn blue eyes. She looked away. I thought of all that had happened; the end of whatever I'd had with Nancy, nearly the end of me. The Black Freighter and the black night on the Gulf Stream, and all of it in that terrible August heat.

It was too much. I could not live through all that so quickly and still have feelings, too. No human being could. Maybe that was

Anna's point.

"In here is empty right now," I said. I touched her hand. "I've been through too much. I still feel too bad, too close to dead." I closed my eyes and saw it again; the burning skeleton, the snake, the sound of the flesh flaking off my bones. The drums. I opened my eyes. Anna was looking at me, concerned and—I don't know, something else, too. "Or maybe I'm just too doped up. Maybe I can't think straight." I wrapped my fingers around hers and held her hand tightly. "I want to be with you. I'm pretty sure of that. I feel better when I see you. I think I need you to bring some kind of feeling back."

"And so I am to be your medicine?"

"Yes," I said.

She didn't flinch. She looked back at me without blinking.

"There's nothing wrong with that. That's what two people do for each other. They fill in the blank spots, help each other heal. I'm not sure I can do it alone this time. I don't think you can, either. I can help, Anna. We can help each other. What else do you want from me?"

"But we are neither of us knowing, this is just the thing. This is why I say, is too much and also is not enough." She put my hand carefully back onto the bed and stood up. "And so," she said. "I am thinking one more thing."

I closed my eyes and let it all whip through me. Through the layers of pain and frustration and medicine I could just barely make out that she was saying something about how we needed to find a way to be ourselves without distractions and be very sure and not jump into something that trapped us and on and on. *Sure, Anna,* I thought. *Let's be friends.* I waited for her careful words of rejection, knowing they were coming, but not really listening. I couldn't take it, not now.

And then she stopped talking and stroked my hand and what she had said finally filtered through. I blinked my eyes open and looked at her. She was smiling a funny smile I hadn't seen before, and blushing bright red at the same time.

"What?" I said. "What did you say?"

"I say," she said, trying hard to meet my eye, "perhaps we are knowing better if we try to be together with nothing else, and so can you get from your friend for a little while a sailboat?"

CHAPTER THIRTY-TWO

November brought cool winds down from Canada and the awful heat of August was finally gone. People started to remember why they lived in Florida. It was a time of long and mild days, spectacular sunsets and crystal clear evenings cool enough for a light blanket, a real luxury after the sweaty misery of the summer.

We left Miami in another of Bert's rebuilt sailboats, a 36-foot Hunter this time. The first days were just for relaxing. We didn't push it. We both had some serious sorting-out to do, and this was the first chance we'd had to do it. I was still troubled by a few short spells where I couldn't remember what I was supposed to do. I'd look down and see a rope in my hand and be filled with terrible anxiety. The feeling would fade after a few minutes, but it was bad while it lasted. The doctor had said it would probably go away, but he wouldn't say when.

So we sailed, we ate simple meals, we slept side by side without touching in the big double bunk, and we tried as hard as we could to wake up from the nightmares we had come through, wake up to each other in the small separate world of a sailboat.

Our fourth day out was beautiful, but this was Florida. By noon a smudge of black clouds had appeared low on the horizon. By 1:30, the wind had gone from a pleasant ten knots to thirty, gusting higher, and the buffed green surface of the water had turned choppy grey, carpeted with white caps. We dropped the jib sail. The clouds blew closer, and soon we heeled far over under the surge of wind known as a squall breeze, which was just Nature's way of saying, "Here I come."

Within moments we felt the first stinging drops of rain, and then abruptly everything forward of the mast disappeared into a sheet of rain. We were leaning at a dangerous angle and taking on water from the rain and the waves. I shouted at Anna to take the tiller and jumped to the mast to double-reef the mainsail, something Betty had explained to me but I had never done before. It left us with only half the sail area for the wind to hit. We slowed a bit and lost the worst edge of our heel-over almost immediately.

For the next hour we fought the squall and couldn't have seen the *Queen Mary* if it was lashed to the mast. According to the chart we had plenty of open water and good depth, so I wasn't worried— until a quick break in the squall opened the sheet of water pouring down on us and I saw a sandy beach straight ahead.

Trying hard not to scream, I put the boat about and ran parallel to where I thought I'd seen the island. The storm tore at us, and even with our tiny scrap of sail we flew across the water like a foam cup. I saw breakers flash off to the right, put her over again, and suddenly the water was calm and the wind was about half the strength it had been. I turned our nose into the wind, ran up to the bow, and dropped the anchor.

I let the line play out fast, trying to gauge the depth; between ten and fifteen feet. I gave us enough scope, set the hook with a hard yank, and looked around, straightening my creaking back and taking my first breath of the last two hours.

We were lying in a lagoon sheltered by two fingers of sandy beach, each with a row of pine trees stretching back from the shore. The squall still blew furiously, lashing the waves with stinging rain, but inside our lagoon I would have felt safe riding out a hurricane.

The storm didn't last very long. Another fifteen minutes and it had blown itself out, moved on to hassle Cuba. I went below with Anna and pulled on a dry shirt and waited it out. When the sun broke through we went up on deck to look over our harbor.

It was a small island, just big enough for a game of catch. There was a good sand beach, trees to block the wind, and a line of shrubbery and weeds leading into the interior. Off to our left a spit of beach curved around to form the sheltering arm of the little harbor. I couldn't see any litter on the beach; no soda or beer cans, no broken coolers, old T-shirts, oil containers, pizza boxes, plastic bags, coffee cups, six-pack holders, candy wrappers—nothing.

"Paradise," I said.

"Hmmp," said Anna. "And if so where is ice machine?"

That night we made a driftwood fire on the beach and as it died to the embers we watched the sky, counting six falling stars and one moving light we couldn't identify. We talked, sitting close but not touching, passing a bottle of wine back and forth between sentences. We hit an easy tone and just rambled, saying whatever popped into our heads, playing out mock debates about things that didn't matter, just for the pleasure of hearing each other.

And with the gentle breeze, the dying fire, and the enormous Florida sky above us, everything that had happened on the Black Freighter started to seem like last summer's blockbuster movie. When we finally rowed the small inflatable dinghy back to the boat Anna was giggling and I felt my face stretching into a smile for the first time since August.

• • •

In the night the snake came for me again and rattled my bones, bearing down on me with its huge rubbery grin. I tried to fly away but it ate my wings and as I smoldered and fell it moved closer, smiling, smiling—

"Billy!" Anna said. She slapped me and I blinked awake. She moved to slap me again.

"I'm okay," I said, but she hit me anyway.

"Of all damn-ness," she said. "Wake now!" And she moved her hand back to hit me again.

I grabbed her wrist and held it. "I'm okay," I said again.

"Is not okay, to make such a noises," she said. She sounded mad. "You are jumping this way, then that way, then you are saying no no no, then making such a noise as—Gikk-gahhhkk." She made a face of strangling. "And the entire you is going flap, flap, all over."

I closed my eyes again. The entire me felt battered, thrashed with steel rods and dipped in glue. "Bad dream," I said.

"The snake," she said.

"Yes."

She was quiet for a long minute. "I also have this dream," she said. "Perhaps both we will always have it." She pulled her hand away from mine and dropped it onto my chest.

"No," I said. "Not always. But it takes time."

She made no answer and I became aware of the weight and heat of her hand against me. After a moment it was all I could think about.

Then a small wet drop hit me beside Anna's hand. I looked up at her face. A quiet tear slid out of her eye. Then some inner wall broke down and the tears came in a flood, along with great, ratchety sobs that shook her whole body. I held her for a long time, until the shaking stopped, and the sobs had slowed to huge, ratcheting breaths. And gradually the rough breathing smoothed and slowed, and soon she was asleep in my arms.

I held her, not wanting to move for fear of waking her. And at some point the sound of the wind, the slap of water against the hull and the easy rocking of the boat did their job. I fell asleep under the soft warm weight of her.

When I woke up her weight had shifted, and so had her breathing. Her head was nestled against my neck and her hand was now on my face, softly stroking it. And as I blinked awake I realized one other change.

Anna's shirt was off.

Her bare breasts pressed against me, the nipples hard. My hand moved up to cup her as if it had a life of its own, and she trembled.

I hesitated, but this time the trembling was not fear, or old dreams coming back. It was eagerness.

It had been a long wait for both of us and we made love with a fire hotter than any I could remember. It was not enough and we drove ourselves further, and further still, moving up on deck to be under the bright Florida stars, and further still, until the sun came up on two exhausted and happy people stretched out together on the cushions in the cockpit of the sailboat.

The breeze stayed out of the north for three days, which meant it would have been just a little too much work to push our boat back to Key West. Besides, we weren't in any hurry. The anchorage we had found was a good one, in the lee of an island that wasn't even on the charts. But it protected us from the wind. No other boat had found our spot so far, and that made us a little bit lazy about things like clothing.

There was a reef to explore within easy reach of the dinghy, and a small cut nearby stocked with uneducated mangrove snapper. They grilled beautifully, painted with lime juice and a few grains of salt and pepper.

And so there were days of sun, swimming, fishing, long lazy naps, and exploring the reef and the nearby island; and there were nights of strange rum drinks made with no ice and whatever supplies we had left; star-gazing, quiet contentment, and other explorations. My ribs and arm were still sore, and every now and then I would have to think a little too hard to remember a word like "potato," but that didn't seem important. There was the sun and the healing water and above all there was Anna, and it was as near a perfect time as I could remember.

We made that good time last as long as we could. All too soon we would have to go back, back to the everyday pain and hassle of the real world. I didn't want to. Neither did Anna. Maybe we were afraid that what we had worked so hard to find with each other, what we had finally found only by being here, away from everything but each other—maybe that couldn't live anywhere else. It was so new, special, delicate—maybe it couldn't live in a place like Key West.

So we stayed there, anchored in the lee of our little island. We swam, snorkeled, and fished. We built bonfires on the beach until we ran out of driftwood, and then we just sat under the stars and held hands like a couple of kids. We stayed, and we were down to a box of crackers and a quart of grapefruit juice when we finally pulled up the anchor and headed south to Key West. We would have stayed longer if we could. You don't find perfection very often. You don't let go of it if you have a choice. But there never is a choice. Something disguised as need always pries it out of your fingers, and tells you it's time, you had your piece of wonderful, and anyway, nothing lasts forever. Especially perfection.

I just hoped we were taking some of it back with us. I hoped it would be enough. Here at the end of that hot summer of death and nightmares, I hoped Anna and I had found just enough in our time together, and that it would turn into something we could hold onto together as much as we shared the bad dreams.

When we came in to Key West at last, even the crackers were gone and the only thing left of the grapefruit juice was the awful bitter aftertaste. It didn't matter. We could have dropped the sails and motored home a lot quicker. We didn't. We made it last. We kept the sail up until we had the dock in sight, and then I motored on in at dead slow. Neither one of us wanted this trip to end. We both knew that coming back to Key West would change things. Would it kill what we had? There was no way to know, except by stepping onto the dock and finding out what happened next. A big part of me didn't want to risk that, a nasty, dark-edged little voice that came at me from the shadows, that deep and powerful place where the drums still played and the snake writhed and reached for me with smiling coils.

I told myself it was only fear, and I'd lived with that same fear since Nicky woke me up in the broom closet on the *Petit Fleur*. But the closer I got to the dock, the stronger it became, and this time, it was based on something real.

What had we really found together, Anna and me? Was it real?

Or just something that had happened because we were on a boat all alone and we both needed something to hold onto until the nightmares rolled away? I didn't know. I only knew that whatever it was, I didn't want to lose it.

I looked at Anna. There was a slight frown on her face, a face now nearly as tanned as mine. I knew the feel of that face—its texture, its taste, and I wanted to keep knowing it for a good long time. I wanted to see it when I went to sleep at night, and when I woke up in the morning, and as often as possible in between.

Anna must have felt me staring. She turned her head, and for just a second there was nothing in the world but the endless deep blue of her eyes. And then her small frown fell away, replaced by a smile, and not just any smile. It was the smile she wore after lovemaking, the smile that had been on her face each night as the motion of the waves rocked us to sleep, still holding onto each other. It was a smile that stopped time and nearly made me turn the boat back around and head for that little island again. I was willing to live on sand and salt water if I could keep looking at that smile.

Anna put her hand on top of mine, where it rested on the sailboat's tiller, and she gave it a little squeeze.

I looked away from her, back to the dock, now only twenty-five feet away. I still didn't know what we had or how long it would last, but I knew we were both in it, together, until we found out. That was enough for now. Nothing is ever guaranteed in this life except that sooner or later it ends. Until then, you have to live like it matters, and hold on as tight as you can to the people that make it seem like it does. No guarantees. In the end, you can only try, and if you can manage it, try together, with somebody that matters. Maybe it works, and maybe it doesn't, but you try. Anna and I were going to try. It might last fifty years and it might be over by lunch tomorrow. But we were through the hard part, and the time for those bad dreams was over, too. They might come back now and then, but we would deal with that when it happened.

I thought about that word: we. It had a brand new feeling

to it, and a kind of strength that made me think it just might be enough to see us through. I might turn out to be wrong about that. I didn't think so.

I took Anna's hand and held it as I brought us in to the dock. Only time would tell. But for now, I didn't mind the wait.

JEFF LINDSAY is the *New York Times* bestselling author of the Dexter novels, which debuted in 2004 with *Darkly Dreaming Dexter*. They are the basis of the hit Showtime and CBS series, *Dexter*. He lives in South Florida with his family.

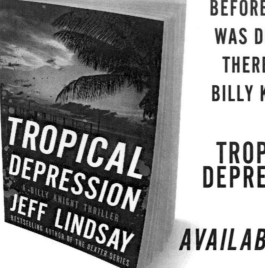

BEFORE THERE WAS DEXTER, THERE WAS BILLY KNIGHT.

TROPICAL DEPRESSION

AVAILABLE NOW!

New York Times bestselling author Jeff Lindsay mastered suspense with his wildly addictive *Dexter* series. Before that, however, there was former cop and current burnout Billy Knight. When a hostage situation turns deadly, Billy loses everything—his wife, his daughter, and his career. Devastated, he heads to Key West to put down his gun and pick up a rod and reel as a fishing boat captain. But former co-worker Roscoe McAuley isn't ready to let Billy rest.

When Roscoe tells Billy that someone murdered his son, Billy sends him away. When Roscoe himself turns up dead a few weeks later, however, Billy can't keep from getting sucked back into Los Angeles, and the streets that took so much from him.

Billy's investigations into the death of a former cop, and his son, will take him up to the highest echelons of the LAPD, finding corruption at every level. It puts him on a collision course with the law, with his past, with his former fellow officers, and with the dark aftermath of the Civil Rights Movement. Jeff Lindsay's considerable storytelling gifts are on full display, drawing the reader in with a mesmerizing style and a case with more dangerous blind curves than Mulholland Drive.